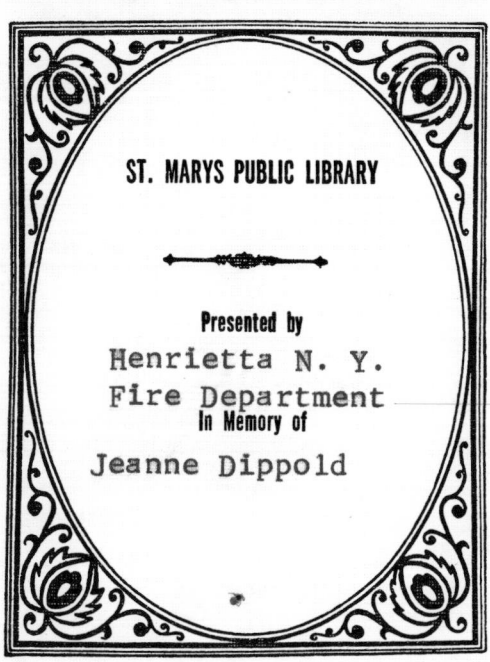

COYOTE WAITS

Books by TONY HILLERMAN

◁◁◁ *FICTION* ▷▷▷

Talking God

A Thief of Time

Skinwalkers

The Ghostway

The Dark Wind

People of Darkness

Listening Woman

Dance Hall of the Dead

The Fly on the Wall

The Blessing Way

The Boy Who Made Dragonfly *(for children)*

◁◁◁ *NONFICTION* ▷▷▷

The Great Taos Bank Robbery

Rio Grande

New Mexico

The Spell of New Mexico

Indian Country

TONY HILLERMAN

COYOTE WAITS

1817

HARPER & ROW, PUBLISHERS, New York

Grand Rapids, Philadelphia, St. Louis, San Francisco
London, Singapore, Sydney, Tokyo, Toronto

FIRST LARGE PRINT EDITION

ISBN 0-06-016423-9 (large print edition)

Designed by Alma Orenstein

The Library of Congress has cataloged the standard edition as follows:
Hillerman, Tony.
    Coyote waits / Tony Hillerman.—1st ed.
      p. cm.
    ISBN 0-06-016370-4
    1. Navaho Indians—Fiction. I. Title.
  PS3558.I45C69 1990
   813'.54—dc20   89-46098

---

90 91 92 93 94 CC/HC 10 9 8 7 6 5 4 3 2 1

For my great friend and brother-in-law,
Charles Unzner,
          and
For our world-class next-door neighbors—
Jim and Mary Reese,
and Gene and Geraldine Bustamante

All characters and events in this book are figments of my imagination.

OFFICER JIM CHEE was thinking that either his right front tire was a little low or there was something wrong with the shock on that side. On the other hand, maybe the road grader operator hadn't been watching the adjustment on his blade and he'd tilted the road. Whatever the cause, Chee's patrol car was pulling just a little to the right. He made the required correction, frowning. He was dog-tired.

The radio speaker made an uncertain noise, then produced the voice of Officer Delbert Nez. ". . . running on fumes. I'm going to have to buy some of that high-cost Red Rock gasoline or walk home."

"If you do, I advise paying for it out of your pocket," Chee said. "Better than explaining to the captain why you forgot to fill it up."

"I think . . ." Nez said and then the voice faded out.

"Your signal's breaking up," Chee said. "I don't read you." Nez was using Unit 44, a notorious gas hog. Something wrong with the fuel pump, maybe. It was always in the shop and nobody ever quite fixed it.

Silence. Static. Silence. The steering seemed to be better now. Probably not a low tire. Probably . . . And then the radio intruded again.

". . . catch the son-of-a-bitch with the smoking paint gun in his hand," Nez was saying. "I'll bet then . . ." The Nez voice vanished, replaced by silence.

"I'm not reading you," Chee said into his mike. "You're breaking up."

Which wasn't unusual. There were a dozen places on the twenty-five thousand square miles the Navajos called the Big Rez where radio transmission was blocked for a variety of reasons. Here between the monolithic volcanic towers of Ship Rock, the Carrizo Range, and the Chuska Mountains was just one of them. Chee presumed these radio blind spots were caused by the mountains but there were other theories. Deputy Sheriff Cowboy Dashee insisted that it had something to do with magnetism in the old volcanic necks that stuck up here and there, like great black cathedrals. Old Thomasina Bigthumb had told him once that she thought witches caused the problem. True, this part of the Reservation was notorious for witches, but it was also true that Old Lady Bigthumb blamed witches for just about everything.

Then Chee heard Delbert Nez again. The voice was very faint at first. ". . . his car," Delbert was saying. (Or was it ". . . his truck"? Or ". . . his pickup"? Exactly, precisely, what had Delbert Nez said?) Suddenly the transmission became clearer, the sound of Delbert's delighted laughter. "I'm gonna get him this time," Delbert Nez said.

Chee picked up the mike. "Who are you getting?" he said. "Do you need assistance?"

"My phantom painter," Nez seemed to say. At least it sounded like that. The reception was going sour again, fading, breaking up into static.

"Can't read you," Chee said. "You need assistance?"

Through the fade-out, through the

static, Nez seemed to say "No." Again, laughter.

"I'll see you at Red Rock then," Chee said. "It's your turn to buy."

There was no response to that at all, except static, and none was needed. Nez worked up U.S. 666 out of the Navajo Tribal Police headquarters at Window Rock, covering from Yah-Ta-Hey northward. Chee patrolled down 666 from the Shiprock subagency police station, and when they met they had coffee and talked. Having it this evening at the service station–post office–grocery store at Red Rock had been decided earlier, and it was upon Red Rock that they were converging. Chee was driving down the dirt road that wandered back and forth across the Arizona–New Mexico border southward from Biklabito. Nez was driving westward from 666 on the asphalt of Navajo Route 33. Nez, having pavement, would have been maybe fifteen minutes early. But now he seemed to have an arrest to make. That would even things up.

There was lightning in the cloud over the Chuskas now, and Chee's patrol car had stopped pulling to the right and was pulling to the left. Probably not a tire, he thought. Probably the road grader operator had noticed his maladjusted blade and overcorrected. At least it wasn't the usual washboard effect that pounded your kidneys.

It was twilight—twilight induced early by the impending thunderstorm—when Chee pulled his patrol car off the dirt and onto the pavement of Route 33. No sign of Nez. In fact, no sign of any headlights, just the remains of what had been a blazing red sunset. Chee pulled past the gasoline pumps at the Red Rock station and parked behind the trading post. No Unit 44 police car where Nez usually parked it. He inspected his front tires, which seemed fine. Then he looked around. Three pickups and a blue Chevy sedan. The sedan belonged to the new evening clerk at the trading post. Good-looking girl, but he couldn't come up with her name. Where was Nez? Maybe he actually had caught his paint-spraying vandal. Maybe the fuel pump on old 44 had died.

No Nez inside either. Chee nodded to the girl reading behind the cash register. She rewarded him with a shy smile. What was her name? Sheila? Suzy? Something like that. She was a Towering House Dineh, and therefore in no way linked to Chee's own Slow Talking Clan. Chee remembered that. It was the automatic checkoff any single young Navajo conducts—male or female—making sure the one who attracted you wasn't a sister, or cousin, or niece in the tribe's complex clan system, and thereby rendered taboo by incest rules.

The glass coffee-maker pot was two-thirds full, usually a good sign, and it smelled fresh. He picked up a fifty-cent-size Styrofoam cup, poured it full, and sipped. Good, he thought. He picked out a package containing two chocolate-frosted Twinkies. They'd go well with the coffee.

Back at the cash register, he handed the Towering House girl a five-dollar bill.

"Has Delbert Nez been in? You remember him? Sort of stocky, little mustache. Really ugly policeman."

"I thought he was cute," the Towering House girl said, smiling at Chee.

"Maybe you just like policemen?" Chee said. What the devil was her name?

"Not all of them," she said. "It depends."

"On whether they've arrested your boyfriend," Chee said. She wasn't married. He remembered Delbert had told him that. ("Why don't you find out these things for yourself," Delbert had said. "Before I got married, I would have known essential information like that. Wouldn't have had to ask. My wife finds out I'm making clan checks on the chicks, I'm in deep trouble.")

"I don't have a boyfriend," the Towering House girl said. "Not right now. And, no. Delbert hasn't been in this evening." She handed Chee his change, and giggled. "Has Delbert ever caught his rock painter?"

Chee was thinking maybe he was a little past dealing with girls who giggled. But she had large brown eyes, and long lashes, and perfect skin. Certainly, she knew how to flirt. "Maybe he's catching him right now," he said. "He said something on the radio about it." He noticed she had miscounted his change by a dime, which sort of went with the giggling. "Too much money," Chee said, handing her the dime. "You have any idea who'd be doing that painting?" And then he remembered her name. It was Shirley. Shirley Thompson.

Shirley shuddered, very prettily. "Somebody crazy," she said.

That was Chee's theory too. But he said: "Why crazy?"

"Well, just because," Shirley said, looking serious for the first time. "You know. Who else would do all that work painting that mountain white?"

It wasn't really a mountain. Technically it was probably a volcanic throat—

another of those ragged upthrusts of black basalt that jutted out of the prairie here and there east of the Chuskas.

"Maybe he's trying to paint something pretty," Chee said. "Have you ever gone in there and taken a close look at it?"

Shirley shivered. "I wouldn't go there," she said.

"Why not?" Chee asked, knowing why. It probably had some local legend attached to it. Something scary. Probably somebody had been killed there and left his *chindi* behind to haunt the place. And it was tainted by witchcraft gossip. Delbert had been raised back in the Chuska high country west of here and he'd said something about that outcrop—or maybe one nearby—being one of the places where members of the skinwalker clan were supposed to meet. It was a place to be avoided—and that was part of what had fascinated Officer Delbert Nez with its vandalism.

"It's not just that it's such a totally zany thing to do," Delbert had said. "Putting paint on the side of a rocky ridge, like that. There's a weirdness to it, too. It's a scary place. I don't care what you think about witches, nobody goes there. You do, somebody sees you, and they think you're a skinwalker yourself. I think whoever's doing it must have a purpose. Something specific. I'd like to know who the hell it is. And why."

That had been good enough for Chee, who enjoyed his own little obsessions. He glanced at his watch. Where was Delbert now?

The door opened and admitted a middle-aged woman with her hair tied in a blue cloth. She paid for gasoline, complained about the price, and engaged Shirley in conversation about a sing-dance somebody was planning at the Newcomb school. Chee had another cup of coffee. Two teenaged boys came in, followed by an old man wearing a T-shirt with DON'T WORRY, BE HAPPY printed across the chest. Another woman came, about Shirley's age, and the sound of thunder came through the door with her. The girls chatted and giggled. Chee looked at his watch again. Delbert was taking too damned long.

Chee walked out into the night.

The breeze smelled of rain. Chee hurried around the corner into the total darkness behind the trading post. In the car, he switched on the radio and tried to raise Nez. Nothing. He started the engine, and spun the rear wheels in an impatient start that was totally out of character for him. So was this sudden sense of anxiety. He switched on his siren and the emergency flashers.

Chee was only minutes away from the trading post when he saw the headlights approaching on Route 33. He slowed, feeling relief. But before they reached him, he saw the car's right turn indicator blinking. The vehicle turned northward, up ahead of him, not Nez's Navajo Tribal Police patrol car but a battered white Jeepster. Chee recognized it. It was the car of the Vietnamese (or Cambodian, or whatever he was) who taught at the high school in Shiprock. Chee's headlights briefly lit the driver's face.

The rain started then, a flurry of big, widely spaced drops splashing the windshield, then a downpour. Route 33 was wide and smooth, with a freshly painted centerline to follow. But the rain was more than Chee's wipers could handle. He slowed, listening to the water pound against the roof. Normally rain provoked jubilation in Chee—a feeling natural and primal, bred into dry-country people. Now this joy was blocked by worry and a little guilt. Something had delayed Nez. He should have gone looking for him when the radio blacked out. But it was probably nothing much. Car trouble. An ankle sprained chasing his painter in the dark. Nothing serious.

Lightning illuminated the highway ahead of him, showing it glistening with water and absolutely empty. The flash lit the ragged basalt shape of the formation across the prairie to the south—the outcrop on which Nez's vandal had been splashing his paint. Then the boom of thunder came. The rain slackened, flurried again, slackened again as the squall line of the storm passed. Off to the right Chee saw a glow of light. He stared. It came from down a dirt road that wandered from 33 southward over a ridge, leading eventually to the "outfit" of Old Lady Gorman. Chee let the breath whistle through his teeth. Relief. That would probably be Nez. Guilt fell away from him.

At the intersection, he slowed and stared down the dirt road. Headlights should be yellow. This light was red. It flickered. Fire.

"Oh, God!" Chee said aloud. A prayer. He geared the patrol car down into second and went slipping and sliding down the muddy track.

2

UNIT 44 WAS PARKED in the center of the track, its nose pointed toward Route 33, red flames gushing from the back of it, its tires burning furiously. Chee braked his car to a stop, skidding it out of the muddy ruts and onto the bunch grass and stunted sage. He had his door open and the fire extinguisher in his hand while the car was still sliding.

It was raining hard again, the cold drops splashing against his face. Then he was engulfed in the sickening black smoke of burning rubber, burning oil, burning upholstery. The driver's-side window had been shattered. Chee fired the extinguisher through it, seeing the white foam stream through the smoke, and seeing through the smoke the dark shape of Nez slumped over the steering wheel.

"Del!"

Chee snatched at the door handle, barely conscious of the searing pain. He jerked the door open and found himself engulfed in a gust of flames. He jumped back, whacking at the fire burning his uniform shirt. "Del," he shouted again. He sprayed the extinguisher foam into the car again, dropped the extinguisher, reached through the open door, clutched the arm of Officer Delbert Nez and pulled.

Nez was wearing his seat belt.

Chee fumbled for the catch, released it, pulled with all his strength, aware as he did that his palm was hurting in a way he had never experienced before. He tumbled backward into the driving rain, he and Delbert Nez. He lay for a moment, gasping, lungs full of smoke, conscious that something was wrong with the hand, and of the weight of Delbert Nez partly across him. Then he was aware of heat. His shirt sleeve burning. He put it out, struggled out from under the weight of Nez.

Nez lay on his back, arms and legs sprawled. Chee looked at him and looked away. He picked up the extinguisher, sprayed the burning places on the officer's trousers. He used what was left in the tank to put out the fire. "Running on fumes," Nez had said. That was lucky. Chee had seen enough car fires to know what a full tank would do. Lucky? Fumes had provided enough fire to kill Delbert Nez.

He was on the radio, calling this in to Shiprock, asking for help, before he was fully aware of the pain of his own burns.

"There was blood, too," Chee was saying. "He might have been shot. I think blood on the back of his shirt, and blood on the front, too."

Captain Largo happened to be in, doing his perpetual paperwork. While Chee was saying that, Largo took over the radio in the Shiprock dispatcher's office.

"We'll send all we have from here," Largo was saying. "And from Window Rock, and we'll see if anybody from Crownpoint is patrolling out your direction. Blood still fresh?"

Chee looked at his hand and grimaced. "It's still sticky," he said. "Somewhere between slick and sticky." A chunk of skin had flapped off the palm of his hand. The door handle, he thought. That had done it. It felt like it had burned all the way to the bone.

"You saw no other car lights?"

"One car. Just as I was leaving Red Rock a white Jeepster was turning off 33 onto the road toward Biklabito. One man in it. I think it was that Vietnamese math teacher at Shiprock High School. I think that's his car, anyway." Chee's throat hurt. So did his lungs. So did his eyes. And his face. He felt with numb fingers. No eyebrows.

"We'll handle that part then," Largo said. "Save any looking for tracks for daylight. Do not mess anything up around the car. You got that?" Largo paused. "Do not," he repeated.

"Okay," Chee said. He wanted to end this. He wanted to go find whoever had killed Delbert Nez. He should have been with Nez. He should have gone to help him.

"You came down 33 from the west? From Red Rock? Get back on 33 and head east. All the way to 666. See if you can pick up anything that way. If the guy had a vehicle that's the only way he could have gone." Largo paused. "Unless he was your Vietnamese schoolteacher."

Chee didn't get all the way to U.S. Highway 666. Three miles east of the intersection, the high beams of his headlights reflected from the back of a man walking down the asphalt. Chee braked and stared. The man was walking erratically down the center of the westbound lane. He was bareheaded, his gray hair tied in a bun, his rain-soaked shirt plastered to his back. He seemed totally oblivious of Chee's headlights, now just a few yards behind him. Without a backward glance, with no effort to move to the side of the road, he walked steadily onward, swinging something in his right hand, zigzagging a little, but with the steady, unhurried pace of a man who has walked great distances, who will walk great distances more.

Chee pulled up beside him, rolled down his window. The object the man was swinging was a squat bottle, held by the neck. *"Yaa' eh t'eeh!"* Chee shouted, the standard Navajo greeting. The man ignored him, plodding steadily down the asphalt. As he moved past the police car and back into glare of the headlights Chee saw he had something bulky stuck under his belt in the back of his trousers. It looked like the butt of a pistol.

Chee unsnapped his own pistol, took it out of its holster, and laid it on the seat beside him. He touched the siren button, producing a sudden howling. The gray-haired man seemed not to hear it.

Chee picked up the mike, raised Shiprock, gave his location. "I have a male, about five feet eight inches tall, elderly, gray-haired, walking down the westbound lane away from the Nez site. He has what appears to be a pistol stuck under his belt and what appears to be a whiskey bottle in his right hand and is acting in a peculiar manner."

"Peculiar manner," the dispatcher said.

"I think he's drunk," Chee said. "He acts like he doesn't hear me or see me."

"Subject is drunk," the dispatcher said.

"Maybe," Chee said. "I will apprehend him now."

Which might be easier said than done, he thought. He pulled the patrol car past the walker and spun it around so its lights shone directly into the man's face. He got out with his pistol in his hand. He felt dizzy. Everything was vague.

"Hold it right there," Chee said.

The walker stopped. He looked intently at Chee, as if trying to bring him into focus. Then he sighed and sat on the pavement. He screwed the cap off the bottle, and took a long, gurgling drink. He looked at Chee again and said:

"Baa yanisin, shiyaazh."

"You are ashamed?" Chee repeated. His voice choked. "Ashamed!" With his good hand he reached over the walker's shoulder, jerked the pistol out of the man's belt. He sniffed the muzzle of the barrel and smelled burned powder. He checked the cylinders. All six contained cartridges, but three of the cartridges were empty. They had been fired. He jammed the pistol under his belt, snatched the bottle out of the walker's hand, and hurled it into the sagebrush beside the road.

"Dirty coyote," Chee said in Navajo. "Get up." His voice was fierce.

The man stared up at him, expression puzzled. The glare of the headlights reflected off the streaks of rainwater running down his face, dripping from his hair, from his eyebrows.

"Get up!" Chee screamed.

He jerked the man to his feet, hurried him to the patrol car, searched him quickly for another weapon, took a pocketknife and some coins from a front pocket and a worn wallet from his hip pocket. He handcuffed him, conscious of the man's thin, bony wrists, conscious of the numbness in his own right hand, and the pain in his left palm. He helped the man into the backseat, closed the door behind him, and stood for a moment looking through the glass at him.

"Shiyaazh," the man said again. *"Baa*

yanisin." My son, I am ashamed.

Chee stood with his head bowed, the rain beating against his shoulders. He wiped the back of his hand across his wet face and licked his lips. The taste was salty.

Then he walked into the sagebrush, looking for the bottle. It would be needed as evidence.

3

THERE WAS NOTHING Lieutenant Joe Leaphorn dreaded more than this—this unpleasant business of pretending to help people he could not possibly help. But those involved today were a family in Emma's clan, his in-laws, people from Bitter Water clan. By the Navajos' extended definition of kinship, they were Emma's brothers and sisters. He'd rarely heard Emma speak of them but that was beside the point. It was beside the point, too, that Emma would never have asked him to interfere. Certainly not in this case, with one of their own policemen murdered. She would have tried to help them herself, though. Tried very quietly—and she would have been no less impotent than Leaphorn. But Emma was dead now and that left only him.

"We know he didn't kill that policeman," Mary Keeyani had said. "Not Ashie Pinto."

By the white man's way of reckoning kinship, the Keeyani woman was Ashie Pinto's niece. In fact, she was the daughter of Ashie's sister, which gave her among the Turning Mountain People the same status as a daughter. She was a small, bony woman dressed in her old-fashioned, traditional, going-to-town best. But the long-sleeved velvet blouse hung on her loosely, as if borrowed from fatter times, and she wore only a single bracelet of narrow silver and a squash blossom necklace which used very little turquoise. She sat stiffly upright in the blue plastic chair across from Leaphorn's desk, looking embarrassed and uncomfortable.

While Mary Keeyani explained her relationship to Ashie Pinto, and therefore to Hosteen Pinto's problem, in the proper fashion of a traditional Navajo, Louisa Bourebonette had not explained herself at all. She sat next to Mary Keeyani, looking determined.

"There is absolutely no doubt that this is all some sort of mistake," Louisa Bourebonette said in a slow, precise, slightly southern voice. "But we haven't had any success talking with the FBI. We tried to talk to someone at the Farmington office and then we went to Albuquerque. They simply won't discuss it. And we don't know who to get to look for evidence to prove he's innocent. We thought we could hire a private detective. We thought maybe you could recommend someone who would be reliable."

Louisa Bourebonette had given Leaphorn her card. He picked it up now and glanced at it again.

LOUISA BOUREBONETTE, PH.D.
ASSOCIATE PROFESSOR, AMERICAN STUDIES
NORTHERN ARIZONA UNIVERSITY
FLAGSTAFF, ARIZONA

This wasn't the information he wanted. He wanted to know how this trim, gray-haired, sharp-eyed woman was connected to the sorrowful business of Delbert Nez, a young man murdered and an old man destroyed. It was partly the wisdom Leaphorn had accumulated in a long life of police work that people have reasons for whatever they do—and the more effort required, the stronger the reason must be. Among Navajos, family is an overpowering reason. Bourebonette was not Navajo. What she was doing required a lot of effort. He put the card in his desk drawer.

"Have you talked to Hosteen Pinto's attorney?"

"She didn't seem to know much," Bourebonette said. She made a small, self-deprecatory face and shook her head. "Of course, they turned Mr. Pinto over to someone brand new in the job. She'd just moved in from Washington. Had just been hired. She told us the Federal Public Defender's office had two investigators who might be helpful. But . . ."

Professor Bourebonette let the sentence trail off, intending to let the skepticism in her tone finish it. Leaphorn sat silently behind his desk. He glanced at her. And away. Waiting.

Bourebonette shrugged. "But I got the impression that she didn't think they would be very helpful. I don't think she knew them well yet. In fact, she didn't give us much reason to believe that Mr. Pinto will be well represented."

Leaphorn knew one of the federal defender cops. A good, solid, hardworking Hispano named Felix Sanchez. He used to be with the El Paso police department and he knew how to collect information. But there wasn't much of anything Sanchez could do to help these women. And nothing Leaphorn could do, either. He could give them the names of private detectives in Farmington, or Flagstaff, or Albuquerque. White men. What could they do? What could anyone do? An old man had been turned mean by whiskey and had killed a policeman. Why waste what little money his family might have? Or this abrasive white woman's money. How did she fit into this?

"If you hire a private detective it's going to be expensive," Leaphorn said. "He would want some money in advance as a retainer. I'd guess at least five hundred dollars. And you'd be paying his expenses. Mileage, meals, motels, things like that. And so much an hour for his fee."

"How much?" Professor Bourebonette asked.

"I'm not sure. Maybe twenty-five, thirty dollars an hour."

Mrs. Keeyani sucked in her breath. She looked stricken. Dr. Bourebonette put a comforting hand on Mrs. Keeyani's arm.

"That's about what I'd expected," Professor Bourebonette said, in a stiff, unnatural-sounding voice. "We can pay it. Who would you recommend?"

"It would depend," Leaphorn said. "What do you—"

Professor Bourebonette interrupted him.

"One would expect, or should expect if she didn't know better, that you people would take care of this yourselves. That the family wouldn't have to hire someone to find out the facts in a murder case."

The anger left Leaphorn with nothing to say. So he said the obvious.

"In a case like this, a felony committed on a reservation, the jurisdiction . . ."

She held up her hand. "The Federal Bureau of Investigation has the jurisdiction. We know that. We've already been told, and we knew it already, being reasonably intelligent. But after all, one of your own men was killed." A trace of sarcasm crept into Bourebonette's tone. "Aren't you a little bit curious about who actually killed him?"

Leaphorn felt himself flushing. Surely this arrogant white woman didn't expect him to answer that. Not in the presence of the murderer's niece.

But the professor was waiting for an answer. Let her wait. Leaphorn waited himself. Finally he said: "Go on."

"Since you don't seem to be investigating, and since the Federal Bureau of Investigation is content to simply bring Ashie Pinto to trial without any effort to find the actual criminal, we hope you can at least give us some advice about who to hire. Somebody honest."

Leaphorn cleared his throat. He was trying to imagine this haughty woman in the beautifully finished office of the agent-in-charge at Albuquerque. Nothing but politeness and good manners there, he was sure.

"Yes," he said. "That's what we were discussing. And to give you that advice I must know some things. What do you have to tell this private detective? What can you give him to work on? Would it be leads he'd be following on the Reservation— around where Hosteen Pinto lived? Or around Shiprock and Red Rock where the—where it happened? In other words, what do you know that can help? What do you know that would help him find a witness, something to prove, for example, that Hosteen Pinto was somewhere else when this crime happened? What can you give him to give him a place to start looking?"

Leaphorn paused, thinking he shouldn't pull himself into this. It was not his case, not his business. Interfering was certain to cause offense in a department that wanted the death of a brother officer balanced with a conviction of his killer. He shouldn't open the door he was about to open. He should simply tell these women he couldn't help them. Which just happened to be the sad truth. Still, Mary Keeyani was Emma's kin. And, still, there were some unanswered questions in that Nez business—as much as he knew about it.

"As a matter of fact," he said, "if you have any useful information—any witnesses, anything that would lead to concrete evidence that the FBI wouldn't listen to—you can tell me. I'll see to it that the Bureau pays the proper attention. Anything you know."

"We know he didn't do it," Bourebonette said. But the anger was used up now. She attempted a small, wan smile. "All we can tell you is *why* we know he couldn't have killed the policeman, and that's nothing more concrete than telling you about the kind of man Ashie Pinto is. Always has been."

But he did kill a man, Leaphorn was thinking, *a long time ago. If I remember what I read in that report, he was convicted, years ago, went to prison for killing a man.*

"Are you a relative?" he asked Bourebonette.

"I am a friend," Bourebonette said.

Leaphorn looked at her over his glasses, waiting for more than that.

"For twenty-five years," she added. "At least."

"Ah," Leaphorn said.

Professor Bourebonette looked impatient, as if it probably wasn't worth her time to explain. But she decided to.

"My interest is in comparative mythology. The evolution of myth inside cultures. The evolution of myth as cultures meet and intermix. The relationship of a society's mythology with its economic base. Its environment. Mr. Pinto has been one of my informants. For years." She paused.

Leaphorn glanced at her. Was she finished? No. She was remembering.

"He wouldn't kill anyone," she added. "He has a great sense of humor. A great memory for the funny things. A great memory for everything." She looked into Leaphorn's eyes and said it slowly, as if he was the judge. As if he was the jury. Could whiskey not make a killer out of a funny man, just as it did of sad men and angry men?

"He has a great sense of humor," Bourebonette repeated.

It didn't prove anything, Leaphorn thought. But it was interesting. It was also interesting that she was telling him this. A long way to come, a lot of time used, a lot of money to be spent if she was serious about hiring an investigator. And a very flimsy explanation of why she was doing it.

And so Leaphorn had asked the Turning Mountain woman and the professor to wait. He called downstairs and asked for the file marked HOMICIDE; DELBERT NEZ.

He had been away when it happened, waiting in a motel room in Phoenix to be called as a witness in a case being tried on appeal in the federal court there. Even so, he remembered a lot of it. He had read about it every day in the Phoenix *Gazette* and the *Arizona Republic,* of course. He had called the Shiprock subagency station and talked to Captain Largo about it. The Navajo Tribal Police included only about 110 sworn officers, making the murder of any one of them not only memorable but close and personal. He had barely known Delbert Nez and remembered him as a small, quiet, neat young officer. But, like Leaphorn, Nez had worked out of the Window Rock office and Leaphorn had seen him often. Nez had been trying to grow a mustache. That was not an easy task for Navajos, with their lack of facial hair, and his sparse growth had provoked teasing and ribald jokes.

Leaphorn had known the arresting officer much better. Jim Chee. He had run across Chee several times on other investigations. An unusually bright young man. Clever. Some good qualities. But he had what might be a fatal flaw for a policeman. He was an individualist, following the rules if and when they agreed with him. On top of that, he was a romantic. He even wanted to be a medicine man. Leaphorn smiled at the idea. A Tribal Policeman-Shaman. The two professions were utterly incongruous.

Leaphorn found himself wondering if he had been Chee's first client. After a tough case, in the awful malaise that had followed Emma's death, he'd hired Chee to do a Blessing Way for him. An impulsive decision—unusual for him. He'd done it partly to give the young man a chance to try his hand as a shaman and partly as a gesture toward Emma's people. The Yazzies were Bitter Water clansmen and traditionalists. The ceremony would be sort of an unspoken apology for the hurt he must have caused them. He'd left Emma's mother's place on the second morning after they'd carried the body out into the canyon—unable to endure the full four days of silent withdrawal among her relatives that tradition required. It had been rude, and he'd regretted it. And so he had called Agnes and told her he'd hired a singer. He asked her to arrange the ceremony. She had gladly done it, not needing a reminder that his own clan, the Slow Talking Dinee, was now scattered and almost extinct, or that there was little left of his own family. He'd been uneasy around Agnes. Agnes had never married and, as Emma's sister, he would have been expected to marry her under the old tradition.

He glanced up at the two women waiting patiently across the desk and then looked back at the report. But he was thinking of Officer Chee, his hair tied in a knot at the back of his head arranging his equipment on the swept earthen floor of the Yazzie hogan. Chee had been nervous, showing Leaphorn where to sit with his back against the west wall of the hogan, spreading a small rug in front of him. Then Chee had extracted from his deerskin *jish* the little leather sack that was his Four Mountain bundle, two pairs of "talking prayersticks," a snuff can containing flint arrow points, and a half dozen pouches of pollen. He had solemnly formed the shape of footprints on the earth and marked on them with the pollen the symbols of the sunrays on which Leaphorn would walk. Beyond Chee, through the hogan doorway to the east he could see the rugged ramparts of the Carrizo Mountains reflecting the rosy twilight. He had smelled the piñon smoke from the cooking fires of Emma's kinfolks and of his own friends who had come to join him in this venture into the spirit world of his people.

At that moment he had wished desperately for a way to call it all off. He was a hypocrite. He did not believe that the ritual poetry that Officer Jim Chee would chant, or the dry paintings he would form on the hogan floor, would control the powers and force them to restore Joe Leaphorn to a life with "beauty all around him." The beauty had gone somewhere up in the canyon rocks with Emma's body. Gone forever. He wanted only to follow her.

But there had been no way out of it. And on the second dawn, after the long night of chanting, he had sucked in the four great ceremonial breaths of cold morning air feeling different than he had felt for weeks. It had not cured him, but it had started the healing. He could thank Shaman Jim Chee for that, he guessed. Or for part of it. But Officer Jim Chee was another matter. If Officer Chee had done his duty, Delbert Nez might still be alive.

"Shot high in the left chest," the report

said. "Apparently at very close range."

Leaphorn glanced up at Mary Keeyani and the professor. "Sorry I'm taking so long," he said.

"There is time enough," Mary Keeyani said.

Captain Largo had told him that Chee wanted to resign after the homicide. Getting Nez out of the car, Chee had been burned on both hands, one arm, one leg, and the chest. Largo had gone to the hospital at Farmington to see him. Largo was an old friend. He'd told Leaphorn about it.

"He didn't just offer to resign," Largo had told Leaphorn. "He insisted on it. He gave me his badge. Said he'd screwed up. That he should have gone to assist Nez when he knew Nez was in pursuit. And of course he should have gone."

"Why the devil didn't he go?" Leaphorn had asked. "The silly son-of-a-bitch. What was his excuse?"

"He didn't offer any excuses," Largo had said, his voice resenting Leaphorn's judgmental tone. "But I reminded him that his report showed Nez had been laughing. From what little he heard on the radio Nez wasn't taking it seriously. Like it was a joke. And I told him he couldn't resign anyway. He can't resign until we get Pinto tried."

Thinking of that conversation now as he turned the page in the report, Leaphorn remembered that Largo had some sort of vague clan kinship link with Officer Chee. At least he'd heard that. Navajo Tribal Police regulations prohibited nepotism in the chain of command. But the rules were just picked up from *biligaana* personnel regulations. The white rules didn't recognize clan connections.

The next sheet was the report of Sergeant Eldon George. When George arrived he had found Chee sprawled in the front seat of his vehicle, half-unconscious from shock. Pinto was asleep on the back seat, handcuffed. George had attempted to treat Chee's burns with his first aid kit. Another Navajo Police unit had arrived, and a San Juan County Sheriff's car, and a New Mexico State Police patrolman and then the ambulance that Chee had called to pick up Nez. Instead, it had taken Officer Chee. Pinto had been transported to the county jail at Aztec and booked on an assault charge—the toughest rap possible for a crime committed on federal trust land until the federals got involved and filed their felony homicide complaint.

Leaphorn glanced up at Mrs. Keeyani. She sat with her hands clenched in her lap, lower lip caught between her teeth, watching him.

"I must refresh my memory before I can tell you anything," he said.

Mrs. Keeyani nodded.

The next page reminded Leaphorn that Ashie Pinto had not made a statement. When apprehended, he had said, according to the report:

"Officer, I have done something shameful."

Sounded stilted. Leaphorn considered it. Pinto would have spoken to Chee in Navajo, probably. Chee, probably no better than half-conscious, would have passed along a translation to George. George had jotted it into his notebook, retyped it into his report. What had Pinto actually said?

According to the report, nothing else. He had admitted nothing, denied nothing, remained absolutely silent, refusing to answer any question except to confirm his identity with a nod, declining to call a lawyer, to name anyone who he might wish to be informed of his arrest. When asked to submit to the taking of a blood sample, "Subject Pinto was seen to nod in the affirmative."

The test showed a blood alcohol level of 0.211. The percentage of alcohol in the blood that made one formally and legally drunk in New Mexico was 0.10.

There followed the Federal Bureau of Investigation report dated eleven days following the arrest. Leaphorn scanned it. Ballistics confirmed that the bullet fired into the chest of Nez had come from the pistol confiscated from Pinto, a .38 caliber revolver. It confirmed that holes in Pinto's trousers were caused by burns. There was more, including the autopsy. Leaphorn knew what it said. Nez had been alive when the fire suffocated him. Probably unconscious, but alive. Leaphorn sighed, turned to the next page. It summarized a statement taken from Chee at the hospital. He scanned it quickly. Familiar stuff. But wait. He lingered on a paragraph. Reread it.

"Officer Chee said that for several weeks Nez had been interested in apprehending an unidentified subject who had been vandalizing and defacing a basaltic outcrop east of Red Rock and south of Ship Rock. Chee said he believed from what he heard on the radio that Nez had seen this person and expected to apprehend the subject. He said the radio signal was breaking up but that he heard Nez laughing and Nez did not appear to want a backup."

Leaphorn snorted, an angry sound and unintentionally loud. He glanced up to see if the women had noticed. They had.

He covered his embarrassment with a

question. "Did anyone tell you about the circumstances?"

"They said he was arrested out there where it happened," Mrs. Keeyani said. "They said he had the gun that killed that policeman."

"Did they tell you that he hasn't denied it?" Leaphorn asked. But he was thinking of Jim Chee. Irritated. Nez did not appear to want a backup. Whether he wanted one or not, the rules said Chee should be there. But that was Chee's reputation. He made his own rules. Smart. Unusually smart. But not a team player. So he was sitting in the trading post at Red Rock drinking coffee while Nez, alone, was dealing with a homicidal drunk armed with a pistol.

"I don't know what my uncle told them," Mary Keeyani said. She shook her head. "But I know he didn't do it. Not Hosteen Pinto. He wouldn't kill anybody."

Leaphorn waited, watching her face, giving her a chance to say more. She simply sat, looking down at her hands.

Finally she said: "A long, long time ago, before I was born. . . . He got in a fight then, when he was young, and a man was killed. But he was a wild boy then, and drunk. Now he is an old man. He doesn't drink now. Not for years."

It was not something to argue about.

Instead Leaphorn said, "He won't tell them anything at all. That's what I'm told. Not a word. Not even to his lawyer."

Mrs. Keeyani looked at her hands. "That wasn't his gun," she said. "My uncle had an old .22 rifle. A single-shot rifle. He still has that. It's in his hogan."

Leaphorn said nothing. This interested him. That pistol Pinto had was a Ruger, an expensive model and not what you would expect a man like Pinto to own. On the other hand, there could be a thousand explanations of why he did own it.

"Perhaps you didn't know about this pistol," Leaphorn said.

Now it was Mrs. Keeyani's turn to be surprised. "He is my mother's brother," she said. "He never got married. His place was there at our grandmother's place behind Yon Dot Mountain."

Leaphorn needed no more explanation. If Ashie Pinto had owned an expensive Ruger revolver, his relatives would have known it. He glanced back at the FBI report, looking for the name of the investigating officer. Agent Theodore Rostik. He'd never heard of Rostik, which meant he was a newcomer to the Gallup office—either fresh and green from the FBI Academy, or an older agent exiled as a lost cause. Up-and-comers in the agency were not sent to places like Farmington, or

Fargo, or Gallup, or other towns considered Siberian by the Bureau hierarchy. These were the billets for new men without political connections in the agency, or those who had fallen from grace—perhaps having caused bad publicity (the agency's mortal sin) or shown signs of original thinking. For Leaphorn the point was that Rostik might be unusually stupid, or unusually smart—either of which might cause his exile. But most likely he was simply green.

"I'll tell you what I think you should do," he said to Mrs. Keeyani without looking up from the report. "Hosteen Pinto has a lawyer who may be green but will be smart. The Federal Public Defender just hires the smart ones. Work with her. Tell her the strange things that trouble you. She will send out one of the investigators to learn the facts. I know one of them personally, a very good man. You should work with them."

Leaphorn read on, not looking up, waiting for a response. He heard Mrs. Keeyani shift in her chair. But the voice he heard was Dr. Bourebonette's. "Are they Navajos?" she asked. "Would they understand that Hosteen Pinto's family would certainly know if Hosteen Pinto owned that pistol?"

"Maybe not," Leaphorn said. He didn't

look up because he didn't want to show his resentment. Mrs. Keeyani he could tolerate. He respected her reason for being here—even though it wasted her time and his. Professor Bourebonette was another matter. But it was an astute question. "Probably they wouldn't understand that," he agreed.

He was looking for something in the report that would tell him how Ashie Pinto had gotten from his place behind Yon Dot Mountain to Navajo Route 33 south of Shiprock, New Mexico. Two hundred miles, more or less. Nothing in the report mentioned an abandoned car or pickup.

Dr. Bourebonette cleared her throat politely. "Does that report tell how Hosteen Pinto got over into New Mexico?"

"I was looking for that," Leaphorn said, glancing up at her. "Do you know?"

"Someone came and got him," she said.

"Who?"

Dr. Bourebonette glanced at Mary Keeyani.

"I don't know," Mary Keeyani said. "But I know somebody came and got him. I had gone over to the store at the Gap to get some kerosene for the light. And my husband, he was out with the sheep. Everybody was gone somewhere except my youngest daughter. She had come home on the school bus and she'd gone out to catch her horse and go help with the sheep and she saw dust from the car."

"It wasn't Pinto's car?"

Mrs. Keeyani laughed. "Hosteen Pinto's car broke a long time ago," she said. "The chickens sleep in it." Her amusement left as quickly as it had come. "She was up on the side of the hill with the horse and all she saw was the dust and maybe just a glimpse. It had come from Hosteen Pinto's shack. The road, it runs right by my mother's hogan and past our house and then out toward Twentynine Mile Canyon and connects up with the road to Cedar Ridge Trading Post. She said it might be a light-colored car, or maybe a pickup, or maybe it was just dusty."

"When was this?"

"It was the evening before Hosteen Pinto got arrested over in New Mexico."

Leaphorn flipped back through the report. He found nothing about any of this.

"Did a policeman come to talk to you?"

"A young white man," she said. "With those little spots on his face. And a Navajo to translate for him."

Freckles, Leaphorn thought. A culture unafflicted with freckles has no noun for them. "What did they want to know?"

"They asked about the pistol. They

asked about what Hosteen Pinto was doing over there. Where did Pinto get the pistol? Where did he get the two fifty-dollar bills he had in his pocket? Did Hosteen Pinto know Delbert Nez—the man they say he shot? They asked questions like they thought Hosteen Pinto was bootlegging wine. Like how did Hosteen Pinto act when he was drunk? Did he get into fights? How did he make a living? Was he a bootlegger?" Mrs. Keeyani had been looking down at her hands. Now she looked up. "They seemed to think for sure he was a bootlegger." She shook her head.

"How did you answer?"

"I said maybe the fifty-dollar bills were his fee. From the one who came and got him."

"Fee?"

"He had his crystals with him," Mrs. Keeyani said. "When he was younger he used to work finding things for people. When I was a little girl they would come from as far away as Tuba City, and even Kayenta and Leupp. He was pretty famous then."

"He was a crystal gazer," Leaphorn said. He leaned forward. If this man was working as a shaman, maybe there was more to this than just another senseless, sordid whiskey killing. "He still worked at it?"

"Not much." She thought about it. "Last year he found a horse for a man who works over at Copper Mine, and then he did a little work for a white man. And he would work with Dr. Bourebonette." She nodded at the professor. "That was about all I know about."

"What had the white man lost?"

"I think he was hunting old-time stories."

Leaphorn wasn't sure what she meant. He waited for an explanation. None came.

"Was Hosteen Pinto someone the anthropologists came to see to learn the old stories? Like Professor Bourebonette?"

"Yes. Many times in the old days. Not so much now. He learned most of them from Narbona Begay, I think. The brother of his mother."

"You think it was this white man looking for stories who came for him the day before the shooting?"

Mrs. Keeyani shook her head. "I don't know who it was. Maybe."

Or maybe not, Leaphorn thought. And how does it help anyway? His mind kept returning to Dr. Bourebonette's reason for being here. She knew the man, obviously. She said she liked him, had worked with him. But being here involved a lot of time and effort if you worked in Flagstaff. And she also seemed ready to pay for the expense of a private investigator.

"Are you still working with Hosteen Pinto?" he asked her. "I mean something current? Going on right now?"

She nodded. "We have been collaborating on a book," she said.

"About mythology?"

"About the evolution of witchcraft beliefs," she said. "Ashie Pinto had noticed it himself. How the stories had changed since his boyhood. He went to Albuquerque with me and we listened to the tapes. . . ." She paused. Decided this needed explanation. "The oral history tapes in the University of New Mexico collection. Interviews with elderly Navajos. And not just Navajos. With the other Native American cultures and the Spanish-American old people. Tapes that were made back in the thirties and forties that were recording memories that go way back into the 1880s. And if you allow secondhand, second-person memories—what we call grandfather stories—some of the memories went back before the Long Walk. We'd listen to these and look at the transcripts and that would refresh Hosteen Pinto's memories of the tales he had been told."

Dr. Bourebonette had an austere face. The only expressions Leaphorn had identified in it were skepticism, anger, and determination—the face of a woman used to getting her way who doubted she would get it from him. Now Bourebonette's face had changed. As she talked of this book there was animation and enthusiasm.

Leaphorn decided he might know what motivated Dr. Bourebonette.

". . . It's remarkable," she was saying. "What Hosteen Pinto can remember. How well he commands the little nuances of those old stories. The differences in attitudes of the teller toward the witch, for example. The shift in importance if the variation came from outside the Navajo culture. For example, from the Zuni sorcery tradition. Or the Hopi 'two-heart' legends, or—" Dr. Bourebonette stopped, midphrase. She looked embarrassed.

"You were still working with Hosteen Pinto? You hadn't finished?"

"More or less. I was to pick him up later that week. The week it happened. In fact that's how I found out he was arrested. I had read about the crime, but they hadn't released Hosteen Pinto's name. So I went out to his place and Mrs. Keeyani told me he was in jail."

In jail, Leaphorn thought. Unavailable to answer professorial questions. A book put on hold. Perhaps never to be finished.

Professor Bourebonette's motivations seemed much less mysterious.

"Can the book be finished without him?" Leaphorn asked. His voice was as neutral as he could make it. But Professor Bourebonette read him exactly. Her sharp blue eyes stared into his. "Of course," she said. But she nodded, conceding his point and accepting the accusation. "But it might not be as solid a work."

Leaphorn looked away from her, back at the report, impressed with her astuteness and feeling slightly guilty. If he told Emma of this exchange, as he would have, she would have clucked her tongue, disapproving of his conduct. He turned the page, looking for the answer to the obvious question these women had posed. How had the old man gotten from the west side of the Reservation to Ship Rock country? At least he could try to find that out for them.

"It was mostly his book," Professor Bourebonette said, as if to herself.

Leaphorn glanced up, directly into her eyes. And saw what? Anger? Disappointment?

He flipped through the remaining pages. The question that seemed so obvious to him and his visitors had not seemed so intriguing to Agent Rostik. It simply wasn't dealt with. Well, perhaps there was some simple, irrelevant answer.

He had intended to ignore the Manila envelope of photographs in the back of the folder. They weren't the sort of images he'd want to share with these women. But now he was curious. He slid the stack out on his desk.

Nez's body beside the burned car. More burned car, with Chee's fire extinguisher lying beside it. The pistol, shiny and new looking. A half-dozen shots of the locale taken in daylight, with the tortured, ugly shape of a basaltic outcrop rising in the background over the grassy ridge, a liquor bottle, a pocketknife, odds and ends that the police photographer, or the officer running the investigation, thought might be relevant.

Relevant. Leaphorn picked up the photograph of the bottle. A typical Scotch bottle—nothing to distinguish it from most any other, except the cost. He put on his glasses and examined the label.

DEWARS WHITE LABEL

He turned over the photograph. The label on the back confirmed that this was the bottle Ashie Pinto was carrying when apprehended by Officer Chee. "One quart capacity," the notation added, "approx. five sixth empty."

Scotch. Expensive Scotch.

"Mrs. Keeyani," Leaphorn said. "Do you know what Hosteen Pinto likes to drink? Wine? Whiskey?"

Mrs. Keeyani's face said she resented the question. "He doesn't drink," she said.

"He had been drinking that night," Leaphorn said. "Alcohol was in his blood."

"He used to drink," Mrs. Keeyani said. "Just now and then. He'd say if he took one little spoonful he just couldn't stop. For a long time, he wouldn't drink, and then somebody would have to go into Flagstaff or Winslow or some place and bring him home from jail. And then he wouldn't drink any more for a long time. For months. But finally four-five years ago, he did it again, and he got sick in the jail at Flag. Had to go to the hospital and the doctor said it would kill him. And after that—" She paused, shook her head. "No more drinking after that."

"But when he drank, what did he drink?"

Mrs. Keeyani shrugged. "Wine," she said. "Anything. Whatever was cheap."

"How about Scotch?"

Mrs. Keeyani looked puzzled. "Is it sweet?"

"No. It's very strong and expensive, but not sweet. Why?" Leaphorn asked.

Mrs. Keeyani smiled, remembering. "My uncle had a sweet tooth," she said.

"We used to call him Sugarman. Anything sweet, he loved it. If she saw Hosteen Pinto's pickup coming, my mother would say, hurry up children, hide that cake I baked. Hide the candy. Hide the sugar sack. Here comes my brother the Sugarman." She chuckled at the memory. Then, not wanting her mother misjudged, added, "She'd give him a piece of cake."

"But you don't know if he drank Scotch?"

"If it was sweet, he drank it. If it was cheap."

Leaphorn glanced at the photograph of the bottle. The Scotch that came in that was definitely not cheap.

Leaphorn sighed. After a lifetime in police work, he understood himself well enough to know he wouldn't tolerate this apparent violation of the natural order. He had been curious about how Pinto came to be two hundred miles away from home with no way of getting there, or getting back. But that could be explained by hitch-hiking. He could think of no such easy explanation for this bottle of Dewars Scotch. Or two fifty-dollar bills. Or how he got that pistol.

Leaphorn stood.

"Ladies," he said, "I will see what I can find out."

4

JIM CHEE CAME slouching out of the Burn Doctor's examining room at the University of New Mexico Hospital Burn and Trauma Center feeling distinctly down. Predictions concerning his hand had been ambiguous. Then he noticed the woman sitting against the wall in the waiting room. Something about her reminded him of Janet Pete. She was immersed in a *Newsweek,* her sleek, dark hair visible above the cover and her very nice legs neatly crossed. He stared. She turned the page of the magazine, giving him a look at more than her forehead.

Depression vanished, replaced by delight. It *was* Janet Pete.

"Hey," Chee said. "Janet. What are you doing here?"

"I was waiting for you," Janet Pete said, grinning at him. "I wanted to see how you look toasted."

"Not much improvement," Chee said, displaying the bandage on his hand. He used his good arm to hug her.

Janet hugged back, hard against Chee's damaged chest.

"Aaagh!"

Janet recoiled. "Oh. I'm sorry."

"Just a play for sympathy," Chee said, breathing hard.

"I didn't notice the bandages under your shirt," Janet said, repentant.

"One on my leg, too," Chee said, tapping his thigh and grinning at her. "The doctor said that altogether if you average it out, I was somewhere between medium rare and medium."

"I just heard about it," she said. "It happened just when I was moving. Back in Washington, they have so much local homegrown homicide that one way out here doesn't make the paper. Not even if it's a policeman."

"I'd heard you'd come back home," Chee said. "Or almost home. I was going to hunt you up when I got all these bandages off." He was looking down at her, conscious that he was smiling like an ape, conscious that the receptionist was watching all this, conscious that Janet Pete had come to see him. "But how did you find me here?"

"I called your office in Shiprock. They told me you were on sick leave. And the dispatcher asked around for me and found out you'd come to the burn center here for a checkup." She touched the bandage with a tentative finger. "Is it better? Are you going to be all right?"

"Mostly just scars. Except for this hand. They think it will be all right, too. Probably. Or close enough so I can use it. But let's get out of here. You have time for coffee?"

Janet Pete had time.

Walking from the university hospital, across the campus to the Frontier Restaurant, Janet touched gently on the death of Nez and deduced that Chee wasn't ready to talk about it. Chee touched on Janet's coming home from her law-firm job in Washington, and sensed this was a subject better returned to later. And so as they walked through the mild Albuquerque morning, they skipped further back in time and reminisced.

"Remember that day we met?" Janet said. "At the San Juan County jail. You were trying to keep my client locked up without charging him with anything. And I was being righteously indignant about it. Remember that?" She was laughing.

"I remember how I outsmarted you," Chee said.

"Like hell you did," Janet said. She stopped laughing. She stopped walking. "How? What do you mean?"

Chee looked back at her, grinning.

"What do you mean?" Janet demanded.

"Remember, you were getting your man out of lockup, and you had gotten his sack of stuff from the booking desk, and you got sore at me, thinking I was trying to worm some incriminating information out of him in the interrogation room. So when you went to call the FBI to complain about my conduct and get me called off, you took your client to the telephone with you."

Janet was frowning. "I remember that," she said. "The agent-in-charge said you didn't have FBI authorization to talk to the man. What was his name?"

"Bisti," Chee said. "Roosevelt Bisti."

"Yes," Janet said. "I remember he was sick. And I remember the fed said he wanted to talk to you and he told you to butt out. Didn't he? So how did you outsmart me, wise guy?"

"When you went to the phone you took along Bisti, but you left his sack behind."

Janet digested this. She walked toward him, shaking her head.

"You searched through his stuff," she said, accusingly. "Is that what you're telling me? That's not outslicking me. That's cheating."

They were walking again, Chee still grinning. His hand hurt a little, and so did the burn on his chest, but he was enjoying this. He was happy.

"Whose rules?" he asked. "You're a lawyer so you have to play by the *biligaana* rules. But you didn't ask me what rules I was using."

Janet laughed. "Okay, Jim," she said. "Anyway, I got Old Man Bisti out of jail and out of your unfair clutches."

"You enjoyed that job, didn't you? I mean your work out on the Big Rez? Why don't you go back to it? They're shorthanded. I'll bet you could get your job back in a minute."

"I am going back to it."

"With the DNA?" Chee's delight was in his voice. The Dinebeiina Nahiilna be Agaditahe was the Navajo Tribe's version of a legal aid society—providing legal counsel for those who couldn't afford to pay. He'd be seeing Janet Pete a lot.

"Same sort of work but not the DNA," she said. "I'll be working for the Department of Justice. With the Federal Public Defender here in Albuquerque. I'll be one of the court-appointed defense attorneys in federal criminal cases."

"Oh," Chee said. His quick mind formed two conclusions. Janet Pete, being Navajo and being the most junior lawyer on the staff, would have been given Ashie Pinto to represent. From that conclusion, the second was instantaneous and took the joy from the morning. Janet Pete had come to see Officer Jim Chee, not Friend Jim Chee.

"I went to school here, you know," Chee said, simply to have something to say, to cover his disappointment.

They were walking under the sycamores that shaded the great brick expanse of the central mall. A squadron of teenaged skateboarders thundered past. Janet Pete glanced at him, curious about the change of subject and the sudden silence which had preceded it.

"After four years," she said, "a campus starts to feel like home."

"Seven for me," Chee said. "You go a couple of semesters and then run out of money, and come back again when you've stacked some up again. That's the average here, I think. About seven years to get a bachelor's degree. But it never started to feel like home."

"It was different at Stanford," Janet said. "People either had money or they had the big scholarships. You lived around the campus, so you got acquainted, made friends. It's more a community, I guess." She glanced at him again. "What's wrong?"

"Nothing. Everything's fine."

"Your mood changed. A cloud over the sun."

"I shifted from the social mode into strictly business," Chee said.

"Oh?" Puzzlement in her voice.

"You're representing Ashie Pinto. Right?" The tone was a little bleaker than he'd intended.

They walked past the Student Union without an answer to that, toward the fountain formed of a great slab of natural stone. Chee remembered the local legend that the university architect, lacking funds for an intended sculpture, had scrounged the monolithic sheets of rough marble from a quarry and arranged them in something that might suggest Stonehenge, or raw nature, or whatever your imagination allowed. It worked beautifully and usually it lifted Chee's spirits.

"I came to see you because I like you," Janet Pete said. "If you weren't my friend, which you happen to be, I would have come looking for you because you're the arresting officer and it's my job."

Chee thought about that.

"So I had two reasons," she said. "Is that one too many reasons for you?"

"What did I say?" Chee asked. "I didn't say anything."

"Hell you didn't. Then why am I feeling like I'm on the defensive?" Janet said. "And not exactly knowing why." She hurried a little faster. "Boy," she said. "Boy, I can see why that white girl of yours went back to Wisconsin."

Chee caught up with her.

"What was her name? Mary?"

"Mary Landon," Chee said. "Look, I'm sorry. I know how it is. Somebody has to represent Pinto and naturally it would be you. So what do you want to know?"

Janet Pete, still walking fast, was out of the trees now, angling across the parking lot past Popejoy Hall. Chee followed her out under a morning sky that was dark blue and sunny—with just enough of those puffy forenoon clouds to suggest autumn was not too far along to produce afternoon thunderheads.

"FBI's not cooperating, huh?" Chee

said. "What do you want to know?"

"Nothing," Janet said.

"Come on, Janet. I said I was sorry."

"Well," she said. And then she laughed up at him, squeezed his arm.

"I can be as touchy as you are," she said. "I can be a real bitch." She laughed again. "But notice how neatly I put you in the wrong. Did you appreciate that?"

"Not much," Chee said. "Is that something you learn in law school?"

"It's something you learn from your mother."

Jim Chee's taste for coffee had been brutalized by years of drinking the version he used to make for himself in his trailer under the cottonwood trees at Shiprock— recently he'd taken to using little filter things that fit over his cups. The Frontier coffee tasted fresh but weak. Over a second refill they decided that he would cash in his return ticket on the Mesa Airlines flight and ride back to Shiprock with Janet Pete. Tomorrow he'd show her the scene of the crime. By tomorrow, he thought, he would feel like talking about it.

"Did you know Hosteen Pinto still won't say anything about what happened?" Janet asked. "He'll talk to me about other things but not about the crime. He just shuts up."

"What's there to say?"

"Well, everything. Whether he did it, for one thing. Why he did it, if he did. What he was doing out there. Did you know he's a shaman, a crystal gazer? He finds things for people. That seems to be his only income. That and getting fees as an informant. From scholars, I mean. He's sort of an authority on old stories, legends, what happened when. So the history professors, and the mythologists, and the sociologists, and that sort of people are always having him remember things on tape for them. He has a car, but it doesn't run, so how did he get there? I mean where he was when you arrested him. What was he doing about two hundred miles from home? That's what I want him to tell me. And if he did it, why. Everything."

"He did it because he was drunk," Chee said. "Nez picked him up to get him out of the rain, tried to put him in the backseat of the patrol car, and Pinto got sore about it."

"That seems to be the official 'theory of the crime.' I know that's what the U.S. attorney is going to trial with," Janet said.

"And that seems to be pretty much what went on," Chee said.

"But why didn't Nez take that pistol away from him? You guys have a sort of standard procedure for things like that, don't you? For handling drunks?"

Chee had wondered about that himself. "He wasn't arresting him," he said. "We take drunks in for their own protection. So they don't freeze. Or drown." As Janet Pete knew very well.

She sipped her coffee. Her dark eyes looked skeptical over the rim.

"He didn't take the pistol because he didn't see the pistol," Chee added. "The old man had it stuck in his belt, behind him."

Janet sipped. "Come on," she said. "Gimme a break. Isn't that sort of a usual place to stick a pistol?"

Chee shrugged.

"So how did Pinto get there?" she asked.

"I don't know. Maybe the guy in the white car brought him," Chee said. "You've seen the FBI report, haven't you? What did they say?"

Janet had put her cup down. "White car? What white car?"

"When I was driving down from Red Rock, I met a white—anyway a light-colored vehicle. It was raining and getting dark. But I think I recognized it. It's an old banged-up Jeepster that one of the teachers at Shiprock drives. What'd they say about that in the report?"

"They didn't mention it," Janet said. "All news to me."

"They didn't run that down?" Chee said. He shook his head. "I can't believe it."

"I can," Janet said. "You gave them all they needed. Their suspect, arrested at the scene of the crime, holding the murder weapon. All that's missing is the motive. Being drunk takes care of that. He doesn't even deny he did it. So why waste time and complicate things by digging out all the facts?" The question sounded bitter.

"How about that fancy bottle he was carrying? Does the report show where that came from?"

"Nothing. I didn't know it was fancy."

"Like something you'd give a fancy drinker for Christmas. If you wanted to impress him. It wasn't what a drunk would be buying."

Janet finished her coffee, put down the cup, looked at him for a while.

"You know, Jim, you don't have to do any of this. I know how you must feel. And I'm having trouble separating friend from lawyer when . . ."

He held up his right palm, interrupting her.

"When I think I'm hearing a lawyer, I'll shut up," he said. The thing about Janet Pete was that he could talk to her about things that were hard to talk about. She wasn't Mary Landon. No soft, pale hair, no bottomless blue eyes, no talent for making him feel like the ultimate male. But by tomorrow, he thought, he could talk to her about listening to Delbert Nez laughing on the radio. He could talk to her about how the dreadful feeling grew as he sat over his coffee at the Red Rock Trading Post, and waited, and waited, and waited. He could tell her how long it had taken him to sense that he had made an unforgivable, irredeemable mistake. She would understand why, when Ashie Pinto was convicted, he would resign from the tribal police and find some job that he was fitted for. She would understand why he had to see the old drunk convicted. He hadn't done his job. He hadn't kept Delbert Nez alive. But at least he had arrested his killer. Done one thing right.

She'd have to defend the old man, get him a light sentence—or perhaps some sort of an insanity plea bargain that would put him in a hospital for a while. He had no problem with that. It didn't matter to him if the old man was punished. That would do no possible good.

But he needed Janet Pete to understand that a verdict finding Pinto innocent would make Jim Chee doubly guilty.

5

JOE LEAPHORN STOOD at the door of Ashie Pinto's house reexamining his understanding of what the law allowed in a criminal investigation. He was sure that only the most genial judge would tolerate what was going on here. It would be labeled as a search without a warrant, perhaps as downright breaking and entering. However, Mary Keeyani and Louisa Bourebonette had not been impressed with such niceties, nor with Leaphorn's uneasiness.

"I thought we were just going to check around out here," Leaphorn had said. "Ask some questions. See if anyone had seen anything. We don't have any legal right to break into the suspect's house."

"He's my uncle," Mary Keeyani had said. She was using the tire tool from Professor Bourebonette's car, prying at the padlock hasp that secured Ashie Pinto's door.

"It's not as if we were actually breaking in," Bourebonette said. "We're here for his own benefit."

Joe Leaphorn wasn't exactly sure why he was here. Partly curiosity, partly some irrational sense of responsibility to Emma's clan sister—sort of a family gesture to soothe his conscience. Certainly he had no reason to be here that would sound either plausible or professional if this meddling into a federal homicide case caused any complications. True, that seemed extremely unlikely. But he stood aside as Mary Keeyani opened the violated door. The women filed in past him.

"He keeps his papers in a tin box," Mary Keeyani said. "It's in here somewhere if I can find it."

Leaphorn left the women to their questionable task. He walked across the hard-packed earth behind Pinto's house and inspected Pinto's truck. It was a 1970-vintage Ford short-bed pickup with the left front tire flat, the left rear critically low, the glass missing from the driver's-side window, and chicken manure on the seat. He released the hood catch and raised it. The battery was missing—the first thing taken on the back side of the Reservation when a truck gets too worn out to fix. Obviously, Ashie Pinto hadn't driven this truck for a long, long time.

He closed the hood and walked down the slope through the snakeweed to Pinto's outhouse. The raw planks used to build it a lifetime ago had shrunk and warped. Through the gaping cracks Leaphorn admired Pinto's view while he urinated—a grand expanse of tan-silver grass and black-silver sage sloping down Blue Moon Bench toward the cliffs of the Colorado River Canyon. On the way back to the house he made another stop at the hogan that adjoined it. It was round and windowless, built of stone, its tarpaper roof insulated with a layer of earth. Leaphorn pulled open the board door and peered into the darkness. He saw an iron cot, boxes, an old icebox apparently used for storage, nothing that looked interesting.

Nor was there anything interesting under Ashie Pinto's brush arbor—just an old bridle hanging from a crossbar, the bit rusted, the leather stiff and cracked. Leaphorn took it down, looked at it, hung it back where he'd found it, yawned. A wasted day, he thought. The only useful thing Leaphorn could think of that might be found here was something that would tell them how Pinto got from here on the western fringe of the Big Reservation over to Ship Rock territory. Probably at least two hundred miles. Someone with a vehicle must have taken him. Logically they would have sent word they were coming. Probably mailed to Pinto at the Short Mountain Trading Post. Possibly, as Mary Keeyani believed, this letter would have been saved in Pinto's repository of documents.

"When you just get maybe one letter a year—or maybe just eight or ten your whole life—then probably you save them," Mary Keeyani had explained. True enough. He walked back to the house.

In Leaphorn's experience, men who lived alone tended to be either totally sloppy or totally neat—one extreme or the other. Ashie Pinto was neat. From his vantage point leaning against the doorjamb, Leaphorn could see everything in the living room–bedroom of Pinto's two-room house. The bedstead stood on the cracked and worn linoleum, a blue-and-white J. C. Penney blanket folded across it; beside the single window, a three-drawer chest, beside the chest an armchair, the upholstery of its back and seat water-stained; a metal-and-Formica table, two wooden chairs; a tall cabinet with double doors which, since the room had no closet, must hold Pinto's spare clothing. There was nothing on the table, nothing on the chairs, nothing on the bed, but the top of the chest held a cigar box; a framed photograph which seemed, from Leaphorn's viewpoint, to be of Pinto himself; a large wash basin of white ceramic; and something flat, black, and metallic.

Mary Keeyani was looking through the drawers of the chest and Professor Bourebonette was making clattering noises in the kitchen.

"A tin box?" she said. "Square or round?"

"Round," Mary Keeyani said. "I think a fruitcake came in it. Maybe cookies."

Leaphorn struggled with his sense of official decorum on one hand and his curiosity on the other. What was that atop the chest? He reached a compromise.

"Mrs. Keeyani. What's that black thing on top of the chest there? Beside the cigar box."

"It's a tape recorder," Mrs. Keeyani said. She retrieved it, came to the door, and handed it to him with a plastic sack containing five cassettes. "My uncle did a lot of that. Taping stuff for those *biligaana* he worked for."

Professor Bourebonette appeared in the kitchen door. She displayed a round tin can with a cluster of red roses decorating the lid.

"That's it," Mary Keeyani said.

The tape recorder was of the bulky, heavy sort sold about twenty years ago. It contained a cassette. Leaphorn pushed the play button. He heard the faint sound of friction recorders make when running over blank tape. He pushed Stop, and Rewind, waited for the reversing process to stop and pushed Play again.

The speaker produced an old man's voice, speaking in Navajo.

"They say Coyote is funny, some of those people say that. But the old people who told me the stories, they didn't think Coyote was funny. Coyote was always causing trouble. He was mean. He caused hardship. He hurt people. He caused people to die. That's the way the stories go that I was told by my uncles when I was a boy. These uncles, they say . . ."

Professor Bourebonette was standing beside him. Leaphorn pushed the stop button, looked up at her.

"He was doing that for me," she said. "I asked him for that story. I wonder how far he got."

"Ashie Pinto? For your book?"

"Not really. He told me he knew the original correct version of one of the Coyote myths. The one about the red-winged blackbirds and the game they play with their eyeballs. Throwing them up in the air and catching them, and Coyote forcing them to teach him the game." She glanced at Leaphorn, quizzical. "You know the story?"

"I've heard it," Leaphorn said. He looked at the tin she was holding. "Are you going to open Mr. Pinto's box?"

Bourebonette read into Leaphorn's tone some hint of disapproval. She looked at the box and at Leaphorn and said, "I'll just give it to Mary. She's his niece."

Mary Keeyani had no qualms. She worked off the lid. Inside Leaphorn could see a jumble of papers: envelopes, receipts, what seemed to be a car title, odds and ends. She put it on the table where she and Bourebonette sorted through it.

"Here's a letter from me," Bourebonette said, extracting an envelope. "And another one." She glanced at Leaphorn. "That's all of them. We didn't do much business by mail."

Mary Keeyani stopped sorting. "Here's all he has in here for this year," she said. She displayed two envelopes. "No use going back any further than that." She extracted a single sheet of notepaper from one envelope, read it, slipped it back into the envelope, and dropped it back into the box. She repeated the process, put the lid on the box, and stood, looking disappointed.

"Nothing helpful?" Bourebonette said.

Nothing helpful, Mrs. Keeyani had agreed. Nothing that would tell them who had driven out here over this awful rocky track and hauled an old man across the Reservation to commit a murder. Leaphorn drove carefully over that rocky track now, sorting out his reaction to this. It was what he had expected, or should have, and yet he felt disappointed. Why? He hadn't thought a search through Pinto's documents, if he had any, would be revealing. But if you give luck a chance, sometimes it rewards you.

His real hope was in finding a witness. The FBI seemed to have decided its case was made and hadn't looked for one. And strange vehicles came so rarely down these tracks—which were really little more than miles and miles of shared driveways—that people remembered them. A visit from a stranger to anyone on your side of the mountain was exciting. But, unfortunately, Ashie Pinto's place, even though it was four miles from the road, was the first place on this track. Mary Keeyani's outfit, where he was about to park now, occupied a little cluster of shacks with a shared hogan, out of sight more than a mile down the slope. It was only by chance that one of the children out with the sheep had noticed the dust raised by the vehicle that took Pinto away. There had been no one else to see it.

Leaphorn stifled a yawn. It was almost sundown. A long day. He was tired. He had driven more than two hundred and fifty miles, and two hundred and fifty miles with two strange women is more exhausting than that distance in the relaxing solitude to which he was accustomed. And before he was done with this day, he had to drive another four hours back to Window Rock. A day wasted. Nothing accomplished. Well, almost nothing. He stopped the car beside Mrs. Keeyani's house, a weathered mobile home set on concrete blocks. At least, he would get rid of this sense of family responsibility—and get rid of these two women—when he wrapped this up.

So wrap it up.

"Mrs. Keeyani," he said, "who all had Hosteen Pinto worked with? I mean in recent years. Besides Dr. Bourebonette."

Mrs. Keeyani was sitting beside him, getting her stuff together.

"He used to work with a man from Tucson. Somebody named Dr. Drabner. But not this year, I think. And then there was an old professor from the University of Utah. I don't remember his name but he spoke pretty good Navajo."

"I think that was a Dr. Justin Milovich," Bourebonette said. "He was into linguistics."

"Milovich," Mrs. Keeyani said. She climbed out of the car, where three dogs greeted her with much tail wagging, jumping, and rowdy enthusiasm. "That was him."

"Anyone else? That's it?"

"Nobody else I knew of."

"How about that history professor from the University of New Mexico?" Bourebonette said. "Tagert. How about Tagert? Hosteen Pinto used to work with him a lot."

"Not no more he don't," Mary Keeyani said.

Her tone and her face raised a question and Professor Bourebonette asked it. "Something happened?"

"He would give my uncle whiskey."

"Oh," Bourebonette said. "The son-of-a-bitch." She turned to Leaphorn. "When he drinks he just about kills himself."

Or someone else, Leaphorn thought.

"I told that man not to ever give my uncle any whiskey but he did it anyway," Mary Keeyani said. "So when the last time he wrote my uncle a letter about working for him, when my uncle brought it to me, I wouldn't even read it for him. I just tore it up. And I made my uncle promise not to work for him any more."

"When was that?" Leaphorn asked.

"Last year. Way last spring a year ago."

"When was the last time he heard from Milovich or Drabner? Can you remember?"

"Long time for Milovich," she said. "Drabner, I think it was last winter. Maybe even last fall. It was that letter in the box."

They were back on U.S. 89, Bourebonette and he, rolling southward toward the Tuba City junction, when the turnoff to Short Mountain reminded Leaphorn of Old Man McGinnis and his Short Mountain Trading Post.

He slowed, looked at Bourebonette. "I'm thinking of that bottle of whiskey Ashie Pinto had. The bottle he had when

Chee arrested him. Remember what Mary Keeyani said about that New Mexico historian giving him booze?"

"I thought about that, too," she said. "Maybe Pinto picked up his mail himself, and there was a letter from Dr. Tagert and Ashie didn't let Mary see it. Maybe he got somebody else to read it for him and help him answer it."

"Exactly," Leaphorn said, pleased with her. "Maybe not, too. But didn't the Pintos do their trading at Short Mountain?"

"That was his mailing address."

"Let's go check."

The road from Highway 89 to Short Mountain Trading Post was a little better than Leaphorn remembered it from his days as a patrolman working out of Tuba City. It had been improved by gravel and grading from terrible to fairly bad. Leaphorn maneuvered the patrol car back and forth across its washboard surface, avoiding the worst of the bumps such roads develop. It was twilight when they dropped down into Short Mountain Wash and parked on the hard-packed earth that formed the trading post yard.

It was empty. Leaphorn parked near the porch, turned off the ignition and sat. He had brought Emma here once, long ago, to see this place and to meet Old John

McGinnis. He'd described McGinnis as he'd known him, honorable in his way but notoriously grouchy, pessimistic, perverse, quick with insults and overflowing with windy stories and gossip. Over the front door nailed to the porch beam a faded sign proclaimed:

THIS ESTABLISHMENT FOR SALE
INQUIRE WITHIN

The sign had been there at least fifty years. According to local legend, McGinnis had hung it there within weeks after he'd bought the store from the Mormon who'd established it. The legend had it that young McGinnis had been outsmarted in the deal. Those who knew him found that incredible.

"He's rude," he'd told Emma. "No manners at all and he may snap at you. But look him over. I'd like to know what you think of him."

So, of course, McGinnis had been courtly, charming, full of smiles and compliments, showing Emma the best of his pawn goods and his collection of lance points, pots, and assorted artifacts—perverse as always. Emma had been charmed.

"I don't see why you say those bad

things about him," she'd said. "He's a good man."

As always when it came to judging people, Emma was correct. In his prickly, eccentric way, John McGinnis was a good man.

Leaphorn was aware that Professor Bourebonette had glanced at him and glanced away. He supposed she was wondering why he was just sitting here. But she said nothing, and made no move to open her door. Willing to wait, sensing the value of this moment to him. He found himself favorably impressed with the woman. But then this sort of sensitivity would be something one in her profession would polish—part of their technique for establishing rapport with those they need to use. How long would her formula cause her to wait?

Cold evening air settling into Short Mountain Wash pushed a breeze across the yard, moving a tumbleweed languidly toward the porch. A water barrel stopped it. The buildings here had looked tired and decrepit the first time he'd seen the place. In the red light of the sunset they looked worse. A plaster-and-stone building behind the main post had been partially burned and left unrepaired, the shed where hay was stored leaned to the left.

Even the porch seemed to have sagged under the weight of age and loneliness.

Now a naked light bulb hanging over the trading post door went on, a feeble yellow glow in the twilight.

"Well," Leaphorn said. "He's ready to receive a customer. Let's go talk to him."

"I only met him once," Bourebonette said. "He helped me find some people. I remember he seemed fairly old."

"He knew my grandfather," Leaphorn said. "Or so he claims."

Bourebonette looked at him. "You sound skeptical."

Leaphorn laughed, shook his head. "Oh, I guess he really did know him. But with McGinnis—" He laughed again.

The front door opened and McGinnis stood in it, looking out at them.

"After closing time," he said. "What you want?"

He was smaller than Leaphorn remembered—a white-haired, bent old man in faded blue overalls. But he identified Leaphorn as soon as he climbed out of the car.

"Be damned," McGinnis said. "Here comes the Sherlock Holmes of the Navajo Tribal Police. And I betcha I can guess what brought him out here to the poor side of the Reservation."

"Yaa' eh t'eeh," Leaphorn said, "I think you know Dr. Bourebonette here."

"Why, yes indeed I do," McGinnis said. To Leaphorn's amazement, he made something like a bow. "And it's good to see you back again, Ma'am. Can you come on in and have something to drink? Or maybe join me at my supper. It's only some stew but there's plenty of it."

Professor Bourebonette was smiling broadly. "Mr. McGinnis," she said, "I hope you got my letter, thanking you for your help." She held out her hand.

McGinnis took it, awkwardly, his face expressing an emotion Leaphorn had never seen there before. Shyness? Embarrassment? "I got it," McGinnis said. "Wasn't necessary. But much appreciated."

He ushered them through the gloomy dimness of his store toward his living quarters in the back. Not much stock, Leaphorn noticed. Some shelves were bare. The case where McGinnis had always kept his pawn goods locked behind glass held only a scattering of concha belts, rugs, and the turquoise and silver jewelry by which the Navajos traditionally measured and preserved their meager surplus. There was a sense of winding down in the store. Leaphorn felt the same sensation when he stepped through the doorway into the big stone-walled room where McGinnis lived.

"You want to talk about Hosteen Pinto," McGinnis said. "What I know about him." McGinnis had removed a pile of *National Geographic*s from a faded red plush chair for Bourebonette, motioned Leaphorn toward his plastic-covered sofa, and lowered himself into his rocking chair. "Well, I don't know why he killed that policeman of yours. Funny thing for him to do." McGinnis shook his head at the thought of it. "They say he was drunk, and I've seen him drunk a time or two. He was a mean drunk. Cranky. But no meaner than most. And he told me he'd quit that drinking. Wonder what he had to burn up that officer for. What did he say about that?"

Leaphorn noticed that Professor Bourebonette looked surprised and impressed. He was neither. McGinnis was shrewd. And why else would Leaphorn be coming here to talk to him? Now McGinnis was pouring water from a five-gallon can into his coffeepot. He struck a match to light his butane stove and put the pot on it.

"I understand he won't talk about it," Leaphorn said.

McGinnis stopped adjusting the flame. He straightened and looked at Leaphorn.

He looked surprised. "Won't say why he did it?"

"Or whether he did it. Or didn't do it. He just won't talk about it at all."

"Well, now," McGinnis said. "That makes it interesting." He sorted through the odds and ends stacked on a shelf above the stove, extracted two cups and dusted them. "Won't talk," McGinnis said. "And old Ashie was always a forthcoming man."

"That's what the FBI report says. He won't admit it, won't deny it, won't discuss it," Leaphorn said. Professor Bourebonette stirred in her chair.

"What was he doing way over there anyhow?" asked McGinnis. "Didn't his folks know? Mary Keeyani keeps a close eye on him. He don't get away with much that she don't know about."

"Mary doesn't know," Bourebonette said. "Somebody came and got him. Must have been that."

"But Mary don't know who?" McGinnis chuckled. "I know who then. Or, I'll bet I do."

"Who?" Leaphorn said. He tried to make it sound casual, resisted the impulse to lean forward. He remembered how McGinnis loved to drag things out and the more you wanted it, the longer he made you wait.

"If it was somebody he was working for, that is," McGinnis said. "He'd been working for Professor Bourebonette here—" he nodded toward her "—and for somebody from the University of New Mexico. I think his name was Tagert. And for a couple of others off and on. People who wanted his folk tales like the professor, or wanted to put down some of his memories."

McGinnis stopped, tested the side of the coffeepot for temperature with the back of his finger and looked at Leaphorn. Waiting.

"Which one was it?"

McGinnis ignored Leaphorn's question. "You sure Mary didn't know?" he asked Bourebonette.

"Absolutely sure."

"Had to be Tagert then." He waited again.

"Why Tagert?" Leaphorn asked.

"Tagert used to give him whiskey. Mary found out about it. She wouldn't let him work for Tagert any more."

Leaphorn considered this. It fit with what Mrs. Keeyani had said. And it made a certain amount of sense, even though the way McGinnis told it, it seemed nothing more than a guess. But McGinnis knew more than he'd told. Leaphorn was sure of that. He was also tired, with hours of driving ahead of him. He didn't want to sit here while McGinnis amused himself.

"Did you write a letter for him? For Hosteen Pinto?"

McGinnis tested the coffeepot again, found the heat adequate, filled one cup, handed it to Professor Bourebonette.

"If you like sugar in it, I can get you that. I'm all out of milk unless I have some condensed out in the store."

"This is fine," she said. "Thank you."

"You known Lieutenant Leaphorn long? If I might ask such a question."

"You may. We met just this morning."

"Notice how he gets right to the point. That's unusual in a Navajo. Usually they're more polite about it." McGinnis glanced at Leaphorn. "We got plenty of time."

"Pinto got a letter from Tagert here," Leaphorn said. "He happened to pick it up himself, didn't he? You read it to him and then you answered it for him. That about right?"

McGinnis poured Leaphorn's coffee into a mug that bore the legend JUSTIN BOOTS. It reminded Leaphorn that the boots Emma had bought him for his birthday after they were married were Justins. They couldn't afford them then. But he'd worn them almost twenty years. Emma. The sure knowledge that he would never see her again sat suddenly on his shoulders, as it sometimes did. He closed his eyes.

When he opened them, McGinnis was holding the mug out to him, expression quizzical.

Leaphorn took it, nodded.

"You had it about right," McGinnis said. "He was in the store when the mail came, as I remember it. Tagert wanted to interview him about something. He wanted to know if he could come and get him on some date or other. He asked Ashie to let him know if that date was all right or to name another if it wasn't."

"Anything else?" Leaphorn asked. He sipped the coffee. Even by the relaxed standards of the Window Rock Tribal Police headquarters it was bad coffee. Made this morning, Leaphorn guessed, and reheated all day.

"Just a short letter," McGinnis said. "That was it."

"What was the date?"

"I don't remember. Would have been early in August."

"And Pinto agreed?"

"Yeah," McGinnis said. He frowned, remembering—the plump, round face Leaphorn remembered from a decade ago shrunken now into a wilderness of lines and creases. Then he shrugged. "Anyway, the upshot was he asked me to write Tagert back and tell him he'd be ready in the afternoon."

Professor Bourebonette, either politer or more starved for caffeine than Leaphorn, was sipping her coffee with no apparent distaste. She put down the cup.

"So now we know how he got to Shiprock," she said. "Tagert came and got him."

But Leaphorn was studying McGinnis. "Pinto said something about it, or something like that? He didn't just immediately say write him back?"

"I'm trying to remember," McGinnis said, impatiently. "I'm trying to get it all back in my mind. We was in this room, I remember that much. Ashie's getting too damn old to amount to much but I've known him for years and when he comes in we usually come back here for a talk. Find out what's going on over by the river, you know."

He rocked forward in his chair, got up clumsily. He opened the cabinet above the stove and extracted a bottle. Old Crow.

"The lieutenant here don't drink," McGinnis said to Professor Bourebonette.

He glanced at Leaphorn. "Unless he's changed his ways. But I will offer you a sip of bourbon."

"And I will accept it," the professor said. She handed McGinnis her empty coffee cup and he poured the whiskey into it. Then he fumbled at the countertop, came up with a Coca-Cola glass and filled it carefully up to the trademark by the label. That done, he sat again, put the bottle on the floor beside him, and rocked.

"I didn't offer Hosteen Pinto a drink. I remember that. Wouldn't be the thing to do, him being alcoholic. But I poured myself one, and sat here and sipped at it." McGinnis sipped his bourbon, thinking.

"I read the letter to him and he said something strong." McGinnis examined his memory. "Strong. I think he called Tagert a coyote, and that's about as strong as a Navajo will get. And at first he wasn't going to work for him. I remember that. Then he said something like Tagert paid good. And that's what had brought him in here in the first place. Money. You notice that belt out in the pawn case?"

McGinnis pushed himself out of the rocker and disappeared through the doorway into the store.

Leaphorn looked at Bourebonette. "I'll tell the FBI about Tagert," he said.

"You think they'll do anything?"

"They should," he said. But maybe they wouldn't. Why would they? Their case was already made. And what difference did it make anyway?

McGinnis reappeared carrying a concha belt. The overhead light reflected dimly off the tarnished silver.

"This was always old Pinto's fallback piece. The last thing he pawned when he was running low." McGinnis's gnarled hand stroked the silver disks. "It's a dandy."

He handed it to Professor Bourebonette.

Leaphorn could see it was indeed a dandy. An old, heavy one made of the turn-of-the-century silver Mexican five-peso pieces. Worth maybe two thousand dollars from a collector. Worth maybe four hundred in pawn credit.

"Trouble is he'd already pawned it," McGinnis said. "Not only pawned it. He'd been in twice to bump up the loan. He wanted another fifty dollars in groceries on it and we was jawing about that when the mail truck came up."

McGinnis was rocking while he remembered, holding the Coca-Cola glass in left hand, tilting it back and forth in compensation for the rocking motion. Exactly as he'd seen him do it when Leaphorn was twenty years younger, coming in here to learn where families had moved, to collect gossip, just to talk. Leaphorn felt a dizzying sense of dislocation in time. Everything was the same. As if twenty years hadn't ticked away. The cluttered old room, the musty smell, the yellow light, the old man grown older, as if in the blink of an eye. Suddenly he knew just what McGinnis would do next, and McGinnis did it.

He leaned, picked up the Old Crow bottle by the neck, and carefully recharged his glass, dripping the last of the recharge until it was exactly up to the trademark.

"I've seen Pinto poor before. Many times. But that day he was totally tapped out. Said he was out of coffee and cornmeal and lard and just about everything and Mary wasn't in any shape to help him with her own bunch to feed."

McGinnis fell silent, rocking, tasting the whiskey on his tongue.

"So he took the job," Professor Bourebonette said.

"So he did," McGinnis said. "Had me write Tagert right back." He took another tiny sip, and savored it in a silence that made the creaking of his rocker seem loud.

A question hung in Leaphorn's mind: *Why had Pinto called Tagert a coyote?* It was a hard, hard insult among the Navajos—implying not just bad conduct but the evil of malice. Mary Keeyani said Tagert had given him whiskey. Would that be the reason? Leaphorn noticed his interest in this affair growing.

"But I know he didn't want to," McGinnis added. "I said, What's wrong with this fella? He looks all right to me. He pays you good money, don't he? He's just another one of them professors. And old Ashie said Tagert wants me to do something I don't want to do. And I said what's that, and he said he wants me to find something for him. And I said well hell, you do that all the time, and he was quiet a while. And then he said, you don't have to go looking for Coyote. Coyote's always out there waiting."

Professor Bourebonette had offered to share driving on the way home and Leaphorn had explained to her that Tribal Police rules prohibited it. Now, about fifty miles east of Tuba City, Leaphorn began wishing he hadn't. He was exhausted. Talking had helped keep sleep at bay for the first hour or so. They talked about McGinnis, about what Tagert might have wanted Hosteen Pinto to find, about Pinto's reluctance. They discussed how Navajo mythology related to the origin story of the Old Testament, and to myths of the Plains Indians, and police techniques in criminal investigations, and civil rights, and academic politics. She had told him about the work she had done studying mythology in Cambodia, Thailand, and Vietnam, before the intensifying war made it impossible. And now Leaphorn was talking about his days as a graduate student at Arizona State, and specifically about a professor who was either weirdly absent-minded or over the hill into senility.

"Trouble is, I'm beginning to notice I'm forgetting things myself," he concluded.

The center stripe had become double, waving off in two directions. Leaphorn shook his head, jarring himself awake. He glanced at Bourebonette to see if she'd noticed.

Professor Bourebonette's chin was tilted slightly forward, her head leaned against the door. Her face was relaxed in sleep.

Leaphorn studied her. Emma had slept like that sometimes on late night returns. Relaxed. Trusting him.

6

THE BATTERED white Jeepster proved remarkably easy to locate. It sat in space number seventeen in a weedy parking lot guarded by a sign that declared:

SHIPROCK HIGH SCHOOL
TEACHER/STAFF PARKING ONLY

Janet Pete parked her little Toyota two-door beside the jeep. She'd changed out of her go-see-a-sick-friend skirt into jeans and a long-sleeved blue shirt.

"There it is. Exactly as you planned," she said. "You want to wait here for the owner?" She motioned to the cars streaming out of the teacher/staff parking lot, a surprising number it seemed to Chee. "It shouldn't be long."

"I want to know who I'm talking to," Chee said, climbing out. "I'll go ask."

The secretary in the principal's office looked at Jim Chee's badge, and through the window to where he was pointing, and said "Which one?" and then said, "Oh."

"That's Mr. Ji's," she said. "Are you going to arrest him?" Her voice sounded hopeful.

"Gee," Chee said. "How does he spell it?"

"It's H-U-A-N J-I," she said, "so I guess if you pronounced it the way we pronounce 'na-va-*ho*' it would be 'Mr. Hee.' "

"I heard he was a Vietnamese. Or Cambodian," Chee said.

"Vietnamese," the secretary said. "I think he was a colonel in their army. He commanded a Ranger battalion."

"Where could I find him?"

"His algebra class is down in room nineteen," she said, gesturing down the hallway. "School's over but he usually keeps part of them overtime." She laughed. "Mr. Ji and the kids have a permanent disagreement over how much math they are going to learn."

Chee paused at the open door of room nineteen. Four boys and a girl were scattered at desks, heads down, working on notebooks. The girl was pretty, her hair cut unusually short for a young Navajo woman. The boys were two Navajos, a burly, sulky-looking white, and a slender Hispano. But Chee's interest was in the teacher.

Mr. Huan Ji stood beside his desk, his back to the class and his profile to Chee, staring out the classroom window. He was a small man, and thin, rigidly erect, with short-cropped black hair and a short-cropped mustache showing gray. He wore gray slacks, a blue jacket, and a white shirt with a tie neatly in place and looked, therefore, totally misplaced in Shiprock High School. His unblinking eyes studied something about level with the horizon. Seeing what? Chee wondered. He would be looking across the tops of the cottonwoods lining the San Juan and southwestward toward the sagebrush foothills of the Chuskas. He would be seeing the towering black shape of Ship Rock on the horizon, and perhaps Rol-Hai Rock, and Mitten Rock. No. Those landmarks would be beyond the horizon from Mr. Ji's viewpoint at the window. Chee was creating them by looking into his own memory.

Mr. Ji's expression seemed sad. What was Huan Ji seeing in his own memory? Perhaps he was converting the gray-blue desert mountains of Dinetah into the wet green mountains of his homeland.

Chee cleared his throat.

"Mr. Ji," he said.

Five students looked up from their work, staring at Chee. Mr. Ji's gaze out the window didn't waver.

Chee stepped into the classroom. "Mr. Ji," he said.

Mr. Ji jerked around, his expression startled.

"Ah," he said. "I'm sorry. I was thinking of something else."

"I wonder when I might talk to you," Chee said. "Just for a moment."

"We're about finished here," Ji said. He looked at the five students, who looked back at him. He looked at his watch. "You can go now," he said. "If you have finished, give me your papers. If not, bring them in tomorrow—finished and corrected." He turned to Chee. "You are a parent?"

"No sir," Chee said. "I'm Officer Chee. With the Navajo Tribal Police." As he said it, he was conscious of Mr. Ji noticing the thick bandage on his hand, his denims, his short-sleeved sport shirt. "Off duty," he added.

"Ah," Mr. Ji said. "What can I tell you?"

Chee heard hurrying footsteps—Janet Pete coming down the hallway toward them. Hosteen Pinto would be legally represented in this conversation, he thought. Well, why not? But it bothered him. Where does friend end and lawyer start?

"Mr. Ji?" Janet asked, slightly breathless.

"This is Janet Pete," Chee said. "An attorney."

Mr. Ji bowed slightly. If Mr. Ji ever allowed confusion to show, it would have shown now. "Is this about one of my students?" he said.

The last of Mr. Ji's students hurried past them, the urge to be away overcoming curiosity.

"Miss Pete represents Ashie Pinto," Chee said.

It seemed to Jim Chee that Mr. Ji momentarily stopped breathing. He looked at Janet Pete, his face showing no emotion at all.

"Is there a place we could talk?" Chee asked.

Someone was in the teachers' lounge. They walked out to where Janet's Toyota was parked.

"Is this your car?" Chee pointed to the Jeepster.

"Yes," Ji said.

"It was seen out on Navajo 33 the night Officer Delbert Nez was killed."

Ji said nothing. Chee waited.

Ji's face was blank. (The inscrutable Oriental. Where had Chee heard that? Mary Landon had used it once to describe him. "You are, you know. You guys came over the icecap from the steppes of Mongolia or Tibet or someplace like that. We came out of the dark forests of Norway.")

"What was the date?" Ji asked.

Chee told him. "That was the night of the rain. Good hard rain. It would have been between seven-thirty and eight. But getting dark because the storm was coming."

"Yes," Ji said. "I remember it. I was there."

"Did you see anyone? Anything?" Janet Pete asked.

"Where?" Ji asked.

Chee suppressed a frown. It seemed a stupid question.

"Where you were. Out beyond Ship Rock," he said. "East of Red Rock on Route 33."

"I don't remember seeing anything," Ji said.

"How about after you turned north on Route 63?"

"Route 63?" Ji looked genuinely puzzled. Not too surprising. Not many people, including those who routinely drove that dusty, bumpy route, would know its map number.

"The gravel road close to Red Rock that goes north toward Biklabito and Shiprock."

"Oh," Ji said, nodding. "No. I saw nothing. Not that I remember."

"You didn't see the fire, Nez's car burning?"

"I think I saw a glow. I thought it was the lights of a car. I really don't remember much about that now."

"Do you remember what you were doing out there?"

Ji smiled and nodded. "I remember that," he said. "It looked like it might rain. Rain clouds back over the mountains. It rains a lot in my country and I miss it out here. I thought I would drive out and enjoy it."

"How did you go?" Chee asked.

Ji thought. "I drove south on U.S. 666 toward Gallup, and then I turned west on that paved road over to Red Rock, and then circled back on the gravel road."

"Did you see a Tribal Police car?"

"Ah, yes," Ji said. "One passed me."

"Where?"

"On the Red Rock road."

That would have been Delbert's Unit 44. "Did you see it again?"

"No."

"You would have passed it," Chee said. "It had pulled off the left side of the road and driven down a dirt track."

"I didn't notice it," Ji said. "I think I would have remembered that."

"Did you meet anyone, I mean on your way home?"

Mr. Ji thought about it. "Probably," he said. "But I don't remember."

And that was exactly all they learned.

From the parking lot, they drove southward down 666, across the San Juan bridge.

"You want to go see where it happened?" he asked Janet.

She looked at him, surprised. "Do you?"

"Not exactly," he said. "But yes, I guess I do."

"You haven't been back?"

"I was in the hospital in Albuquerque for weeks," Chee said. "And then, I don't know, there just wasn't any reason."

"Okay," Janet said. "I think I should see it."

"You have a better reason than I do," Chee said. "I've got nothing to do with it anymore. It's FBI business. I'll just testify as the arresting officer."

Janet nodded. She saw no reason to comment on any of this. Chee knew she already knew it.

"I didn't do any of the investigating," he added, knowing she would have known that, too.

"Do you think the FBI took a statement from Mr. Ji?"

Chee shook his head. "He would have mentioned it."

"Doesn't it surprise you that they didn't?"

He shook his head. "Not now. Remember? You explained it to me. They have all they need for a conviction. Why waste their time?"

She was frowning. "I know I said that. But they'd seen your statement. They knew you'd met that car driving away from the scene. You described it as a white Jeepster, said who owned it. I'd think just simple curiosity . . ." She let it trail off.

"They had their man, and their evidence," Chee said. "Why make things complicated?"

Janet thought about that. "Justice," she said.

Chee let it pass. Justice, he thought, wasn't a concept that fit very well in this affair. Besides, the sun was just dipping behind the Chuskas now. On the vast, rolling prairie that led away from the highway toward the black shape of Ship Rock every clump of sagebrush, every juniper, every snakeweed, every hummock of bunch grass cast its long blue shadow—an infinity of lines of darkness undulating across the glowing landscape. Beautiful. Chee's spirit lifted. No time to think of justice. Or of the duty he had left undone.

Janet's Toyota topped the long climb out of the San Juan Basin and earth sloped away to the south—empty, rolling gray-tan grassland with the black line of the highway receding toward the horizon like the mark of a ruling pen. Miles to the south, the sun reflected from the windshield of a northbound vehicle, a blink of brightness. Ship Rock rose like an oversized, free-form Gothic cathedral just to their right, miles away but looking close. Ten miles ahead Table Mesa sailed through its sea of buffalo grass, reminding Chee of the ultimate aircraft carrier. Across the highway from it, slanting sunlight illuminated the ragged black form of Barber Peak, a volcanic throat to geologists, a meeting place for witches in local lore.

They did the right turn off 666 onto Navajo 33, driving into the setting sun.

"Here's probably about where he was

when we first made radio contact," Chee said. "Just about here." His voice sounded stiff in his own ears.

Janet nodded.

He slowed, pointing. "I was way over there, twenty-five, thirty miles behind Ship Rock, driving south on the road from Biklabito. I was back there behind the rock. Something like that screws up radio communication. It keeps fading in and out."

Chee cleared his throat. He pulled down the sunshade. Janet flipped down the one on the driver's side, found she was too short to be helped by it, and fished out her sunglasses. She was thinking that Chee wasn't as ready to talk about this as he'd thought he was.

"Going to be quite a sunset," she said. "Look north."

North, over Sleeping Ute Mountain in Colorado, over Utah's Abajo Mountains, great thunderheads were reaching toward their evening climax. Their tops, reflecting in the direct sun, were snowy white and the long streamers of ice crystals blown from them seemed to glitter. But at lower levels the light that struck them had been filtered through the clouds over the Chuskas and turned into shades of rose, pink, and red. Lower still, the failing light mottled them from pale blue-gray to the deepest blue. Overhead, the streaks of high-level cirrus clouds were being ignited by the sunset. They drove through a fiery twilight.

"There's where it happened," Chee said, nodding to the left. "He pulled off the pavement right up there, and the car was burning over by that cluster of junipers, way off there."

Janet nodded. Chee noticed her forehead, her cheeks rosy in the reflected light. Skin as smooth as silk. Her eyes were intense, staring at something. An intelligent face. A classy face. She frowned.

"What's that over on those rocks?" She gestured. "Those white marks up in that formation over there?"

"That's what was bothering Delbert," Chee said, and made a chuckling sound. "That's the artwork of our phantom vandal. Delbert noticed somebody had been painting those formations maybe six weeks ago. He wanted to catch the guy."

"It bothered him? I don't guess there's a law against it. Nothing specific anyway," she said. "But it bothers me too. Why ugly up something natural?"

"With Nez, I think it was a mixture of being bothered and thinking it was sort of weird. Who would climb up in there and waste all that time and paint turning black basalt into white? Anyway, Delbert was always talking about it. And that night, it sounded like he thought he'd seen the guy. He was laughing about it."

"Maybe he did see him," Janet said. She was staring out at the formation. "What caused all that? I know it must be volcanic but it doesn't look like the normal ones. Frankly, they don't teach you anything about geology in law school."

"In anthropology departments either," Chee said. "But from what I've been told, the volcanic action that formed Ship Rock lasted for tens of thousands of years. The pressure formed a lot of cracking in the earth's surface, and every thousand years or so—or maybe it's millions of years—there would be another bubbling up of melted rock and new ridges would form. Sometimes right beside the old ones."

"Oh," Janet said.

"These run for miles and miles," Chee said. "Sort of parallel the Chuska Mountains."

"Is there a name for them?"

Chee told her.

She made a wry face. "My parents wanted me to speak perfect English. They didn't talk Navajo much around me."

"It means something like 'Long Black

Ridges.' Something like that." He glanced at Janet, not knowing where she stood on the issue of Navajo witchcraft. "Lot of traditional Navajos wouldn't want to go around those lava formations—especially at night. According to Navajo mythology, at least on the east side of the Reservation, those lava flows are the dried blood of the monsters killed by the Hero Twins. I think that's one of the things that got Nez so interested. You know. Who was breaking that taboo?"

"Maybe Nez caught whoever it was, and the guy killed him," Janet said.

"And gave the pistol to Hosteen Pinto," Chee said. "You're going to have trouble selling that one."

Janet shrugged. "It's as good as anything else I've thought of," she said. "Let's take a look at it." She glanced at Chee, looking suddenly doubtful. "Or would there be a lot of snakes this time of year?"

"Always some snakes in places like that," Chee said. "But they're no problem if you use your head."

"Just thinking about snakes is a problem," Janet said. But she turned the Toyota off the asphalt.

Getting to part of the formation where the painter worked involved maneuvering the little Toyota across about a mile of trackless stone, cactus, Russian thistle, buffalo grass, sage, and snakeweed. After dropping a wheel with a rattling jolt into a little wash, Janet switched off the ignition.

"It's easier to walk," she said. "Especially easier on my poor car."

It wasn't quite as easy as it looked. As with all large objects seen through the thin, dry, high desert air, the outcrop was bigger and more distant than it seemed. The sun had dipped well below the horizon when they climbed the steep final slope toward its base. Overhead the high clouds had faded from rose to dark red. Far to the west across Arizona, clouds over the Kaibito Plateau were blue-black, outlined by fiery yellow.

Janet stopped to stare.

"Did you miss these sunsets in Washington?" Chee asked.

"I'm looking at that car," she said, pointing.

Pulled behind a clump of junipers was a dark green Ford Bronco II, dirty, dented, and several years old. They detoured to walk behind it. It wore a New Mexico vanity license plate.

"REDDNEK," Janet read. "You think the irony was intended?"

Chee shrugged. He didn't catch the

irony. The vehicle was empty. What was it doing here? Where was the driver?

"A redneck who can't spell it," she explained.

"Oh."

On the ridge beyond the vehicle, Janet stopped again. She stood, head tilted back, staring up at the massive, unbroken slab of basalt which confronted them here.

"I don't see any sign of paint," Janet said. The red light changed the color of her shirt, and her faded jeans, and her face. Her hair was disheveled, her expression intent, and, taken all together, she looked absolutely beautiful to Jim Chee. It would be a lot better, he thought, if friends didn't look like that.

"Let's see if we can find where he climbed up," he said.

That wasn't easy. The first upward possibility dead-ended on a shelf that led absolutely nowhere except up a vertical face of stone. The second, a pathway that opened inside a split in a basaltic slab, took them perhaps seventy-five yards upward and in before it finally dwindled away into an impossibly narrow crack. They found the third atop a sloping hump of debris by ducking under a tilted roof of fallen stone.

"I haven't brought up the subject of

snakes," Janet said. She was brushing the dirt from her hands on her pant legs. "If I do, I hope you'll try to say something positive."

"Okay," Chee said. He thought for a minute, catching his breath. "If you like snakes, this is a fine example of the places you come to find them."

"I don't like snakes," Janet said. "I know all that BS about Navajos and snakes being friends, but I don't like them. They scare me."

"We're not supposed to be friends," Chee said. "The way it goes in the legend, First Man and Big Snake learned to respect one another. The way you do that is by not putting your hand, or your foot, or any other part of you where you can't see. That way you don't step on your little brother, or sit on him, or poke him in the eye. And in return, he buzzes his rattlers to tell you if you're getting in dangerous territory. Very efficient."

"I still don't like them," Janet said, but she was staring up into the formation. "Look. I think that's paint."

It was. Above them and to their left, Chee could see a face of the basalt cliff reflecting white. Reaching it involved climbing up a deep crack into a long, narrow pocket. But eons of erosion had filled it with enough fallen rocks and blown dust to form a floor. There Chee leaned against the stone, breathing hard, the bottom level of the paint just above his head.

"Look here," Janet said. She was kneeling on the dirt. "Can you believe this? I think somebody carried a ladder in here."

If Janet was breathing hard it didn't show. But Chee was, and was embarrassed by it. It was being out of shape, he thought. Too long in the hospital bed. Too many weeks without exercise. Climbing with one hand in a bandage hadn't been easy. He would have to get back into doing some exercises.

He took a long, deep breath and squatted beside her. Two narrow, rectangular shapes had been pressed into the earth, the proper distance apart to have been made by the feet of a ladder.

"A determined painter," Janet said. "With a plan, obviously. Why else haul a ladder way up in here? He had to know he was going to be reaching up somewhere where he'd need it."

Chee was examining the holes the ladder had left. He was wishing they'd climbed in here when the light was better.

"I think that's interesting," Janet said.

He stood and brushed off his jeans with his good hand, wondering if Nez actually caught the son-of-a-bitch. Did Nez chase him? Did he even know Nez was after him?

"Did this crazy rock painter kill Nez?" Janet asked.

"Ashie Pinto shot Nez in the chest," Chee said. "But did this nutty rock painter have anything to do with it? Did he see it happen?"

"He seems nutty all right," Janet said. She had climbed halfway out of the pocket and was staring up into the broken, slanted wilderness of slabs, crags, boulders, and cliffs of the upthrust. "You can see several painted places back in there. One big squarish place, and a narrow vertical strip and some other small places."

Chee climbed up beside her.

"If he saw it happen, and I can find him, then you could just plead Pinto guilty," Chee said. "No use letting it go to trial. Just make a deal for him."

Janet let it pass, staring up into the formation. "Odd," she said.

"It doesn't seem to form any pattern," Chee agreed. "Or communicate anything or make any sense." With his knife, he scraped at the painted stone where they were standing, collecting a sample from the lower edge of the brush mark. Then he bent close, examining it in the dimming red glow of the twilight.

"He's sending some sort of signal to flying saucers," Janet said. "Or when the Mesa airliner comes over here flying down to Gallup, this says 'YOU'RE LOST' to the pilot. Or the guy who is doing it, they lost his luggage and when you look down from the airplane this is some sort of awful obscene insult."

"Look at this," Chee said.

Janet bent closer. "What?"

"It washed down a little," Chee said, indicating the flow with his finger.

"So?"

"So I think the paint was fresh when it started raining. He was still painting when the rain began."

"Ah," Janet Pete said. "So maybe there was a witness. Maybe..." Her voice trailed off, turning squeaky. She shrank away from the slab where she had been leaning, away from a buzzing sound.

"Jim," she whispered. "Don't tell me that's what I think it is."

"Only if you don't think it's a rattlesnake," Chee said. "Move back toward me. It's under the edge of that slab. See it?"

Janet made no effort to see it. "Let's go," she said. And went, and it was still light enough to see that the old green Bronco II was no longer parked behind the junipers.

She rolled the Toyota to a halt under the cottonwood tree that shaded Jim Chee's home—a well-scuffed and dented aluminum trailer parked on the low north bluff of the San Juan River. Chee made no move to get out. He was waiting for her to turn off the ignition. She left the motor running and the headlights on.

"The only other time I was here you had a pregnant cat," she said. "Remember that? It seems like a long time ago."

"I didn't have a cat," Chee said. "It was just hanging out here."

"You were looking out after it." She grinned at him. "Remember? You were afraid a coyote was going to get it. And I thought about getting one of those cases they ship animals in on airplanes to use as a cat house. Coyote-proof. And you bought one in Farmington. What happened?"

"You moved away," Chee said. "You followed your boyfriend to Washington and joined his law firm and got rich and came home again."

"I meant what happened to the cat," Janet said.

"I couldn't deal with the cat," Chee said. "It was a *biligaana* cat. Ran away from some tourists I guess. And I thought maybe it could become a natural Navajo Reservation–type cat and live on its own. But it wasn't working."

"But what happened?"

"I put it in the shipping case and sent it to Mary Landon," Chee said.

"Your white schoolteacher," Janet said.

"White schoolteacher, but not mine," Chee said. "She moved back to Wisconsin. Going to graduate school."

"Not yours anymore?"

"I guess maybe she never was."

They sat in the Toyota considering this, listening to the engine run.

Janet looked at him. "You all right now?"

"More or less," Chee said. "I guess so."

They considered that.

"How about you?" Chee said. "How about your ambitious lawyer? I don't remember his name. How about your own ambitions?"

"He's back in Washington. Getting rich, I guess. And here I am, trying to defend a destitute drunk who won't even tell me he didn't do it."

Chee, who had been listening very, very carefully, heard nothing much in her voice. Just a flat statement.

"You're all right now? Is that the message you're sending me?"

"We don't write," she said, voice still flat. "I guess so. Except it leaves you feeling stupid. And used. And confused."

"I'll make some coffee," Chee said.

No response. Janet Pete merely looked out the windshield, as if she was seeing something in the darkness under the cottonwoods.

"Maybe somebody told you about my coffee," Chee said. "But I don't boil it anymore. Now I've got some of these things where you put a little container on top of the cup, and coffee grounds in the container, and pour boiling water through. It's much better."

Janet Pete laughed and turned off the ignition.

The coffee was, in fact, excellent. Hot and fresh. She was tired and she sipped it gratefully, surveying Jim Chee's narrow quarters. Neat, she noticed. That surprised her. Everything in place. She glanced at his bed—a blanket-covered cot suspended from the wall. Monastic was the word for it. And above it, a shelf overflowing with books. She recognized Joseph Campbell's *The Power of Myth*, Buchanan's *A Shining Season*, Momaday's *The Way to Rainy Mountain*, and Zolbrod's *Dine Bahane*, which had seemed to her to be the best translation of the

Navajos' origin story. Odd that Chee would be reading a white man's version of the Navajo Bible.

"You still planning to be a medicine man?" she asked.

"Someday," Chee said. "If I live long enough."

She put down her cup. "It's been a long day," she said. "I don't think I learned much useful. I don't think I answered any questions about Ashie Pinto. Like how he got there. Or why. Or who killed Officer Nez."

"That's the only one I can answer," Chee said. "Your client did it. I don't know why. Neither does he, exactly. But the reason was rooted in whiskey. The Dark Water. That's what the Navajo word for it means in English."

Janet let all that pass. "How about you?" she asked. "You think we solved any mysteries?"

Chee was leaning against the stove, holding his cup clumsily in his left hand. He sipped. "I think we added a new one. Why Mr. Ji lied to us."

"How?"

"He said he didn't meet anyone on the way home. He must have seen me coming toward him, just as he was turning off Route 33 onto the gravel."

"Maybe he forgot," Janet said. "It's been weeks."

"I had my siren going and my cop lights blinking."

Janet considered that. "Oh," she said. "You'd think he'd remember that."

"He would have just driven past a fire. A big one not far off the road. Then here comes a cop car, siren going. This isn't Chicago. Nothing much happens out here. He would have remembered."

She frowned. "So what does it mean— that he was pretending he was there when he actually wasn't? Or pretending he didn't see your patrol car? That wouldn't make sense. Or, maybe somebody else was driving his car and he was covering for them. Or . . . what?" She rubbed the back of her hand across her forehead, picked up the cup again and drained it. "I'm too damn tired to think about it," she said. "And I've got to go. Got to drive down to Window Rock tonight."

"That's too far," Chee said. "Two hard hours. Just stay here." He paused, gestured. "I'll roll my sleeping bag out on the floor."

They looked at each other. Janet sighed.

"Thanks," she said. "But Emily's expecting me."

Emily. Chee vaguely remembered the name. Someone Janet had shared an apartment with when she worked in Window Rock.

He stood in the doorway watching the Toyota on its climb back up to the road, then sat on the bunk and removed his shoes. He was tired, but the coffee would keep him awake. He unbuttoned his shirt and slipped it off over the bandage, yawning.

Three new questions added today, he thought. Not just why Mr. Ji had lied. There was also the methodical insanity of the painter to puzzle over. And most important of all, there was Janet Pete.

7

THE VOICE OF ASHIE PINTO had an odd sort of singsong quality through the earphones Jim Chee was wearing. It rose and fell, recounting the time in myth when Changing Woman had her second menstrual period.

"They say that much time had passed but I don't know how much in days as we count them now. The old men would tell about this very carefully. Careful not to make any mistakes, they would tell it, but if they told the number of the days I do not remember that now. They told how First Man had instructed Changing Woman, and First Woman had watched after her, and I think they must have told Changing Woman to tell them when her second period began. And when it did, Talking God came to the place there where the Holy People were staying near Huerfano Mesa. He came to the hogan First Man had built east of the mesa. They say that Calling God came with him but they say Talking God was in charge of it."

Pinto's voice shifted from singsong into a creaky-voiced chant. Chee recognized one of the Talking God songs from the Blessing Way. He had memorized that ceremonial himself, and given it twice when his ambition to be a medicine man had been alive and thriving.

" 'e ne ya! Now I am the child of Changing Woman. My moccasins are of white shell . . ."

The earpiece of the tape player was hurting Chee's earlobe. He listened to another couple of minutes of the tape, noticing that Pinto's version was just a little different in phrasing from the chant Frank Sam Nakai had taught him. His maternal uncle was Hosteen Nakai, and he was a medicine man of good reputation. Chee tended to consider Nakai's versions correct and to disapprove of variations. He pushed the fast-forward button and looked around him.

The reading room of the Reserve Section of the University of New Mexico Library was almost empty. The row of tables was vacant except for him and a skinny, middle-aged man working his way methodically through boxes that seemed to be filled with old postcards and letters. In the silence, the sound of the tape racing over the reel seemed loud. Chee stopped it sooner than he had intended and listened again.

". . . way out there north of Ladron Butte. That's what my grandfather told me. He said that the Utes used to cross the San Juan River upstream from where Montezuma Creek is now, and they'd come down Tsitah Wash. That's the route they liked to take in those days. They'd ride up the wash and come out there where Red Mesa school is now, and then go east of Tohatin Mesa and try to catch the people who lived around Sweetwater. He said a lot of the Mud Clan People used to grow corn and beans and peaches there in those days, and the Utes would try to kill the men and steal the horses and the women and children. He said in those days when his father was a boy the Mexicans used to pay sometimes a hundred dollars for a Navajo child there in Santa Fe where they sold them. And then when the *biligaana* came in the price got higher and . . ."

Chee took off the headset and pushed the rewind button. He was wasting his time. All he had accomplished by coming here was to confirm what Janet Pete had told him. Ashie Pinto had been discovered long ago by the academic world as a source of what academics treasure. He knew the old tales that contain the history of the Dinee. And he knew the story of how the Holy People had created the humans who were to become the Navajo clans. Wonderful. But what did it have to do with the murder of Delbert Nez?

Chee shifted his weight in the hard chair, stretched his legs and thought about that—reexamining the thinking that had led him here. The question that troubled him most wasn't motive for murder. He knew the motive. Whiskey. *Todilhil,* the Navajos had named it. Water of Darkness if you translated that word into *biligaana* language. But Navajos sometimes mispronounced it. *Todilhaal,* they'd say. Making it mean "sucking in darkness," and enjoying the wry irony of the pun. The savagery of whiskey erased the need for a motive. No Navajo policeman—or any policeman—had to relearn that message. Death slept in the bottle, only waiting to be released, and every policeman knew it. The question that nagged at Chee was a different one. What motivated the old man to come halfway across Arizona into New Mexico to an empty place beside a lonely road? There had to be a reason for that. And how the devil did he get there? Pinto made tapes for the scholars. Maybe he had been working for a scholar that day. Maybe a check of scholars who harvested Ashie Pinto's vast memory would provide a list of names. Leads. Maybe listening to the tapes these harvesters of memory collected would tell him what attracted Pinto to the Ship Rock country. Maybe not. Whatever the truth of that, Chee now had his list of who had made these tapes.

He looked at the notebook.

Professor Christopher Tagert, University of New Mexico, Department of History.

Professor Roger Davenport, University of Utah, Department of Anthropology.

Professor Louisa Bourebonette, Northern Arizona University, Department of American Studies.

Professor Alfonso Villareal, University of New Mexico, Language and Linguistics.

Perhaps there were others. These names simply represented tapes of Pinto's recollections available in this library. If others existed in any library they could be found, copied, and sent here. The very pleasant woman at the Special Collections desk had assured him of that. Chee decided not to bother. The only thing that seemed even vaguely promising was one of the Tagert tapes. In it, Pinto was remembering what his grandfather had told him about two white men being killed somewhere south of the San Juan and east of the Chuska. Tagert's cross-examination focused on where the two had come from, when it had happened, and where they had died. Pinto's answers had seemed vague but Tagert hadn't pursued it.

Perhaps there was a later tape. He'd look Tagert up in the faculty directory, call him, and ask about it.

He checked in the tapes and the tape player at the desk.

"I noticed you didn't sign the register," the woman at the desk told him. "We ask people to do that." She pointed to the ledger open on the table beside the door.

Chee filled in his name and address, left the space for "academic department" blank, and jotted "Ashie Pinto tapes" in the "material required" space, and then noted the date and the hour checked out and in. The name on the line above was John Todman. He noticed the old pictures Todman was examining were listed as "Golightly mining camp photographs."

Who else, he wondered, would be interested in Ashie Pinto's old tapes? Probably no one. He turned the page, scanned it. Turned it again. And again. And again. Six pages back, on a page where the first dates were mid-July, he found the legend "Navajo language tapes—Pinto."

The person who signed for them was William Redd.

Chee pursed his lips. He turned the page again. William Redd had also required the same tapes the previous day, and the day before, and the day before that. He jotted the name and address in his notebook and glanced at his watch.

It was still early. He would drive past that address and see if an old green Bronco II was parked there with REDDNEK vanity plates.

8

JIM CHEE IN ALBUQUERQUE was Jim
Chee separated from his vehicle—a duck
out of water. He had left his pickup at the
Farmington airport yesterday, flown Mesa
to Albuquerque, and taken a taxi to his
motel. This morning he'd called a cab
again to get to the University Medical Center for his appointment at the Burn and
Trauma Center. His medical insurance
would pay for all that. But taxis were expensive and, like all cities of the trans-
Mississippi West, Albuquerque had grown
on the presumption that humans over
fourteen were driving themselves around

in their own cars. There was some bus service if you understood how to use it. Chee didn't, and taxicabs made Chee uneasy.

Now, afoot at the university library, Chee did a typical Western thing. He called a friend to ask for a ride.

"I'm supposed to be working," Janet Pete said.

"This will be working. Pick me up in the parking lot behind Zimmerman Library and we'll go work some more on the Ashie Pinto business."

"Like what?" Janet sounded suspicious.

"Remember you noticed that REDDNEK vanity plate on the Bronco parked out by the lava? Well, I was in the Reserve Room listening to Ashie Pinto tapes and I noticed a guy named Redd had been checking them out. R-E-D-D. Like on the plate. He'd checked them out for four consecutive days just about a week before the murder."

As Chee said it, it sounded monumentally trivial. He expected Janet to say something like "So what?" Instead she said nothing at all.

"Well?" Chee said. "Is that a good enough excuse?"

"I can't right now, Jim. I'm right in the middle of finishing something. With people waiting. Can I pick you up in an hour? Hour and a half?"

"Good enough," Chee said, trying to keep from feeling disgruntled, thinking that Janet was doing something important while he was killing idle time, wondering what she was thinking. "I'll walk over to the Union and drink coffee."

Walking across the brick-paved mall he had another idea. Since he couldn't check on Redd now, he'd go find Professor Tagert, while he was waiting, and see if Tagert could tell him anything.

The Department of History had moved since Chee's days on the campus. He found it in a handsome old building he remembered as a dormitory.

The woman at the desk in the department office looked at him curiously, taking in the bandage on his hand first, and his being a Navajo second. "Dr. Tagert?" she said, and chuckled. She sorted quickly through papers on the desk and extracted what looked like a list. "He has office hours this afternoon. Right now in fact. And his office is room 217." She gestured down the hallway and chuckled again. "I wish you luck."

The door of 217 was open.

Chee looked into a cluttered room, lit by two dusty windows, divided by two long desks placed back to back in its center. Books were everywhere, jamming bookcases that occupied the walls, stacked on chairs, tumbled out of untidy piles on the desks. Behind the nearest desk, her back to Chee, a woman was typing.

Chee tapped at the door.

"He's still not here," the woman said without looking around at him. "We haven't heard from him."

"I'm looking for Professor Tagert," Chee said. "Any idea where I could find him?"

"None," she said, and turned around, looking at Chee over the tops of reading glasses. "Which class are you in?"

"I'm a cop," he said. He fished out his identification and handed it to her. Not a worry in the world if the Bureau bitched about him nosing into an FBI case. He was going to quit anyway.

She looked at the identification, at him, at his damaged hand. She was a plump woman in her late twenties, Chee guessed, with a round, good-natured face and short brown hair.

"On duty?"

Shrewd, Chee thought. "More or less," he said. "I'm working on a case that involves a man Dr. Tagert did some business with. I wanted to see what Dr. Tagert could tell me about this guy."

"Who is it?" She smiled at him,

shrugged. "None of my business, maybe. But I'm Tagert's teaching assistant. Maybe I could help."

"Where would Tagert be, this time of day?"

She laughed. "I can't help you with that. He's supposed to be sitting right there—" she pointed across the desk "—having his office hours. And he was supposed to be here all last week, meeting his classes. And the week before that, attending the presemester faculty meetings. Nobody knows where the hell he is." She pointed across the desk at a stack of envelopes overflowing a wire basket on the adjoining desk. "Unopened mail," she said.

Chee looked at the stack. A lot of mail.

"From when? How long has he been gone?"

"I saw him at the end of summer session." She laughed again but there was no humor in it. "Or almost the end. He usually manages to quit a little early. Had me grade his papers for him and turn in his grades. He said he had to get going on some research."

Chee found himself a lot more interested. "My name's Jim Chee," he said.

"Oh," she said. "I'm Jean Jacobs." She held out her hand.

Chee shook it.

"Can I sit down?"

She gestured toward a chair. "Move the books."

He sat. "Doesn't anybody know where he is? How about Mrs. Tagert?"

"They're separated," Jacobs said. "I called her when the department chairman first got excited about finding him. She said she didn't know and she didn't want to know and if I found him to please not tell her about it."

"Strange," Chee said.

"Not really," Jacobs said. "Dr. Tagert wouldn't be a happy man to live with. In fact . . ." She let that trail off, unfinished.

"I meant strange nobody knows where he is," Chee said. "You'd think he'd keep the department informed."

"No you wouldn't," Jacobs said. "Not if you knew him."

Chee was remembering his own days as an undergraduate here. Usually things had been fairly well organized, but not always. And it had seemed to him that the tenure/academic freedom system made faculty members almost totally independent.

"What's the chairman doing about it?"

"He's pissed off. He got me to start Tagert's Trans-Mississippi West class. And I met with his seminars just to tell those poor souls what he'll expect, hand out the reading lists, and all that. And then the dean called and wanted to know when he'd be back, and what he was doing—as if it was my fault." Jean Jacobs's expression soured at the memory. "I hope the Navajos got him," she added.

"Is that where he was going? To the Navajo Reservation?"

"Who knows?" she said. "Or gives a damn. But that's where he'd been working."

"You know what he was working on?"

"Vaguely. It had to be cops and robbers. That's his field. 'Law and Order in the Old West.' He's The Authority in that particular category." She paused. "Or so he tells everybody."

"Do you know if he was working on that with a Navajo named Ashie Pinto?"

"Sure," she said. "Pinto was one of his informants this summer. For old stories and things like that." Her eyes went from Chee's hand to his face. "Chee," she said, recognition dawning. "You're the one who arrested Mr. Pinto. You got yourself burned trying to pull that other policeman out of the car."

Clearly Jean Jacobs was impressed.

"I'm on leave," Chee said, indicating

the hand and feeling embarrassed. "But I'm trying to find out what Pinto was doing out there. Where the crime was committed. How he got there. So forth. And Pinto won't talk about it."

Jean Jacobs had another question. "Why did he kill the policeman?"

"He was drunk," Chee said. It irritated him that it didn't sound like a convincing motive. "Very drunk."

Jean Jacobs was looking at Chee. Smiling. Approving.

"I thought maybe Professor Tagert could tell me something helpful. Maybe he was doing something for Tagert. Working with him on something."

"It might show in his calendar," Jean Jacobs said. "Let's look."

Tagert's desk calendar was open to the second week in August. The spaces below Monday through Thursday were mostly filled with jottings—Friday, Saturday, and Sunday were blank except for a diagonal line drawn across them and the legend "Go hunting." Just above the Wednesday space the words "pick up Oldfart" were written in a neat, precise hand.

Chee indicated it with his finger.

"I don't know who that means," Jacobs said. "I'm not his TA because I like him," she explained. "He's chairman of my dissertation committee. I'm trying to get a doctorate in history. Doing it on the impact of the trading post system on the Western tribes. That falls into Doctor Tagert's field so he's chairman of my committee—like it or not."

"He was here when I was a student," Chee said. "I remember now. One of my friends told me to avoid Professor Tagert."

"Good thinking," Jacobs said. "Sound advice."

"Except now. Now it looks like he had himself scheduled to pick up somebody, maybe Mr. Pinto, the day before Mr. Pinto shot a policeman. Now I think Tagert could tell me a lot."

"Well," Jean Jacobs said, "I wish I could help you find him." She sorted aimlessly through the papers on the desktop, as if some clue to Tagert's whereabouts might be among them. Chee flipped forward in the desk calendar. The next week was blank. The following page was cluttered with notations of committee meetings, luncheon engagements, numbers to be called. "Looks like he intended to get back before classes started," Chee said.

"I noticed that."

He flipped the pages backward, reentering August, moving out of the time when Nez was dead, to the day Nez died because Chee hadn't done his job. That page was blank.

Jean Jacobs must have been watching his face.

"What's wrong?"

"Nothing," Chee said. "Just remembering."

He turned the pages back to the date where Tagert had left it, and back another page to a week when Chee had been a happy man. That week, too, was cluttered with the busy Tagert's notations.

Among them, near the bottom, in the space left for Friday, Tagert had written: "Find out what Redd wants." That and a telephone number.

9

REDD ANSWERED the telephone.

"Jim Chee?" he said. "Chee. Are you the cop who arrested Old Man Pinto?"

"Right," Chee said. He was surprised. But after all, there had been a lot in the paper about it. And Redd seemed to be involved, somehow, in this odd affair. "That's what I'd like to talk to you about. What you know about Pinto."

"Damn little," Redd said. "But go ahead and ask. What do you want to know?"

"How about me coming over? I hate to talk on the telephone."

"Sure," Redd said, and he gave Chee his address.

Janet Pete was waiting in the lot behind Zimmerman Library, with the unhappy, nervous look of people who are parked in loading zones.

"You're late," she said. "You said an hour. The cops already made me move twice."

"It was you who said, and you said an hour and a half or so," Chee said. "By Navajo time it is now just a tiny bit past the so."

Janet snorted. "Get in," she said. "You're sure getting a lot of mileage out of that sore hand."

Redd's address was in Albuquerque's student ghetto—a neighborhood of small frame-stucco bungalows left over from the 1940s with weedy yards and sagging fences. Redd's residence was behind such a bungalow in what had once been a double garage. The rusty Bronco II with the REDDNEK plate was parked beside it, and Redd himself was standing in the door watching them as Janet Pete pulled up.

He was a tall man with athlete's shoulders, but the first thing Chee noticed was red hair, a red mustache, and a long, narrow face sprinkled with freckles.

"Yaa' eh t'eeh," he said, handling the Navajo glottal sounds perfectly. "William Odell Redd," the man said, holding out his

hand to Janet Pete, "but people call me Odell. And you'd be?"

"Janet Pete," she said, "and this is Jim Chee."

Odell Redd was grinning broadly at Chee. "That's the hand you got burned," Redd said. "I read about that. But come on in. You want a drink?"

The interior of Redd's apartment was jammed but orderly. Except for books. Most of them concerned linguistics. Dictionaries were everywhere, English and foreign, ranging from French to Quechua. There was a Cherokee dictionary and beside it *Navajo Tonal Syntax.* Books were stacked on all flat surfaces. There was even a dictionary on the battered table in the center of what served as both Redd's living room and bedroom. But that was an incongruous *Dictionary of Stamps.* Other books cluttering the tabletop involved coins. The *Macmillan Encyclopedic Dictionary of Numismatics* was open, surrounded by tidy rows of pennies. More pennies were piled into three cigar boxes.

"Take that there," Redd told Janet, pointing to an overstuffed chair in the corner. The burden of books it had once held now stood in a tidy stack on the linoleum floor beside it—cleared away, Chee guessed, to make room for his coming. "I'll fix a place here for Mr. Chee to sit."

Redd lifted a huge Spanish-English dictionary and two smaller ones from a kitchen chair and pushed aside enough pennies to make room for them on the table. Then he sat down himself, reversed on a kitchen chair, leaning across its wooden back, looking first at Janet Pete and then at Chee.

"Didn't I see you two out there south of Ship Rock the other evening? Out there south of Highway 33?"

"That's right," Chee said.

"Interesting country," Redd said. "You probably know more about it than I do—being Navajos. All those lava flow ridges and outcrops and things. There's supposed to be a place out there somewhere where witches get together. Initiate people as skinwalkers. That sort of thing."

"You have any idea what Pinto was doing out there?" Janet asked.

Redd smiled at her. "I'll bet you're his kinfolks," he said. "Pinto, he's Mud Clan. Are you related?"

"I'm his lawyer," Janet said.

"Won't he tell you, then? I mean what he was doing out there that night. When he shot the policeman."

Janet hesitated. She glanced at Chee, uncertain. Chee said: "Pinto won't talk about it."

"I sort of got that impression from the papers," Redd said. "It said he was drunk. Said double the legal level. Maybe he just doesn't remember."

"Maybe not," Chee said. "Any idea how he could have gotten out there?"

Redd denied it with a shake of his head. "But the old man had to get there some way or other. Two hundred miles, more or less, is too far to walk. Even for a Navajo. You wouldn't think somebody would just drop him off way out there and leave him. And otherwise, you'd think the cops would have seen somebody driving away."

"Nobody saw anything as far as we know," Janet said. "Jim got there just after it happened and he didn't see anybody. And Mr. Ji came by just about before that, and he didn't either."

Redd looked puzzled. "Mr. Gee?"

"Mr. Ji," Janet said. "J-I but it sounds like 'Gee.' It's Vietnamese. He's a teacher at Shiprock."

"Oh," Redd said. "Anyway, the best I can do about what Pinto was doing out there is guess at it. I think he was working for Professor Tagert."

Chee waited for some expansion of that. None came.

"Like how?" he asked. He held up his hand. "But first answer me another one.

What were you doing out there when you saw Janet and me?"

Redd laughed. "I was exercising my curiosity. I kept thinking there'd be more in the papers. You know, after the police finished their investigation, explaining what the hell was going on. There wasn't, and I kept thinking about it and I came up with a theory. So I went out to take a look and it didn't pay off."

"What's the theory?"

"I had the notion that Pinto had found Butch Cassidy for Tagert," Redd said.

He smiled at them, waiting.

Finally, Janet said: "Butch Cassidy?"

Redd nodded. "What do you know about Western history?" he asked. "I mean about the academic politics of Western history."

"Little bit of the history. No politics," Chee said.

"Well, the guru for years in that field was Frederick Jackson Turner. He died back in the thirties, I think. Taught at Harvard and way back at the end of the nineteenth century he came up with this theory that the wide open western frontier had free land, gold, silver, grazing for anybody who could take it—" Redd paused, looking slightly abashed "—take it away from the Indians, I mean. Anyway, he thought this changed European immigrants into a new kind of people. Made democracy work. Turner and his followers dominated academic Western history down through this century. The Anglo white man was the hero and there wasn't much attention paid to the Spanish, or the French, or the Indians. But now there's a new wave. Donald Worster at the University of Kansas, Patricia Limerick at Colorado University, Tagert here, a guy named Henderson at UC Berkeley, and a few others are the leaders. Or, at least Tagert would like to be one."

Redd paused, looking from one to the other. "This takes a little time to explain."

"No rush," Janet said.

"Well, the way I understand this feud started, this Dr. Henderson wrote a textbook, and Tagert did a paper criticizing part of it, and then Henderson took a whack in *Western History Quarterly* at a paper Tagert had done about the Hole-in-the-Wall Gang." Redd paused again. "I should have explained that Tagert and Henderson both specialize in law and order—or the lack of it—on the frontier. To get to the point, they hate each other's guts. And Tagert thinks he's onto something that will put Henderson down. It involves something he learned from Pinto."

"You're one of Tagert's students?" Janet asked.

Chee felt his jaw tighten. This interruption broke the flow of whatever Redd was trying to tell them. And, by Navajo standards, such an interruption was rude. One let a speaker finish, and then waited to make sure he was indeed finished, before one spoke. But then Janet Pete was really Navajo only by blood and birth. She hadn't been raised on the Reservation in the Navajo Way. Had never had a *ki-naalda* to celebrate her puberty, had never been taught . . .

"No way," Redd said. "I studied it down at UTEP. But you can't make a living at it. Now I'm working on a doctorate in linguistics. There's a better chance of a teaching job and if you can't get that, you can be a translator. Lot of people need them. Oil companies. Export-import. Law firms. Lots of jobs."

"But you know a lot about history, and Tagert," Janet said.

"I know a lot about Tagert," Redd replied. "A lady who works for him is a good friend of mine."

"Jean Jacobs?" Janet said. "Jim told me he met her today at Tagert's office. She was very helpful."

"Nice gal," Redd said, with an expression that said he meant it. "We go way back."

Chee found himself feeling impatience—a rare emotion with him. Wishing he had left Janet Pete behind. Wanting to get on with it.

"Do you know enough about Tagert to have any idea where he might be?" He noticed his tone wasn't right. So did Redd. So did Pete.

"No," Redd said. "No idea, really." He got up, turned his chair around, and sat again.

The conversation had become formal. Ah, well, Chee thought, I've screwed up. He sensed Janet Pete's eyes on him. Time to pull the rabbit from the hat. But he had no rabbit. He felt disgusted with himself. "You said you'd seen us out near the place where Pinto killed Delbert Nez. You said you were checking on a theory."

"I was just curious," Redd said. "I know Mr. Pinto some. I wondered what he could be doing out there."

"You started to tell us that Pinto was working for Dr. Tagert. To tell us what he was doing. Something about Western history and a professor named Henderson, and—"

"Oh, yeah. I drifted away from the point I was trying to make. Well, this Henderson is out with a new book, about banditry, organized gangs, so forth, but mostly it's about the Pinkerton organization."

Redd paused, glanced at them. "You know about the Pinkertons?"

Chee nodded.

"Well, they're supposed to have hounded Butch Cassidy out of the country. About 1901. Down to Argentina and then to Bolivia. Well, Henderson had gone down there and dug into the records at La Paz, old military records, and established from the official report all the details of how this Bolivian mounted infantry patrol caught the two of 'em in a little village and shot 'em. Nothing much new in it, except the details. Thing is, Tagert doesn't think it happened that way."

Redd paused, awaiting some reaction. In a second or two he got one.

"That's the way it was in the movie," Janet said.

Redd looked surprised. "Movie?"

"*Butch Cassidy and the Sunshine Kid,* I think it was. Robert Redford and somebody-or-other. And the Bolivian army kills them." Janet shuddered. "Blows them all to pieces. Gruesome."

It wasn't the reaction Redd had expected, but he went on. Enjoying the attention, Chee thought sourly, and then was disgusted with himself for his bad temper. Redd could hardly be more cooperative. He seemed to be one of those perpetual graduate students who inhabit the fringes of every university—but a decent sort of fellow.

Redd was telling them that Tagert didn't believe Cassidy had been killed in Bolivia. Tagert believed part of the tale told by Cassidy's kinfolks. The family claimed that Cassidy had slipped back into the United States in 1909, had bought a farm under an assumed name, had lived out his life as a law-abiding citizen, and had finally died as an old, old man about 1932. Tagert believed some of that. But not the law-abiding part.

"He published a paper in *Western Archives* about ten years ago, connecting Cassidy with a 1909 bank robbery in Utah," Redd said. "In stuffy old history faculties that stirred up a controversy, and Henderson blew him out of the water. He found out that Tagert had relied on some old trial testimony that had since been discredited. That infuriated Tagert. And this new book . . ." Redd grinned broadly. "Jean said Tagert was absolutely livid. In a downright rage. Stomping around the office, having a regular tantrum." He laughed, shook his head, savoring the memory.

"I take it that Jean Jacobs doesn't care much for the professor," Janet said.

Redd's delight vanished. "Does the slave love her master?" Redd asked. "That's what we are. Lincoln didn't mention graduate students when he issued the Emancipation Proclamation. We're the Grand Republic's last vestige of indentured labor. We do the master's research for him, or we don't get our dissertation approved. Then you don't get the union card."

Chee swallowed. How did all this Cassidy stuff relate to Ashie Pinto? How could it? But he wasn't going to show impatience again. He would behave like a Navajo. He would endure.

"I remember how it was in law school," Janet said. "If you were working your way through."

"Anyway," Redd said, "old Tagert had dug out an old newspaper account of a train robbery up in Utah. I think it was the newspaper at Blanding. Three men, one of them killed, and the other two getting away and some people on the train claiming one of the robbers was Cassidy. He found a later account reporting that the two bandidos had turned up in Cortez, and got away again, and the posse had chased them south and lost track of 'em south and west of Sleeping Ute Mountain. Again, one of the cops said the blond bandit was

Butch Cassidy. He claimed he'd known him way back when Cassidy was connected with the Hole-in-the-Wall Gang."

Redd paused. Shook his head. "Pretty slim evidence, but it was all Tagert had, and he used it in that paper, along with what Cassidy's kinfolks had said, and—like I said—he got blown out of the water by Henderson's Bolivian stuff." Redd shook his head again, expression wry.

Being raised Navajo, Jim Chee understood how human nature affected storytellers and how they worked an audience. Now, at last, Redd would tell them something pertinent.

"He had nothing but that." Redd looked at Chee. The dramatic pause. "Then Ashie Pinto picked up Butch Cassidy's trail on the Big Reservation."

10

JOE LEAPHORN—a practical man—handled it by telephone. He got Professor Tagert's home number in Albuquerque from information. No one answered. He called the university switchboard for Tagert's office number. There a woman answered. She said her name was Jean Jacobs, Tagert's teaching assistant. From Jacobs, Leaphorn learned two interesting facts.

First, Tagert was two weeks overdue for his academic duties and—if Jacobs knew what she was talking about—no one seemed to know his whereabouts.

Second, the arresting officer in the

Pinto case, Jim Chee, off duty and on convalescent leave, was performing as Chee performed all too often—a mile outside the rules. He had presented himself at Tagert's office asking questions. How could Chee have come to know about Tagert?

Thinking of this, Leaphorn found himself violating one of his own rules. He was allowing his mind to shift back and forth between two problems—Tagert and Chee—and thus getting nowhere on either. Chee could wait. First he would see if he could fit Tagert's absence from his university classrooms into this puzzle.

Leaphorn swiveled his chair to face the map that dominated his wall behind his desk. It was a magnified version of the "Indian Country" map produced by the Automobile Club of Southern California. Smaller versions were used throughout the Four Corners territory for its details and its accuracy. Leaphorn had hired a photographer to copy it and make him a double-sized print on a matte paper. Emma had pasted this to a sheet of corkboard. For years, he had sprinkled it with coded pins, using it, so he said, to reinforce his memory. Actually Leaphorn's memory was remarkable, needing no reinforcement. He used the map in his endless hunt for patterns, sequences, order—something that would bring a semblance of Navajo *hohzho* to the chaos of crime and violence.

From his desk, Leaphorn extracted a box of pins, the sort mapping companies provide. He selected three with large yellow heads—yellow being Leaphorn's code for problems with no priority beyond their inherent oddity. He stuck one in the map between Bekahatso Wash and Yon Dot Mountain, at about the place where Ashie Pinto's hogan stood. Another he placed between Birdsprings Trading Post and Jadito Wash. There Nez had lived. He put the third south of Navajo Route 33 on a line between Shiprock and Beautiful Mountain, the place where Pinto had shot Delbert Nez. Then he leaned back and inspected his work.

The triangle formed by the pins was huge. It emphasized two points in Leaphorn's mind. The Nez home was at least 150 miles south of the Pinto place in a part of the Reservation where intercourse with both the Hopis and the busy world of the *biligaana* was easy if not inevitable. Pinto lived in a different world of the pure, traditional Navajo culture. Everything separated them. Distance. Age. Culture. And yet they had come together violently at the point of the triangle—two hundred miles from either one's home. Duty had taken Nez to that rendezvous. But what had taken Pinto there?

That was the second point. The pins made it clear he could hardly have been there by chance. One could not get from pin A at Pinto's hogan to pin C beside Navajo Route 33 without changing roads a half-dozen times. Pinto could not have simply happened past en route to somewhere else. He had gone there for a purpose. And Leaphorn's reasoning said Pinto's purpose must be linked to why the old man had killed Delbert Nez.

But three pins were not enough to tell him anything. So Leaphorn, being Leaphorn, studied the map to see if they would fit into any other pattern.

He noticed only one thing that interested him. While Leaphorn rejected traditional Navajo witchcraft beliefs and detested them, they were part of his job. Belief in witches, and fear of them, lay at the root of many of the troubles, many of the tragedies, that occupied him as a policeman.

Pin C, where Delbert Nez had died, was very close to a rugged volcanic outcropping, nameless on the map, but which local families called Tse A'Digash. Witchery Rock. Around this long irregular ridge were clustered a measles rash of red pins marked with the letter *a*. The *a* stood for *A'Digash*. Witchcraft. Each pin in the quarter-century accumulation marked some sort of disturbance, assault, threat, or misdemeanor in which fear of these so-called skinwalkers had played some part.

Leaphorn's eyes were on the map but he was seeing Tse A'Digash in his memory—an ugly black ridge of old lichen-covered lava that ran for three or four miles south of Navajo 33. Now a yellow pin stuck out in the cluster of red ones. A coincidence? Perhaps. Leaphorn had learned to be skeptical of coincidences. Perhaps that pin, too, should be red with an *a* in its center.

In fact Leaphorn had learned to be skeptical in general. He took another yellow pin from the desk drawer and stuck it in just south of Flagstaff. Professor Bourebonette had said she lived south of town. Her motivation, so she said, was merely friendship. He had absolutely no way to calculate how she actually fit into this.

Then Leaphorn picked up his phone, dialed the records office downstairs, and asked for the file on the Delbert Nez homicide.

While he waited for it, he shuffled

through the folders Bolack Travel had sent him on China. One concerned a tour sponsored by the Audubon Society, which would focus on visits to bird sanctuaries. He reread parts of that. Emma had been an amateur bird watcher—keeping three feeders stocked in their backyard. The others on the trip would be interesting people, probably. But he would have nothing to talk to them about. Nothing in common. Another tour simply involved visits to cities. That left him cold. His best alternative seemed to be going alone. He would see if any of his old professors were left on the anthropology faculty at Arizona State. It wasn't likely, but it was possible. If not, maybe someone else there would help him. He'd explain he was an alum, with their master of science in anthropology degree from way back when, and he wanted to go into Asia and see if he could find any roots to his Athabaskan origins. He'd wanted to do that for years, ever since he'd become conscious as an anthropology student that his forebears had probably emerged from Mongolia. It had faded into the subconscious after he'd met Emma and married her. Emma was no traveler. Three days in Albuquerque made her vaguely uneasy, yearning for home. Three days in New York made her miserable.

She would have gone with him without a murmur. But taking her would have been cruel.

When the Nez folder arrived, he was examining a picture of a Shanghai street scene, seeing himself there amid the stampede of bicycles. It depressed him.

He spent almost an hour rereading the file and jotting reminders in the slim notebook he always carried in his uniform pocket.

Chee met car. Was it the schoolteacher's? What did he see?

Expensive whiskey? How? Where bought?

Pistol. Where did he get it?

Two fifty-dollar bills? McGinnis said he was broke.

Did Pinto have his *jish* with him? Where is it?

Then he called the FBI office at Gallup, got Jay Kennedy, and invited him to lunch.

"What do you want this time?" Kennedy asked.

"Wait a minute," Leaphorn said. "Remember. Last time somebody wanted something it was you. You wanted me to check a homicide scene for tracks."

"Which you didn't find," Kennedy said.

"Because there weren't any," Leaphorn said. "Besides, I'll buy."

"I'll have to cancel something," Kennedy said. "Is it important?"

Leaphorn considered. And reconsidered.

"Well?"

"No," Leaphorn said. He considered again. "Probably not."

He heard Kennedy sigh. "So what are we talking about? Just in case I need to look something up. Or dig into something so confidential that it might cost me my job."

"Delbert Nez," Leaphorn said.

"Oh, shit," Kennedy said. "Naturally."

"Why?"

"It was a sloppy job," Kennedy said. "Even worse than usual."

They met at the International Pancake House on old U.S. 66 and sat a while sipping coffee. The autumn sun warmed Leaphorn's shoulders through his uniform jacket and the traffic streamed by off Interstate 40. He noticed how gray Kennedy had become, how—uncharacteristic of FBI agents and of Kennedy himself—he needed a haircut. Old cops, Leaphorn thought. Two old dogs getting tired of watching the sheep. Old friends. How rare they are. The Bureau would be glad to see the last of Kennedy—exiled here years ago for some violation of the old J. Edgar Hoover prohibition against bad publicity, liberalism, or innovative thinking. The story was that Kennedy's ex-wife had been active in the American Civil Liberties Union. She had left him to marry a real estate broker, but the stigma remained.

For that matter, Leaphorn suspected there were those in his Navajo Tribal Police hierarchy who would be happy to celebrate his own retirement. He wouldn't make them wait much longer.

Kennedy had been talking about one of those endless interagency shoving matches which involve public employees—this one an effort of the Bureau of Land Management, the Forest Service, the Bureau of Indian Affairs, and "The Bureau" to make one or another of them responsible for protecting Anasazi ruins under the Antiquities Act. Leaphorn had heard a lot of it before.

Kennedy quit talking. "I'm not holding your attention," he said.

"You ever been to China?" Leaphorn asked.

Kennedy laughed. "Not yet," he said. "If the Bureau opens an office there—say in North Manchuria—I'll get the assignment."

"Think you'd like to go?"

Kennedy laughed again. "It's on my wish list," he said. "Right after Angola, Antarctica, Bangladesh, Lubbock, Texas, and the Australian outback. Why? Are you planning to go?"

"I guess not," Leaphorn said. "Always sort of wanted to. Wanted to go out in the steppe country. Outer Mongolia. The part of the world where they think the Athabaskans originated."

"I used to want to go back to Ireland," Kennedy said. "Where my great-grandfather came from. I outgrew that notion."

"Yeah," Leaphorn said. "Do you know if anybody checked on that pistol Pinto used?"

"Somebody checked," Kennedy said. "It was a common type, but I don't remember the brand. American made, I think it was, and an expensive model. It had been recently fired. The slug in Nez came from it. Check of Pinto's hand showed he'd recently fired something."

"Where did it come from?"

"No idea," Kennedy said. "The old man isn't saying. Totally silent from what I hear. I guess he bought it at some pawnshop."

"I don't think so," Leaphorn said.

Kennedy peered at him, expression

quizzical. "You've been asking around," he said. "Any reason for that?"

Leaphorn made a wry face. "Turns out Ashie Pinto is sort of shirttail, linked-clan kinfolks of mine," he said. "Through Emma's clan."

"You know him?"

"Never heard of him."

"But you got roped in."

"Right," Leaphorn said. "I don't think he bought the pistol because he was broke. Not even eating money. What do you know about those two fifties he had?"

"Nothing."

"Where did Pinto get his hands on them?"

"No idea." Kennedy looked irritated. "How would we know something like that?"

"Did anybody check on the driver of the car Chee met going to the fire?"

Kennedy shook his head. "I told you it was a sloppy job. But damn it, Joe, why would they check on that? Look what you had there. No big mystery. A drunk gets arrested and kills the policeman. Doesn't even deny it. What's to investigate? I know you think we loaf around a lot, but we do have things to do."

"Did Pinto have his *jish* with him? You know where that is?"

"*Jish?*" Kennedy said. "His medicine bundle? I don't know."

"He was a shaman. A crystal gazer. If he was on a job, he'd have his crystals with him, and his *jish.*"

"I'll find out," Kennedy said. "Probably he wasn't working. Left it home."

"We didn't find it at his place."

Kennedy looked at him. "You been out to his place, then."

The waitress delivered the waffles, which smelled delicious. Leaphorn applied butter, poured on syrup. He was hungry and he hadn't been hungry much lately. This Ashie Pinto business must be good for him.

Kennedy had hardly looked at his waffle. He was still looking at Leaphorn.

"We?" he said. "You been out searching Pinto's hogan? Who's we?"

"Pinto's niece," Leaphorn said. And a woman named Bourebonette. A professor at Northern Arizona University. You guys turn up anything about her?"

"Bourebonette? No. Why would we? How would she fit into this?"

"That's what bothers me," Leaphorn said. "She says Pinto was one of her sources for myths, legends, so forth. That's her field. Mythology. She says she's into it because he's a friend. Just that."

Kennedy peered at him. "You sound like you have trouble believing that."

Leaphorn shrugged. "Sophisticated, urbane university professor. Old illiterate Navajo. And she's going to a hell of a lot of trouble."

"You're getting even worse with age," Kennedy said. "Emma used to make you a little more human." He buttered his waffle. "Okay, then. What do you think motivates the woman?"

Leaphorn shrugged again. "Maybe she's working on a book. Needs more out of him to finish it off."

"She could get to him in prison. They're not going to put somebody like that in solitary. Not even for killing a policeman."

"I don't know then. What do you think?"

"Why not just believe she's nuts? Likes the old bastard. She's doing it for humanitarian reasons. You actually went all the way out there and searched the old man's hogan?"

"I didn't search. No warrant."

"You're getting serious about this, aren't you?" Kennedy said. "You think there's something more to it than just Pinto being drunk and killing your man?"

"No," Leaphorn said. "I'm just curious." The waffle was wonderful. He chewed a second bite, swallowed, sipped his coffee. "Have you found that car that Chee saw? The old white Jeepster?"

"Didn't we already cover that? You asked me about the driver."

"And I noticed how you didn't exactly answer. You just sort of nodded, and said it had been sloppy work, and then did your little sermon about why waste time on a made case." Leaphorn was grinning at him. "When the Bureau dumps you I hope you don't get into playing poker for a profession."

Kennedy made a wry face. He chewed for a while.

"It took you longer to get to it than I expected," Kennedy said. "But you never fail to get there. Right to the touchy spot."

"Touchy?"

"How much do you know about the car?"

"Nothing," Leaphorn said. "Just what was in the report. Chee saw an old white Jeepster coming from the direction of the crime, turning on a gravel road toward Shiprock. Chee thought it belonged to an Oriental who teaches at the high school. There was nothing in the report about checking on that car."

"They found it," Kennedy said. He eyed Leaphorn. "This is one of those 'you don't remember where you heard it' times."

"Sure," Leaphorn said.

"The car belonged to a man named Huan Ji. He teaches math at Shiprock High School. Just been there four years. No way he'd have anything to do with this crime. He couldn't have known Pinto or Nez."

Leaphorn waited for more. Kennedy sipped the last of his coffee, signaled the pretty Zuni girl who was their waitress.

"Ready for a refill," he said, indicating his cup.

Kennedy had said all he wanted to say about Juan Gee and the car. Why?

"What was this Gee doing way out there in the rain?" Leaphorn asked. "What did he see? What did he tell you?"

Kennedy grimaced and peered across his coffee cup at Leaphorn.

"You remember the Howard case in Santa Fe. The defrocked CIA agent who was working for the State of New Mexico, and the CIA thought he had sold out to the Russians, and we had him staked out watching him until somebody could get around to filing charges. You remember."

"I remember," Leaphorn said, grinning. "The part I remember best was the ingenious way he slipped away from you guys. Had his wife drive the car."

Kennedy grinned, too, even broader

than Leaphorn. "Embarrassment squared. Embarrassment to the third power," he said. The grin turned into a chuckle. "Can you imagine what it was like in the Albuquerque office when the powers found out Howard was safely behind the Iron Curtain? Hell was raised. Fits thrown. Carefully written reports were sent out explaining why it hadn't occurred to the Bureau that Howard might have his wife driving the car on the escape run."

"I can imagine the CIA people were rubbing it in."

"I think you can be sure of it," Kennedy said.

"Can I be sure that all of this is going to have some bearing on why nobody talked to this Juan Gee?"

"You can," Kennedy said. "It seems the Bureau was aware that Huan Ji was a friend of the Agency. He was a colonel in the South Vietnamese Army. In intelligence, and he was working for Washington as well as Saigon. We have this vague, scuttlebutt impression that he was one of the very hard people, involved with the sort of stuff we used to hear the horror stories about."

"Like dropping Vietcong out of helicopters so the one you didn't drop would be willing to talk?"

"I don't know," Kennedy said. "It was just gossip. But anyway he was a client, so to speak, of the CIA and so when everything went to hell over there in 1975 and the Saigon government collapsed, they got him out and helped him get started in the States."

"A Vietnamese named Juan?" Leaphorn asked.

"It's H-U-A-N and J-I. Sounds like 'Gee.'"

"So why didn't the FBI talk to him?" Leaphorn asked, thinking he already knew the answer.

Kennedy looked slightly defensive. "Why talk to him? The case was all locked up. The arrest was made. We had the smoking gun. No mystery. Nothing to resolve. We didn't really need another witness." He stopped.

"And bothering this guy would look bad to the CIA. Would maybe irritate the CIA, which is already sneering at you guys for letting Howard walk away."

"More or less, I'd say," Kennedy admitted. "I'm not privy to the upper councils, but I'd say that is a close guess."

Leaphorn ate more waffle.

"And what the hell's wrong with that? Why waste everybody's time? Why piss off the Agency? Why bother Mr. Ji?"

"I just wonder what he was doing out there," Leaphorn said. "That's all."

Kennedy finished his waffle. "I've got to go to Farmington," he said. "A hundred bumpy miles up Route 666. And then a night in a Holiday Inn."

"You sure you don't want to go to China?"

"About as much as I want to go to Farmington," Kennedy said. "And don't forget to leave a generous tip."

Leaphorn watched Kennedy leave. He saw his car pull out of the Pancake House parking lot onto old 66, heading for the long drive north to Farmington. He was still wondering what Colonel Ji was doing out in the rain by the rock where the witches gather.

11

THE HAND MAN'S REPUTATION was as good as they get in modern medicine. He had identified himself as an "Indian Indian," smiling as he said it and giving Chee a name which Chee instantly forgot. His voice carried a slight British accent with a trace of lilt in it, and he asked his questions in a soft, gentle voice without looking at Chee, never taking his eyes off the ugly, puckered cavity burned across Chee's left palm. With the Burn Doctor, a woman named Johns, the Hand Man discussed tendon damage, ligament damage, nerve damage, regeneration of tissue, "prognosis for usage," and "viability of surgical techniques."

"You clutched the handle of a car door? Is that how I understand it? And the car was burning?" He glanced at Chee's right hand. "But you are right-handed, is it not true? Why did you use your left hand?"

"I guess because it's natural to open the driver's door that way," Chee said. "If I had another reason I don't remember it."

"It's almost as if your subconscious sensed the forthcoming damage and protected the hand most useful to you." The Hand Man said it in a clipped, didactic tone, still staring at the angry red mass of scarring on Chee's palm, never glancing up. "Would you agree?"

"I doubt it," Chee said. "I'd guess it was also because I was going to pull Delbert out of there with my right hand. But it's all sort of hazy to tell the truth."

"Ah, well," the Hand Man said, no longer interested. And that was that. The Burn Doctor put on a new bandage, using a different wrapping technique. She gave Chee a prescription and instructions, and said she would see him in a week.

"Well, what do you think?" he asked the Burn Doctor.

"Think?"

"About surgery. About how much use

I'll regain of my fingers. Things like that?"

"We'll have to decide," the Burn Doctor said. "You'll be informed."

"Appreciate it," Chee said, but the Burn Doctor didn't notice the irony.

He used the pay telephone again. This time Janet Pete was out. She was in Santa Fe, the receptionist at the Federal Public Defender's office told him. She was involved with picking a jury for a forthcoming trial. Would she be home this evening? The receptionist had no idea.

Chee called Professor Tagert's office. Jean Jacobs answered. No, Tagert still hadn't checked in.

"Can I come over? Do you have time to talk?"

"Sure," Jacobs said. "About what?"

"Mr. Redd told us about Tagert's interest in Butch Cassidy. He said Ashie Pinto had helped Tagert find what might be Cassidy's trail. Out on the Reservation."

"Okay," Jacobs said. "I know he's obsessed with Cassidy but I don't know much about it."

Chee walked, feeling disgruntled. Janet Pete knew he would be back in Albuquerque today. He'd written her a note, telling her. So, maybe she couldn't avoid the Santa Fe duty. On the other hand, maybe she could have. Chee had been around long enough to know how priorities worked when there was a conflict between duty and desire.

He crossed the mall with fallen sycamore leaves blowing around his feet. His hand hurt. His fingers wouldn't respond properly. He felt discouraged. Blue. Bored. Undecided. He found the door of Dr. Tagert's office open. Jean Jacobs sat, elbows on desk, chin on hands, staring out the window. She looked blue, bored, and undecided.

"I'm glad to see you," Jean Jacobs said. "I've got a million things to do." She slapped an angry palm onto a pile of paperwork. "All this goddamn Tagert work, and all my own work and—oh, to hell with it."

"Yeah," Chee said. "Sometimes that's about it."

"So screw it all," she said. "I hope you have just walked in here with something that is not only totally time-wasting but mysterious. We'll figure out how to find the vanished professor of history." She paused. "Even better, we'll figure out where they hid the bastard's body."

"I guess he's not back yet then," Chee said. He decided she wasn't going to ask him to sit down, even though she obviously expected him to stay. So he moved a stack of folders off a chair and sat.

"I think he's dead," Jacobs said. "I'll bet your Mr. Pinto shot him the same time he shot the officer."

"I think that's possible," Chee said. "But then, what happened to his body?"

Jacobs made a "who knows" gesture. "Did Odell tell you anything interesting? Or useful?"

"I'm not sure how useful. He told us all about Tagert's disagreement about Butch Cassidy with that other professor. And he told us that Pinto knew an old story about Cassidy, or some other bandido, coming across the Reservation after a robbery in Utah and getting killed by some of us Navajos. Tagert thought that maybe he could find some proof of that. And he'd given up on trying to prove Cassidy died of old age."

"I heard a little about that yarn," Jacobs said. "Not much. But I think Tagert was excited about it. That was last summer." She paused, looked at Chee, a shy look. "What did you think of him?"

"Of Redd? He seemed like a nice guy. He said you were a friend."

"Ummm," she said. "A friend."

Her expression was so sad, so close to matching Chee's own mood, that he said: "Having troubles?"

And she heard the sympathy in his voice.

"I'm just down today," she said, and laughed a shaky laugh. "You too, I'll bet. You didn't look all that cheerful anyway when you walked in."

"Yeah," Chee said. "It hasn't been one of my better days."

"Hand hurt?"

"A little."

"You look down," Jacobs said. "Troubles?"

"Not really," Chee said. He shrugged. "I was hoping to meet a friend. She had to go to Santa Fe." He considered that. "At least she said she had to go to Santa Fe."

Jacobs was frowning. "She didn't go?"

"Oh, I guess she went. I meant maybe she didn't really *have* to go."

"Oh," Jacobs said. She made a wry face. "I know *exactly* what you mean."

"I'm not sure I do," Chee said.

"I was just guessing. With me, I think it's more important for me to be with Odell than it is for Odell to be with me."

"Okay," Chee said. He laughed. "We're on the same wavelength."

"You've got a bad hand. You fly all the way in from Farmington or wherever, and your girlfriend thinks going to Santa Fe is more important."

"Maybe she couldn't get out of it. And she's not exactly my girlfriend. We're more just friends."

"Uh-huh," Jacobs said. "Like Odell said."

Chee wanted to get off this subject.

"You work for Tagert. Part-time anyway. Did you ever notice anything in the paperwork that would give you any idea what he and Pinto were doing out there?"

"I wasn't that interested, to tell the truth," she said. "You know, it seems pretty mean to me that they still have you working on this when your hand's like that. You should be on sick leave."

"Actually, I am," Chee said. "I'm doing this on my own time."

Jacobs lowered her chin, peering at him over her reading glasses, her smooth, round face furrowed by a frown. "Why? Why are you doing it?"

"I'm curious," Chee said. "I just want to find out how Hosteen Pinto got out there, and what he was doing. Things like that. It doesn't really need to be done. Not for the trial. Pinto doesn't even deny he killed Delbert. I'm just doing it because I don't have anything else to do. And nobody else gives a damn."

"Somebody else is doing it, too," Jacobs said.

"What? Who?"

"I got a call a couple of days ago. From a Navajo tribal policeman in Window Rock. He wanted to talk to Tagert. Wanted to know where he could find him."

"Who was it? You sure it was a Navajo tribal policeman? Not the FBI? Or maybe an investigator from the Federal Public Defender's office."

"It was from Window Rock. He said Navajo Tribal Police."

"What was the name?"

"A funny name. I don't remember. I remember he was a lieutenant."

"Leaphorn!"

"That was it," Jacobs said. "Lieutenant Leaphorn. Do you know him?"

Chee was thinking. He came to the only possible conclusion. "That son-of-a-bitch," he said.

Jacobs looked startled at the bitterness. She looked away, picked up a pen. Put it down.

"Sorry," Chee said.

"It sounds like you know him. Is he your boss?"

"I know him. No, he's not my boss."

"He just asked if Tagert was here. If I knew where to find him." She studied Chee. "Is it bad?"

"No," Chee said. "I don't know. It's just—"

He sighed. "You don't want to hear all this," he said.

"Yes," she said. "I do."

"It's more than curiosity with me," he began, and told her about his radio conversation with Nez, the fading in and out, the nut who painted basalt, the laughter that led him to fail his friend. He told her of arresting Pinto. He told her about Janet Pete back from Washington taking the Federal Public Defender's job and representing Pinto.

"I know she was assigned to do it. It's her job. But Janet lets me know she halfway believes Pinto didn't do it. She sees a lot of unanswered questions. What's his motive, she says. He was drunk, and he'd killed someone before when he was drunk and served time for it. And he was caught red-handed and doesn't even deny it. But for her, that's not enough." Chee shook his head.

"You think it would be kinda nice if it was enough just because you were the one who nabbed him," Jacobs said. "But you've got to consider she's his defense attorney. And she's a woman in a field men have dominated. And so she feels like she's got something to prove. At least I would.

Maybe she feels like she has to prove something to you, too." Jacobs made a wry face. "You know, you've been a cop awhile. Into law enforcement. She's brand new at the game." She shrugged. "I don't know. I'm just talking."

"You are missing the implication," Chee said. He stood up. His voice had sounded stiff, but to hell with it. This woman felt like listening. He felt like letting some of this anger out. "You see, I screwed up on this. If I hadn't screwed up, I would have been there when Nez was making this arrest—or whatever he was doing—and he wouldn't have been killed. But I was over in Red Rock drinking coffee, thinking all was good because I heard Delbert laughing."

He was standing with his arms hanging by his side. That made his hand hurt. He folded his arms.

"But I did get there. Too late to help Delbert, but I got there in time to catch the man who killed him. I was a good enough cop for that."

Jacobs was silent for a while, thinking about it, her face full of sympathy. She was a talented listener. He had noticed it before. When you talked to this woman, she attended. She had all her antennae out, focused on the speaker. The world was shut out. Nothing mattered but the words she was hearing. Listening was ingrained in the Navajo culture. One didn't interrupt. One waited until the speaker was finished, gave him a moment or two to consider additions, or footnotes or amendments, before one responded. But even Navajos too often listened impatiently. Not really listening, but framing their reply. Jean Jacobs *really listened.* It was flattery, and Chee knew it, but it had its effect.

"I can see why you'd want to find Tagert. I can see why you'd want to make sure."

"Sure!" Chee said it louder than he intended. "I *am* sure. How sure can I be? The killer at the scene, drunk, with the smoking gun. He doesn't even deny it. How goddamn sure can you be?"

"It sounds sure to me," Jacobs said.

"And the FBI is happy. They took it to the federal grand jury, and got the indictment. They're ready for trial."

"This Lieutenant Leaphorn, is he—"

"A vote of no confidence," Chee said.

"The tribal police think you got the wrong man?"

"Maybe. More likely Leaphorn is freelancing. He does that some. He's sort of our supercop. Old as the hills. Knows everybody. Remembers everything. Forgets nothing. I worked with him a time or two before. Everybody does sooner or later because he handles the tough investigations wherever they are."

"You didn't get along?"

"I don't think he held me in extremely high regard," Chee said. "But we got along all right. To be fair about it. He even hired me to do a Blessing Way for him."

He saw the question in Jacobs's face.

"It's a curing ceremonial," he explained. "I'm a would-be shaman. A singer. A medicine man. *Hataalii* is the Navajo word for it. I was going to be one of the people who conducts the curing ceremonies to restore people to harmony. Or I was trying to be. Nobody seemed to want my services." He produced a humorless chuckle. "And Lieutenant Leaphorn was my only legitimate patient. Only one outside the family."

"You do sand paintings," Jacobs said. "Is that right? That's about all I know about it."

Even while he was speaking, Chee had the sensation of standing outside himself, watching and listening. He saw self-pity, and heard it. Some anger, yes. But mostly he saw a man who felt sorry for himself. He hated that in others, hated it even more in himself. Now he felt ashamed. And beyond his anger, he was suddenly aware of the implications of Leaphorn's involvement. It couldn't be merely casual. How had the lieutenant found out about Tagert? That must have taken some digging. Chee felt his anger seeping away, replaced by a sense of urgency.

"Sorry about unloading my troubles," he said. "I didn't come in here for that. I came in to see if I could look at some of the paperwork. See if maybe it would tell us what Tagert and Pinto were working on. Tell us if Tagert was with him that day."

"We can look," Jean Jacobs said. "But I don't think it's going to help much."

Look they did. But first Jean Jacobs closed the door. And locked it. "I feel sort of sneaky," she said. "Looking through the old bastard's stuff. Even though I work with a lot of it every day."

"Just remember, I'm the arresting officer," Chee said, and felt his mood improving.

The out-basket was empty. They checked the in-basket.

The mail, the memos, were a month old and, as far as Chee could tell, without relevance.

"How does he file things?" Chee asked.

"By subject, usually. Sometimes mail gets filed by name of the correspondent. Mostly by subject."

"Let's see if he has a Pinto file."

No Pinto file.

"How about a Cassidy file?"

Cassidy folders occupied half a drawer in Tagert's filing cabinet. Chee and Jacobs stacked them on his desktop and started sorting.

"What am I looking for?" Jacobs asked.

"Good question," Chee said. "Anything related to Pinto, I'd say, for starters. Anything that relates to this robbery up in Utah and the chase. Stuff like—"

"Here's stuff about the Utah robbery," Jacobs said. "Copies of newspaper stories."

The headline in the *Blanding Defender* was multiple lines, in turn-of-the-century newspaper fashion:

OLD HOLE IN WALL
GANG BELIEVED
INVOLVED IN
TRAIN ROBBERY

WITNESS SAYS HE SAW
BUTCH CASSIDY AMONG
GANG WHICH BOARDED
COLORADO & SOUTHERN
TRAIN AT FRY CREEK

WOUNDED BANDIT SAYS IT IS TRUE

DEAD BANDIT IS IDENTIFIED
AS RUDOLPH "RED" WAGONSTAFF
HIS FRIENDS SAY HE USED TO
RUSTLE CATTLE WITH CASSIDY
AND THE WYOMING WILD BUNCH

The story below repeated all that with more details and with a rehashing of what happened in the robbery. Three men had boarded the train when it stopped to pick up mail at Fry Creek. They had entered the mail car, and engaged in a gunfight with the two mail clerks. One clerk was killed, the other wounded in the upper chest. The bandit now identified as Wagonstaff was shot in the neck and died the next day in the Blanding hospital.

The bandits had stopped the train north of Blanding where an accomplice was waiting with horses. An off-duty Garfield County deputy sheriff had fired from the train window at the departing robbers. His bullet struck one in the back, causing him to fall from his horse.

The newspaper account continued:

As their bad luck had it, this fellow was carrying the bags which contained most of the loot which had attracted the bandits. He is now in the hospital here in Blanding but the doctor has little hope for him. He told Sheriff Lester Ludlow that his name is Davis and that Butch Cassidy was leading the group.

Sheriff Ludlow said most of the loot taken in the robbery was recovered in the bags Davis had been carrying—which was the payroll money for the Parker Mine. He said the bandits probably got away with no more than three or four hundred dollars—mostly in bank notes, stamps and other supplies being delivered to post offices along the route south from Salt Lake City.

The rest of the story was mostly information about the dead and wounded mail clerks and about the posse formed to pursue the bandits. Chee skipped through it hurriedly and went on to the next item. It was dated a week later. Davis had died. The posse had tracked the two survivors southward. They had been seen by a Mormon rancher near Montezuma Creek— two men with four horses. Sheriff Ludlow expressed optimism. "The Sheriff said in his telegram to this newspaper: 'They will be caught.' "

A week later, Ludlow was not making such optimistic statements. "They have slipped away onto the Navajo Reservation. We have wired authorities throughout Arizona and New Mexico to look for them."

The only mention of the robbery the following week concerned the wounded mail clerk. He was released from the hospital.

"Finding anything?" Jacobs asked. "Reading these old papers is like eating peanuts. You can't stop. Here's a piece about a stagecoach robbery. Imagine!"

"Wonder why he saved that?" Chee was thinking of motivations.

"One of the passengers said it was Butch Cassidy."

Chee was still thinking of motivations, remembering the bandits had gotten away with very little money. That led to a thought of the coin-collector books at Redd's place, the pennies on his table. If coins were involved, they'd be antiques now. And valuable.

"Redd had about a million pennies when we were there," he said. "Do you know what that's all about?"

"It's all about how a graduate student stays alive," Jacobs said. "Pays the rent.

When Odell gets his paycheck, he cashes it at the bank and buys all the pennies he can afford. And then he sorts through them looking for keepers. Some of them are worth something to the collectors. Certain dates, certain mints. Maybe, for example, you find a 1947 penny minted in Baltimore might be worth a dime, or a '54 minted in Denver maybe would be worth twenty cents. He keeps those out and sells them to the coin stores, and takes the others back and buys more pennies."

"Hey," Chee said. "That's smart. How much does he make?"

She laughed. "You don't get rich. One week he found an Indian head worth almost four dollars. That week he made about five dollars an hour for his time."

"What if you found coins taken in that train robbery? Would it be like a gold mine?"

"Not really," Jacobs said. "Odell talked about that—how great it would be to find all those old coins. But he looked it up and it was a bad time for coins. They made tons of silver dollars and five-dollar gold pieces during those years. Scarcity is what makes coins expensive."

"Like how much would a nineteen-hundred silver dollar be worth?"

"Maybe twenty dollars to a coin dealer,

if it was in perfect condition," she said. "And the newspaper said most of the money was bank notes."

So much for that idea. And while he was thinking that, he found what he'd been looking for without knowing he'd been looking for it.

The Manila folder was labeled PINTO/ CASSIDY. In it was a thick sheaf of paper, typed double-spaced.

"They say it was the summer my brother was born. That's when they say this thing happened." Penciled in the margin was the notation "1909/10?"

They say the Utes had been bad
about coming down that year.
They would come down that trail
past Thieving Rock and Blue Hill
and at night they would steal
horses and sheep from the people
around Teec Nos Pos in the flats
around the San Juan River, and
even as far over as Cineza Mesa.
They say this happened several
times, and one time the Utes shot
at a Navajo man over there. He
was out there with his sheep and
those Utes shot at him and he ran
away. They say it was a Piaute
Clan man named Left-handed.

Now Left-handed had a son named Delbito Willie and he had married a woman of the Yucca Fruit Clan and he was living with her over on the other side of the Carrizo Mountains. But he had come over there around Teec Nos Pos to see about his brothers and sisters and everybody told him about the Utes shooting at his father.

They say this Delbito Willie talked to two of his wife's brothers, and some young men in his own Piaute Clan, and he told them they should go up north, go up there around Sleeping Ute Mountain, and they should steal some Ute horses and get all their sheep and goats back.

The Piaute Clan headman over there in those days was an old fellow they called Kicks His Horse and they talked about this idea with him, and he said they should wait. They say he said that because it was in *Yaiisjaastsoh* season, which in the *biligaana* language is Season to Plant Late Crops. They call it July. At that time there is lightning and the snakes are out feeding and then you can have the kind of curing ceremonial they would need before they went on that kind of a raid. And when they got back they would need to have an Enemy Way sing to cure them, and that could not be held either because you can't hold those ceremonials until the Season When the Thunder Sleeps. You can't hold them until the ground is frozen and the snakes are in the ground.

But they say Delbito Willie he was angry about the Utes shooting at his father and he wanted to go anyway. He didn't care what anybody said. They say the Piaute Clan men listened to their headman and wouldn't go, so Delbito Willie went back to his wife's Yucca Fruit people and talked to them about it. He got seven of them to listen to him, mostly young men, they say, but one of them was Old Man Joseph. And so they got their best horses and they went off to the north toward Sleeping Ute Mountain. They say they forded the San Juan there at—

"Find something interesting?" Jean Jacobs was leaning over his shoulder.

"I think this is what Redd was telling us about," Chee said. "Pinto's story that puts Cassidy on the Navajo Reservation. Anyway it's about a raid to steal Ute horses. And the dates would be about right."

Chee flipped through the pages, read about Old Man Joseph being thrown from his horse. Flipped again, read about Delbito Willie deciding that they should take only horses and mules from the pastures west of Sleeping Ute Mountain and not try to drive the goats because the Utes would chase them. Flipped again, read about the two of the men splitting off from the party to head west to Teec Nos Pos, taking eleven of the Ute horses. One of the Piaute Clan men had been shot in the leg somewhere back in one of the pages Chee had skipped. But a fight with the Utes wasn't what he was looking for. He flipped again, scanning rapidly. Then he stopped.

They say there were Hosteen Joseph and Delbito Willie and the young men from the Yucca Fruit People still on their way home then, and they were camped out for the night somewhere between Rol Hai Rock and Littlewater

Wash. They say Delbito Willie had gone out to get some firewood because they were cooking two rabbits they had shot. He saw dust over to the northeast. They put out their fire and watched. These two men were riding toward Beautiful Mountain, leading a mule. It is said that these were white men. They saw where Delbito Willie had left the Ute ponies, on their hobbles down below the cliffs of that place. These two white men, they scouted all around, looking for the people who owned those ponies, but they never did see Delbito Willie or the Yucca Fruit People with him. So they started to steal the horses. They were cutting the hobbles when Hosteen Joseph shot one of them, and the two men got back on their horses and rode away. Delbito Willie and the Yucca Fruit men were chasing them. They were shooting at them and the two men were shooting and one of them, the white man with the yellow mustaches they say it was, he shot Hosteen Joseph. The bullet hit Old Man Joseph in the chest, right below the nipple they say, and it killed him.

After that they chased the two white men. They almost got away once, but the one Hosteen Joseph had shot fell off his horse and the other one had to stop and help him back on. After that they say Delbito Willie shot the other man, but didn't kill him. And then the two white men rode their horses out into a place where there is lava flow. Where it's dangerous to ride a horse even in the daylight. The Yucca Fruit men followed slowly, keeping way back where they wouldn't get shot because that man with the yellow mustaches, they said he was a good shot even riding on a horse. Finally they found where the white men had left their horses and went up into the rocks.

Chee skipped rapidly through the rest of it. The next morning, one of the white men had tried to come out and one of the Yucca Fruit boys shot him again—they thought in the arm this time—and he went back up into the rocks. The Navajos had waited all that day, and the next. They drank up their own water, and the water canteens the white men had left on their horses, and finally—on the morning of the fourth day—Delbito Willie had climbed up into the rocks. He followed the bloody spots back into the formation until he could see the bodies of the two men. Then the group had taken the horses and returned to their place on the other side of the Carrizo Mountains. An Enemy Way was held for all of them because of their contamination with the Utes and the white men.

Chee lingered over the section in which Ashie Pinto had described the ceremonial curing—an Enemy Way and a section of the Ghostway done, apparently, for Delbito Willie alone. It stirred his memory of an Enemy Way he'd attended as a child. The cure had been conducted by a *hataalii* who had been very tall and had seemed to him then to be incredibly ancient. The patient had been Chee's paternal grandmother, a woman he had loved with the intensity of a lonely child, and the event had formed one of his earliest really vivid memories. The cold wind, the starlight, the perfume of the piñon and juniper burning in the great fires that illuminated the dance ground. Even now, he could see it all and the remembered aroma overpowered the mustiness of this office. Most of all, he remembered the *hataalii* standing gray and thin and tall over his grandmother, holding a tortoiseshell rattle and a prayer plume of eagle feathers, chanting the poetry from the emergence story, making Old Lady Many Mules one with White Shell Girl, restoring her to beauty and harmony.

And restore her it had. Chee remembered staying at the old woman's place, playing with his cousins and their sheepdogs, seeing his grandmother happy again, hearing her laughter. She had died, of course. The disease was lung cancer, or perhaps tuberculosis, and people with such diseases died—as all people do. But it had been that cure that had caused him to think that he would learn the great curing ways, the songs and the sand paintings, and become a *hataalii* for his people. Unfortunately, his people showed no sign of wanting him as one of their shamans. He must have laughed because Jacobs asked, "Something funny? You find something interesting?"

"Just thinking," Chee said.

"About what?" Jacobs said. "You're not supposed to be holding out on me."

"I was reading what Ashie Pinto told Tagert about these Navajo horse thieves," Chee said. "They had a curing ceremonial for them when they got home and I was remembering my own boyish dreams about becoming a medicine man."

Jacobs was looking at him, eyes curious. Or perhaps sympathetic. Perhaps both. Their eyes held. Chee made a wry mouth. Jacobs looked down.

"Anything in there that helps get Tagert home so I can quit doing all his work?" she asked.

Chee shrugged. "No," he said. "Or if there is, I don't understand it."

But he was thinking about the Ghostway. He didn't know it. Frank Sam Nakai, who was a respected *hataalii* and Chee's maternal uncle and mentor in all things metaphysical, didn't know it either. Why would part of it have been done for Delbito Willie and for no one else on the raiding party? And why had Ashie Pinto, with his Navajo storyteller's predilection for telling everything in exhaustive detail, skipped so quickly over this?

Maybe Pinto would tell him that, even if he would tell him nothing else.

12

AS WAS HIS FASHION (except when it violated his sense of order), Leaphorn went through channels. The former Vietnamese colonel named Huan Ji lived in Shiprock, which was in the jurisdiction of the Shiprock subagency of the Navajo Tribal Police. Leaphorn dialed the Shiprock Tribal Police office and asked for Captain Largo.

"I've heard of him," Largo said. "He teaches at the Shiprock High School. Math, I think it is, or maybe one of the sciences. But we never had any business with him. What's he up to?"

Leaphorn told him about the conversation with Kennedy.

"I remember now," Largo said. "It was his car Jim Chee met when he was going to the Nez killing. The Bureau had us run it down for them. What'd he tell them?"

"They didn't talk to him," Leaphorn said.

"They didn't?" Largo said, surprised. Then, "Oh, yeah." He laughed—which with Largo was a deep, rumbling sound. "From what I hear he's sort of an untouchable. Supposed to have worked for the CIA in Nam."

"I think somebody ought to talk to the man," Leaphorn said. "I think I'll come and do it."

"You want me to save you the drive?"

"No use you pissing off the Bureau," Leaphorn said. "I'll do it."

"That sounds like you're still thinking of retiring," Largo said, and laughed again.

"One of these days. Anyway, I'm at the point where if a yelling match started with the feds, anybody who decided to fire me would have to move fast."

Largo didn't comment on that. He said, "Let me know when you're coming, and if you need any help. Right now, I'll just look that address up for you."

"I'll probably come this afternoon," Leaphorn said. "Just as soon as I get my paperwork done."

But just as he was moving the penultimate report from in-basket to out-basket, the telephone rang.

"A woman down here to see you," the desk clerk said. "A Professor Bourebonette."

"Ah," Leaphorn said. He thought a moment. "Ask her to come on up."

He put down the telephone, pulled the ultimate report out of the basket, opened it on his desk, and then stared out the window at the sun and shadows on Window Rock Ridge. A question of motive again. What brought the professor here? A long drive from Flagstaff. Either she had risen in the predawn darkness or she had spent the night somewhere. At the Window Rock motel perhaps, or at Gallup. A strong motive. Friendship, she said. Friendship might well be part of it. But what else?

As she came through his door, Professor Bourebonette's words were apologetic. But her expression wasn't.

"I realize we're imposing on your time. Hosteen Pinto isn't your responsibility. But I wondered if you could bring me up to date. Have you learned anything?"

Leaphorn was standing. "Please," he

said, motioning her to a chair. He sat, too, closed the waiting folder. "I haven't learned anything very useful."

"What did Professor Tagert say? I called his office and they told me he wasn't in. They didn't know when to expect him. That seems awfully odd. Their semester started two or three weeks ago. He'd have to be keeping office hours."

"Dr. Tagert seems to have jumped ship," Leaphorn said. "I got the same information you did."

"He's missing?" Dr. Bourebonette sounded incredulous. "Are the police looking for him?"

This was something that always had to be explained. Leaphorn did it, patiently.

"It doesn't work that way with adults. You have a right to be missing if you want to be. It's nobody's business but your own. The police 'look' only if there's some crime involved. Or some reason to suspect foul play."

Professor Bourebonette was frowning at him. "There's certainly a crime involved here. And isn't he what you call a material witness?"

"He might be," Leaphorn said. "If he is, nobody knows it. The crime is the Nez homicide. There's nothing to connect him to that. Absolutely nothing."

Bourebonette absorbed this statement, her eyes on Leaphorn but her thoughts, obviously, on something else. She nodded, agreeing with some inner notion. Leaphorn considered her. What was she thinking? It would be something intelligent, he was sure of that. He wished the thought, whatever it was, would provoke some remark that would give him a clue to what she was doing here.

"Have you considered that Tagert might be dead?" she asked. "Have you considered that whoever killed your officer also killed Tagert? Have you thought of that?"

Leaphorn nodded. "I have."

Bourebonette was silent again, thinking. Long silences didn't seem to bother her. Unusual in a white. From downstairs Leaphorn could hear a telephone ringing. He smelled coffee brewing. Professor Bourebonette was wearing a cologne of some sort. The aroma was very, very faint. So faint it might be his imagination.

"The trial should be postponed," Bourebonette said suddenly. "Until they can find Professor Tagert." She stared at Leaphorn, her eyes demanding. "How can we arrange that? Surely they can't try Mr. Pinto without knowing what's going on.

Nobody knows what actually happened out there."

Leaphorn shrugged. But the shrug wasn't good enough.

"I think we have a right to expect some sort of effort toward simple justice," Bourebonette said. Her voice sounded stiff. "Mr. Pinto has a right to demand that."

"I'll admit I would have liked a little solider investigation," Leaphorn said. "But it's not my responsibility. It's a federal case and the federals have all they need to convince a jury beyond any reasonable doubt. The game is played a little—"

"Game!"

Leaphorn interrupted the interruption with an upraised palm. He, too, could be aggressive. "—a little differently when the defendant does not deny the crime," he continued. "In the first place, that reduces any worry that you have that you might have arrested the wrong person. In the second place, it leaves you without the defendant's story to check. So there's much less the arresting agency can do, even when it has the very best of intentions."

Bourebonette was studying him. "And you think they've done all that's necessary?"

He hesitated. "Well," he said, "I would want to talk to Tagert, and there's another loose end or two."

"Like what? Lack of a motive?"

Leaphorn closed his eyes. Memory has no temporal limits. When he opened them again two seconds later memory had shown him a score of bloody scenes.

"Whiskey is the perfect motive," he said.

"Then what?"

He wanted to turn the question around, to ask this woman to tell him why this drunken shooting was worth so much of her time. It was probably the book. Friendship and the book. She needed Pinto free to finish it. But maybe there was something deeper. If he asked her, she would simply repeat that Pinto was innocent, that Pinto was a friend.

"Well, Officer Chee met a car when he was driving toward the crime scene. This car might have driven past the scene. Perhaps not, but most likely it did. Maybe the driver saw something. Probably not, but I would have found him and asked."

"Of course," Bourebonette said. "You mean nobody did."

"I hear they didn't."

"But why not?"

"Why not? Because they had their case. Smoking gun. Motive. No denial. They have other work to do, stacked on their desks." He made an illustrative gesture at his own desk. Except for the single folder it was uncharacteristically, point-defeatingly clean.

"Too much trouble running him down. Too much trouble finding the car. When an old man is being tried for murder." Her voice was bitter.

"We found the car," Leaphorn said. "It belongs to a schoolteacher at Shiprock. I'm going to talk to him today."

"I'll go with you," Bourebonette said.

"I'm afraid that—" Then he stopped. Why not? No damage to be done. It wasn't his case anyway. If the Bureau got mad, it would get no madder because this woman was along. And he wanted to know what she was after. This business was interesting him more and more.

They took the road that wanders over Washington Pass via Red Lake, Crystal, and Sheep Springs. Winding down the east slope of the Chuskas, Leaphorn stopped at an overlook. He pointed east and swept his hand northward, encompassing an immensity of rolling tan and gray grasslands. Zuni Mountains to the south, Jemez Mountains to the east, and far to the north the snowy San Juans in Colorado.

"Dinetah," he said. She would know the meaning of the word. "Among the People." The heartland of the Navajos. The place of their mythology, the Holy Land of

the Dinee. How would she react?

Professor Bourebonette said nothing at all for a moment. Then: "I won a bet with myself," she said. "Or part of a bet. I bet you would stop here and enjoy the view. And I bet you'd say something about naming this pass after Washington."

This wasn't what Leaphorn had expected.

"And what would I have said?"

"I wasn't sure. Maybe something angry. I would be bitter if I was a Navajo to have anything in my territory named after Colonel John Macrae Washington. It's like naming a mountain pass in Israel after Adolf Hitler."

"The colonel was a scoundrel," Leaphorn agreed. "But I don't let the nineteenth century worry me."

Bourebonette laughed. "If you don't mind my saying so, that's typically Navajo. You stay in harmony with reality. Being bitter about the past isn't healthy."

"No," Leaphorn said. "It's not."

He thought: Professor Bourebonette is flattering me. Why? What will she want from this?

"I would be thinking of the insult," Bourebonette said. "Every time I took this route it would rankle. I would think, why does the white man do this? Why does he honor the man who was our worst enemy and rub our noses in it? The colonel who murdered Narbona, that honorable and peaceable man. The colonel who broke treaty after treaty, and protected the people who captured your children and sold them into slavery in New Mexico and argued for a policy of simply exterminating your tribe, and did everything he could to carry it out. Why take such a bastard and name a mountain pass right in the middle of your country after him? Is that just the product of ignorance? Or is it done as a gesture of contempt?"

There was anger in Bourebonette's voice and in her face. This wasn't what Leaphorn had expected, either.

"I would say ignorance," Leaphorn said. "There's no malice in it." He laughed. "One of my nephews was a Boy Scout. In the Kit Carson Council. Carson was worse in a way, because he pretended to be a friend of the Navajos." He paused and looked at her. "Washington didn't pretend," he said. "He was an honest enemy."

Professor Louisa Bourebonette showed absolutely no sign that she sensed the subtle irony Leaphorn intended in that.

The sun was halfway down the sky when they started down the long slope that drops into the San Juan River basin and

Shiprock town. They had discussed Arizona State University, where Leaphorn had been a student long ago, whether the disease of alcoholism had racial/genetic roots, the biography-memoir-autobiography of Hosteen Ashie Pinto the professor had been accumulating for twenty years, drought cycles, and law enforcement. Leaphorn had listened carefully as they talked about the Pinto book, guiding the conversation, confirming his thought that the Pinto effort was the top priority in this woman's life but learning nothing more. He had noticed that she was alert to what he was noticing and that she had no problem with long silences. They were enjoying such a silence now, rolling down the ten-mile grade toward the town. The cottonwoods along the river formed a crooked line of dazzling gold across a vast landscape of grays and tans. And beyond, the dark blue mountains formed the horizon, the Abajos, Sleeping Ute, and the San Juans, already capped with early snow. It was one of those still, golden days of high desert autumn.

Then Leaphorn broke the mood.

"I told the captain in charge of the Shiprock subagency I'd let him know when I got here," he said, and picked up the mike.

The dispatcher said Captain Largo wasn't in.

"You expect him soon?"

"I don't know. We had a shooting. He went out on that about an hour ago. I think he'll be back pretty quick."

"A homicide?"

"Maybe. We sent an ambulance. You want me to call the captain?"

"Don't interrupt him," Leaphorn said. "When he comes in, tell him I went directly out to the Huan Ji residence. Tell him I'll fill him in if I learn anything."

"Huan Ji," the dispatcher said. "That's where the shooting was reported. That's where we sent the ambulance."

13

THEY MET THE AMBULANCE return-
ing to the Shiprock Public Health Service
Hospital as they turned off onto Huan Ji's
street. The emergency lights were flash-
ing and the siren growling. Leaphorn had
been around violence too long to be de-
ceived by that. The driver was in no
hurry. He recognized Leaphorn as they
passed, and raised a hand in salute. Whoever had been shot at Huan Ji's place was
either in no danger or he was already
dead.

Ji's house was a rectangular frame-
and-stucco bungalow in a block of such

structures. They had been designed long ago by a Bureau of Indian Affairs bureaucrat to house Bureau of Indian Affairs employees. As they had weathered and sagged, they had passed from that existence and become tribal property—occupied now by schoolteachers, hospital clerks, road-grader operators, and similar folk. Ji's house was instantly recognizable. It had attracted a cluster of police cars and a scattering of neighbors watching from their yards. Even without the magnet of this temporary tragedy, it would have stood out.

It was surrounded by a neat chain-link fence and flanked by a tidy gravel driveway that led to an empty carport. Inside the fence was a flower bed, precisely bordered by a perfectly aligned row of bricks. Six rose bushes were spaced on each side of the concrete sidewalk. Autumn had turned the Bermuda-grass lawn gray, but it was trimmed and ready for spring.

The house itself was a clone of its neighbors and as alien as a Martian. In a row of houses frayed, faded, and weary, its fresh white paint and fresh blue trim seemed a reproach to the dusty street.

Captain Largo, as neat as the house but somewhat smaller, was standing on the porch. He was talking to a skinny tribal policeman and a neat young man in a felt hat and a dark gray business suit—which meant in Four Corners country that he was either an agent of the Federal Bureau of Investigation or a young man making his mission for the Church of Jesus Christ of Latter-day Saints. Largo's bulk made them both look unnaturally small. He recognized Leaphorn and waved.

Leaphorn glanced at Bourebonette, thinking of how to phrase his request.

She anticipated it.

"I'll wait in the car," she said.

"I won't be long," Leaphorn said.

On the porch, Largo introduced him. The skinny policeman was Eldon Roanhorse, who Leaphorn vaguely remembered from some affair out of the past, and Gray Suit was Theodore Rostik of the Farmington office of the Federal Bureau of Investigation.

"Mr. Rostik just transferred in this summer," Largo said. "Lieutenant Leaphorn is with our criminal investigation division. Out of Window Rock."

If Rostik was impressed by Leaphorn or his title, he concealed it. He nodded to Leaphorn, turned back to Largo.

"Window Rock," he said. "How'd he know about this? How did he get here so quick?"

Once this rudeness would have irritated Leaphorn. That was a long time ago. He said, "I just happened to be up here on another matter. What do you have?"

"Homicide," Largo said. "Somebody shot the owner here. Twice. No witnesses. Mailman heard him moaning. Looked in and saw him on the floor and turned it in."

"Any suspects?"

"We're talking to neighbors but nobody much seems to have been around when it happened," Largo said.

"This will be a federal case," Rostik said. "Felony on a federal reservation."

"Of course," Leaphorn said. "We'll help any way we can. Interpreting, things like that. Where's his wife?"

"Neighbors say he's a widower," Roanhorse said. "He was a teacher down at the high school. He lived here with his boy. Teenaged kid."

"If we need help—" Rostik began, but Leaphorn held up his hand.

"Just a second," he said. "Where's his car?"

"Car?" Rostik said.

"We've got a call out on it," Largo said, looking solemnly at Leaphorn. "I understand it's an old white Jeepster."

"The son wasn't here?"

"Not unless he did it," Rostik said.

"When the mailman got here there was just Mr. Ji."

"Mr. Rostik," Leaphorn said, "if you don't have any objection, I'd like to look around inside. Nothing will be touched."

"Well, now," Rostik said. He cleared his throat. "I don't see what—"

Captain Largo, who almost never interrupted, interrupted now. "The lieutenant is usually our liaison with the Bureau in cases like this. He'd better see what you have here," he said, and led the way inside.

The homicide team had drawn a chalk outline of where Colonel Huan Ji's body had fallen against the front room's wall. A great splotch of blood drying on the polished hardwood floor made the chalk redundant. Except for that, and a scrabble of reddish marks on the tan wallpaper, the room was as neat as the yard. Immaculate. And cool as the autumn afternoon outside.

Leaphorn avoided the blood and squatted beside the defaced wallpaper.

"He left a message?"

"He left two," Rostik said.

" 'Save Taka,' " Leaphorn read. "Is that what it says?"

"His son's name is Taka," Rostik said. "According to the neighbors."

Leaphorn was far more interested by

the other message. Ji apparently had written them in his own blood by moving a shaky finger across the wall. SAVE TAKA above, and below it: LIED TO CHEE.

"Any theories about this bottom one?" Leaphorn asked.

"Not yet," Rostik said.

Leaphorn pushed himself erect, grunting. He was getting old for the squatting position. He looked at Captain Largo. Largo looked back, expressionless.

"Unfortunately, Chee is a common name among Navajos," Largo said. "Like Smith in Chicago, or Martinez in Albuquerque."

Leaphorn drifted into the kitchen, looking at tidiness, touching nothing. Huan Ji's bedroom was fairly large, but suggested a monastery cell—a narrow bed tightly made, a chair, a small desk, a dresser, a chest of drawers with what seemed to be a camera bag on top of it. Everything tidy. Nothing to suggest someone lived here. He stood at the desk, looking down at the blotter, the little cup holding paper clips, the pen in its holder.

Behind him, Rostik cleared his throat. "Don't touch anything. We'll go through all of this later," Rostik said. "Everything in here. Everything in the house. With trained people."

"Of course," Leaphorn said.

Taka's room was tidy by Leaphorn's standards, if not by Huan Ji's. An identical narrow bed, covers tight. Similar furniture. But the boy's desk was cluttered with books and papers and his dresser was a gallery of photographs. Leaphorn, hands in his jacket pockets, examined these pictures. Most of them were of a girl, a moderately pretty Navajo of perhaps sixteen. One of these seemed to be a school yearbook portrait, rephotographed and blown up to eleven-by-fourteen-inch size. The others were candid shots, apparently taken when the subject wasn't looking. Some included two or three other youngsters, but always with the girl. Many of them had been taken, judging from the compressed background, with a telescopic lens.

The back porch was screened, a repository for stored items. A door opened from it into a side room which Leaphorn guessed had been tacked on as a third bedroom. The door bore the stenciled legend: DARKROOM. KNOCK BEFORE OPENING. He glanced at Rostik, nodded at him, turned the knob. It was dark inside, the windows covered with opaque plastic, the air heavy with the smell of acids. Leaphorn switched on the overhead light. It was a small room, sparsely furnished. Along one side, a table bore a small enlarger, a set of developing tanks, and an array of the inevitable chemical containers. Beside that was another table and on it an open-faced cabinet held boxes which Leaphorn presumed held photographic paper. His gaze wandered over all of this and returned to the developing trays and the electric print dryer beside them. Eight-by-ten prints were stacked in the basket below the dryer.

Leaphorn picked up the top one by the edges. It was a black-and-white photograph of what seemed to be a rugged, irregular outcropping of rock. He replaced the print and picked up the one below it. At first he thought it was identical. Then he saw it was apparently another segment of the same outcropping, with some overlapping. He replaced it and reached for a third print.

Rostik touched his elbow.

"I don't want anything touched," he said. "The experts may want to go over this room."

"Then I will leave it for the experts," Leaphorn said.

On the porch again, he suddenly remembered the professor waiting in the car. He wanted to talk to Largo about Officer Jim Chee, but he didn't want to wash any Tribal Police laundry in front of Agent Rostik of the Federal Bureau of Investigation. First he would explain things to Bourebonette. He'd tell her to start the engine and turn on the heater. He'd tell her that he wouldn't be much longer.

As he started across the street, he saw the old white Jeepster turn the corner. It rolled halfway down the block, stopped, began backing away from the cluster of police cars at the Huan Ji house. Then it stopped again, remaining motionless on the street. Guilt, Leaphorn thought. Or perhaps fear struggling with curiosity. Whatever the driver's motivations, the Jeepster rolled forward again. Leaphorn trotted across the street in front of it to his own car. Bourebonette had rolled down the window. She was watching him.

"It was about what we thought," he said. "Someone shot Mr. Ji twice. Fatally. No one saw it or heard anything. No suspects. And this—" he nodded toward the Jeepster now pulling into the gravel driveway at the Ji residence "—will probably be Taka, who is Mr. Ji's son."

Professor Bourebonette was looking past him at the car. "Does he know?"

"Probably not. Not unless he did it."

Bourebonette looked down. "How sad,"

she said. "How terrible. Is his mother home? Do you think this could—" She stopped.

"Be connected with the Nez homicide?" Leaphorn finished. "Who knows. You don't see anything on the surface, but—" He shrugged.

Across the street, Rostik and Largo were talking to a slender boy in jeans and a black leather jacket. Largo had his large hand on the boy's shoulder. They moved through the front door and disappeared into the house.

"I think I'll go back over there," Leaphorn said.

"Do they need your help?"

Leaphorn chuckled. "The man in charge is the young man in the gray suit," he said. "If he wants my help he has shown absolutely no sign of it. I'll be quick this time."

Roanhorse was waiting on the porch.

"Was that Ji's son?"

"Right," Roanhorse said. "Name's Taka. Something like that."

"He okay?"

"Looked like somebody hit him with a club when Rostik told him," Roanhorse said.

Taka Ji was sitting stiffly on the edge of a recliner chair. Rostik was facing him, perched on the arm of the sofa. Largo leaned against the wall, his round, dark face devoid of expression. Leaphorn stopped just inside the door. Rostik glanced at him, looked irritated, chose to ignore him, continued his questioning.

He was good at it, Leaphorn noticed. Young, obviously. Probably inexperienced. But well trained in the job, and smart. Some of the questions replowed old ground from new angles. Some were new. Huan Ji's son, still looking as if he had been hit by a club, answered them tersely.

He had not seen his father since he'd driven to school with him in the Jeepster. Right?

Taka nodded. "Yes," he said. His voice was so small that Leaphorn could barely hear him.

And how had he gotten the Jeepster?

"My father, he said I could use it after school. He would walk home. He liked to walk. So after my biology class, I got it from the parking lot."

"The key was left in it?"

"I have a key. My father has a key. I have one."

"And where did you go?"

"I drove out toward Ship Rock. I am taking pictures out there. Photographs."

"Pictures of who?"

Taka was looking straight ahead, seeing something in the wallpaper across the room. His face was pale. He closed his eyes. "I take pictures of landscapes," he said.

"Who was with you?"

Leaphorn thought Taka hadn't heard the question. But he had. Finally he said: "No one. I go alone."

A Vietnamese in a Navajo school. A long time ago Leaphorn had been a Navajo in white Arizona State University. He understood what Taka had not quite said. What was it that Colonel Ji had written on the wall in his own blood? "Help Taka." Something like that.

Rostik changed the subject.

"Did your father have enemies?"

Taka shrugged. "He was a man," he said. "A long time ago he was a colonel in the army." He looked up at Rostik. "The Army of the Republic of Vietnam."

"But do you know of any enemies? Had he received any threats?"

Again it seemed Taka wouldn't answer. Then he tilted his head, frowned. "I don't think he would have told me." This knowledge seemed to surprise him.

"No threat you know of then?"

"No."

"Do you know anyone named Chee?"

"Like I told you, there is a boy on the basketball team. There is a girl in my history class."

"Does your father have any friends named Chee? Any enemies?"

"I don't know," Taka said. "There is a teacher. In junior high school. Her name I think is Miss Dolores Chee."

"A friend of your father's?"

"I don't think so," Taka said. "There are lots of Chees."

Leaphorn glanced at Captain Largo and found Captain Largo glancing at him. Largo made a wry face.

And so it went. Leaphorn listened and watched. He assessed Rostik, and reassessed him. A smart young man. He assessed Taka as best he could. This was not the normal Taka. This was a stunned teenager. The death of his father was still unreal, an incredible but abstract fact. Rostik now was covering yesterday. How had Taka's father behaved? What had he said? Leaphorn noticed the boy was shivering.

Leaphorn interrupted.

"Mr. Rostik," he said. "Just a moment, if you don't mind." And he turned to Taka.

"Son. Do you have any relatives here? Anybody to go to?"

"Not here," the boy said. "Not here at Shiprock."

A stranger alone in a strange land, Leaphorn thought. He asked: "Where?"

"My aunt and uncle. They live in Albuquerque."

"Are they the ones you are closest to?" As he asked it, Leaphorn thought how different this would be for a Navajo boy. He would be smothered by family. But maybe it would have been that way for Taka Ji, too, if his people had not been uprooted by war. Perhaps the Vietnamese had not, like the *biligaana,* lost the value of the family.

Taka was nodding. "They are all there is," he said.

"We'll call them when you are finished here," Leaphorn said, glancing at Rostik.

"I'm finished," Rostik said to Taka. "I'll just need to know where we can reach you if we need to know something else."

"How about a friend here? Somebody you can stay with tonight?"

Taka thought. He gave Leaphorn a name, the son of another of the high school teachers.

Rostik left. They made the calls on the colonel's telephone and Roanhorse took Taka in hand. He'd deliver him to the house of the friend.

"I'll lock the place up," Captain Largo said. "We'll keep an eye on it until the feds go over it."

"One last look at the darkroom," Leaphorn said. "No one will ever know."

With Largo peering over his shoulder, he went through the stack of prints in the dryer basket—eleven photographs of segments of the same outcropping of what seemed to be part of a long basaltic ridge. They were taken—or seemed to be—from the same viewpoint, as if the camera with a telescopic lens had been shifted slightly on a tripod for each exposure.

"Landscapes," Largo said. "If those are his landscapes he's not going to get rich with them."

"No," Leaphorn said, and placed them back in the dryer basket. "You recognize the place?"

"They could have been taken any of a hundred places," Largo said. "It just looked like a big bunch of extruded lava. Fairly old. Could be out there around Ship Rock. Could be down in the malpais south of Grants. Could be over east of Black Mesa. Could be lots of places."

On the porch, Largo paused to lock the front door.

"Can you think of any reason those pictures might have been taken?" Leaphorn asked.

"None," Largo said. "No idea why any teenage kid does anything."

"They might have been taken by the colonel," Leaphorn said. "He was a photographer, too."

Largo nodded. "True," he said. But he wasn't particularly interested.

"Odd though," Leaphorn said. "When he feels better I might ask him."

"Maybe the colonel did take them," Largo said. "But so what. People are always taking pictures of rocks. They think they see a shape like a duck, or Ronald Reagan, or God knows what."

"You think the boy did it?"

"The killing? I don't. How about you?"

Leaphorn shook his head. The sort of a shake that avoids an answer.

"I've got another question," Leaphorn said. "While Chee is a common name among us Dinee, unfortunately, it is not all that damn common. How the hell did your Jim Chee get himself mixed up with this?"

Largo's expression was grim. "I intend to find out."

"So do I," Leaphorn said.

14

JANET PETE HAD NOT liked the idea. Basically, no matter what she said, Jim Chee understood that she hadn't liked it because she hadn't trusted him. At worst, she thought he might betray her. Chee doubted that she really believed that, although the possibility that she did lingered in his memory. And rankled. At best, she wasn't certain she could depend on his discretion. On his good judgment. That rankled, too. In a way, that was even worse.

Chee had finally let his temper show. That was a weakness new to him, and he realized it. He explained it to himself as a product of raw nerves; of a hand which, with every twinge, reminded him it might never be fully useful again; of traumatic memories which recalled his failure to perform his duty. However he explained it, he didn't like the way it felt.

"Janet," he said. "Spare me all that lawyer talk. I've told you I won't ask the old man for a confession. I won't ask him what he was doing out there that night. Or how he got there. Or what the hell caused him to shoot Nez. I just want to ask him about the story he told to the professor. Just why he thinks the Enemy Way sing was done for all those horse thieves, and the Ghostway Chant added for one of them. I won't ask him anything that would make any sense to the FBI. Or to you either, for that matter."

That had touched a nerve. Janet's voice turned chilly.

"I'll spare you the lawyer talk. You spare me the 'I'm more Indian than you are' crap. Okay?"

Chee hesitated. "Right," he said. "Sorry about that."

"Okay, then," she said. "But you play by the rules. I'm going to be there every minute. Ashie Pinto only answers what I want him to answer. You two speak better

Navajo than I do, so if I want you to explain a question, you by God explain it until I understand what you're getting at or it doesn't get answered. Understood?"

Chee had understood perfectly.

Janet Pete set it up for three that afternoon and Chee took a cab down to the County Detention Center where federal prisoners were being held. It was a sunny, windless autumn afternoon with a fringe of high clouds drifting in from the northwest, reminding him that the TV weatherman had reported snow in Flagstaff last night and the front—as always—was drifting eastward. He showed his credentials to the desk clerk and a deputy jailer escorted him to the visitors' room.

Janet Pete was waiting. She sat behind a long wooden table in a straight wooden chair looking small and tired and beautiful.

"Yaa' eh t'eeh," Chee began, and swallowed it and said, "Hello, Janet," instead.

She smiled at him. *"Yaa' eh t'eeh,"* she said. "I do know a little Navajo."

"As much as I do," Chee said, which was a blatant lie, but a guard ushered in Hosteen Ashie Pinto before she could say so.

Here, in this still, sterile room lit by a battery of fluorescent tubes, Ashie Pinto was not the man Chee remembered. He remembered a stumbling drunk illuminated in the yellow glare of his headlights, wet with rain, blurred by Chee's own shock and Chee's own pain. Now he was smaller, desiccated, frail, dignified, and terribly old. He sat in the chair next to Janet Pete, acknowledged her with a nod. He looked at Chee, and then at the heavy bandages wrapped on Chee's left hand. Then Ashie Pinto repeated the only thing Chee had ever heard him say.

"I am ashamed," he said, and looked down.

Chee looked down, too. And when he looked up, Janet was watching him. He wondered if she had understood the Navajo phrase.

"I think I told you Mr. Pinto speaks hardly any English at all," she said. "I told him you were coming, of course, so he remembers who you are. He still does not want to say anything at all about the crime and I told him not to answer any questions until I tell him to."

"Okay," Chee said. "The question I want to ask him takes some explaining. Stop me if you get lost."

And so Chee began.

"My uncle," he said, "I think you may have heard of Frank Sam Nakai, who is a singer of the Blessing Way and the Mountain Top Chant and many of the other curing songs. This man is the brother of my mother, and he has tried to teach me to follow him and become a *hataalii*. But I am still an ignorant man. I have much yet to learn. I have learned a little of the Ways of the Holy People. And what I have learned has brought me here to ask you a question. It is a question about something you told to a professor named Tagert."

Chee stopped, eyes on Pinto. The man sat as still as death, waiting. His skin was drawn tight over the skull bones, seeming almost transparent in its thinness. The desiccation made his eyes seem protuberant, larger than they were. They were black eyes, but the cornea of one was clouded by a film of cataract.

Sure now that Chee had finished his statement, Pinto nodded. Chee was to continue.

"You were telling the professor about a time, perhaps before you were born, when some young men of the Yucca Fruit People rode over to Sleeping Ute Mountain to get back some horses the Utes had stolen from them. Do you remember that?"

Pinto remembered.

Chee summarized the rest of the adventure, taking time to tell it carefully. He wanted to draw Pinto's consciousness out of this room, out of his role as prisoner and into his past. Finally he had reached the place which had puzzled him.

"The way the *biligaana* professor wrote down what you told him may not be exactly what you told him. But what he wrote down is like this. That you said the *hataalii* the Yucca Fruit People called decided that an Enemy Way sing should be held for all of those young men. Is that true?"

Pinto considered. He smiled slightly, nodded.

"Then the *biligaana* professor wrote down that you told him that this singer decided he should also hold a Ghostway Chant for the man they called Delbito Willie. Is that true?"

There was no hesitation now. Hosteen Pinto nodded.

"That is the first of my questions," Chee said. "Do you know why this Ghostway was needed?"

Pinto studied Chee's face, thinking. He smiled slightly, nodded again.

"My uncle," Chee said, "will you tell me why?"

"Not yet," Janet Pete said. "I didn't understand a lot of that. What are you driving at?"

"Basically, why a certain cure was prescribed for one of those men and not for the others. That suggests he broke a specific taboo. I wonder what it was?"

Janet Pete was obviously lost. "But how . . . ? Oh, go ahead and answer it."

Hosteen Pinto glanced at Janet Pete, then back at Chee, then at something out the window beside Chee's shoulder. Chee waited. Through the glass came the sound of an ambulance siren, the sound of brakes applied. Somewhere in the building a door slammed, the clang of steel on steel. Chee could smell dust, an astringent floor cleaner, the aroma peculiar to old, old men. Pinto released his breath, a sighing exhalation. He looked at Janet Pete again, smiling. *This man,* Chee thought, *this kindly old man is the man who murdered Delbert Nez. The man who burned my friend in his car. The man whose actions caused this terrible burn across my hand. Why did he do it? Whiskey.* Todilhil. *The Water of Darkness. Twice it had turned this old man into a coyote.*

Hosteen Pinto shifted in his chair, seeking some comfort for old bones. "This young woman has become like a granddaughter to me," he said. "She tells me that she knows you. She says that you are an honorable man. She says you follow the Navajo Way."

He paused to give Chee a chance to respond to that. Then drew a deep breath.

"These things I told Hosteen Professor. I think they wrote these things all down on paper. And you read that paper? Is that right?"

"Yes. I read it all."

Pinto looked puzzled.

"And you know the Navajo Way?"

"I have studied it some," Chee said.

Pinto's expression was slightly skeptical, as if he wondered how much Chee had studied.

"They say there were many skinwalkers then," Hosteen Pinto began. "Even more than now. Do you understand skinwalkers?"

"I know something about them," Chee said. He settled himself in his chair. This was going to take a long time. Pinto would begin in the beginning and talk his way through it. And the longer he talked the better the chance that he'd cast some light on this murky business. If, that is, anything connected with anything.

"They teach us that everything has two forms," Hosteen Pinto said, starting even further back than Chee had expected. "There is the mountain we see there beside Grants, the mountain the *biligaana* call Mount Taylor. That is the outer form. And then they say there is the inner form, the sacred Turquoise Mountain that was there with the Holy People in the First World, the Dark World at the very beginning. And First Man brought it up from the Third World and built it on his magic robe, and decorated it with turquoise. And then there is the yucca. We see the outer form all around us, but it is the inner form of yucca that we offer the prayer plume for when we dig its roots to make the soap to clean ourselves."

He paused, studying Chee. "You understand?"

Chee nodded. This was basic Navajo metaphysics. But he wondered if Janet had ever heard it.

"Bluebird has two forms, and the deer and the beetle. Two forms. They have the form of the *yei* and they have the outer form that we see. All living things. You too. And I. Two forms."

Hosteen Ashie Pinto leaned forward, tiny in the yellow coveralls of the county prisoner, intent on Chee's understanding.

"And then there is Coyote," he said. "Do you know about Coyote?"

"I know something about Coyote," Chee said. He glanced at Janet Pete. She was focused on Pinto, concentrating on what he was saying. Wondering, Chee imagined, where all this was leading. "I know about his tricks. I have heard the stories. How he snatched the blanket and scattered the stars into the Milky Way. How he stole the baby of the Water Monster. How he tricked the sister of the bears into marrying him. How—"

The amusement on Pinto's face stopped him.

"The children are told the funny stories about Coyote so they will not be afraid," Pinto said. The amusement went away. Pinto smiled a tight, grim smile and launched into the explanation—as old as the culture of the People—of why Coyote was not funny. Chee listened, wishing, as he had come to wish many times in such sessions with old taletellers, that Navajos did not have to start everything at the very beginning. He glanced at Janet again. She looked bemused, probably wondering what the devil he was hoping to learn from all this—a wonder Chee was beginning to share. But at least she couldn't accuse him of trying to learn anything incriminating. Unless, of course, the old man talked long enough to tell him what Chee had come here to learn.

Now Hosteen Pinto was talking about how the name for Coyote in the Fourth World was not *atse'ma'ii*, or First Coyote, but *atse' hashkke*, or First Angry, and what that implied symbolically in an emerging culture in which peace and harmony were essential to survival. He talked of Coyote as the metaphor for chaos among a hungry people who would die without order. He talked of Coyote as the enemy of all law, and rules, and harmony. He talked of Coyote's mythic power. He reminded Chee how Coyote always sat in the doorway of the hogan when the Holy People met in Council, neither quite part of these representatives of cosmic power, nor totally allied with the wilderness of evil outside. And finally he reminded Chee that other wise people, like the old men in the Hopi kiva societies, knew that there was a time when humans had two hearts. Thus they were able to move back and forth from one form to the other—from natural to supernatural.

"I think your uncle must have taught you about the power of skin," Pinto said. He looked up for confirmation in Chee's face and, seeing it, went on:

"They say that's how Changing Woman created the first Navajos. From the skin rubbed from her breast, she formed the Salt People, and the Mud Clan, and the Bitter Waters and the Bead People. I have heard of your uncle, of Frank Sam Nakai. They say he is a great *hataalii.* He must have taught you how Coyote transformed First Man into a skinwalker by blowing his hide over him. You know about that? About how First Woman wouldn't sleep with him because now he had all the evil ways of Coyote, smelled like coyote urine, licked himself and tried to lick her, and did all those dirty things that coyotes do. And how the Holy People cured First Man by passing him through the magic hoops to strip away his coyote skin. Your uncle taught you that?"

"Some of it," Chee said. He remembered a little of it. It was something re-enacted in part of the Ghostway ceremony—a cure for the most virulent form of witch sickness.

"So then you know why this fellow had to have the Ghostway sing," Pinto said. "He had to have it because he had been with the *yenaldolooshi.*"

"No," Chee said. "I don't understand that."

Janet Pete raised a hand. "Wait a minute. I don't understand this either. *Yenaldolooshi?* That is the word for animals that trot, isn't it?"

Chee nodded. "Animals that trot on four legs. But it is also used for skinwalkers. Witches."

"Where is this conversation going?" she

asked. "Are you leading Mr. Pinto into something? Do you remember what you promised?"

Pinto was watching, puzzled.

Janet Pete switched to Navajo. "I wanted to make sure that Mr. Chee was not trying to get you to say something that would hurt your chance in the trial," she explained. "I want you to be careful about that."

Hosteen Pinto nodded. "We are talking about something that happened a long time ago," he said.

"I don't understand, my uncle," Chee said. "Why did they do the Ghostway sing for the one they called Delbito Willie when they did the Enemy Way for the others?"

"Because he went in there," Hosteen Pinto said. His tone was patient. "He went in there—into Tse A'Digash. He went in there where the witches gather. He went in there among the corpses and the skinwalkers. He went in to the place where the *yenaldolooshi* do their ceremonies, where they do incest, where they kill their relatives."

Silence. Chee thought about this. He frowned, glanced at Janet Pete. She was watching him. Well, he would ask it anyway.

"My uncle, would you tell me just where this Tse A'Digash is located?"

Pinto's expression changed. "I cannot tell you that."

"Could you tell me if Professor Tagert hired you to show him where it was?"

Hosteen Pinto stared at Chee. "When you arrested me that night, I could smell the fire in your clothing. I could smell where your flesh had burned. I said I was ashamed. I am still ashamed of that. But these things you ask me now, I cannot tell you."

"What's going on?" Janet asked.

Hosteen Pinto stood, limped toward the doorway, his old bones stiff from the sitting.

"Could you just tell me who gave you that whiskey?"

Hosteen Pinto tapped on the glass. The jailer was coming.

"Don't say anything," Janet said. Then to Chee, angrily, "So much for your promises."

"I just want some of the truth," Chee said. "Maybe the truth will make him free."

15

JIM CHEE HAD NOT flown enough to learn to think creatively on an airplane. He spent the time on this Mesa Airlines turboprop flight looking down from his seat by the window at the early snow on the Jemez Mountain ridges below, and the great broken expanse of tan and gray of the Chaco Mesa country and finally, at the ribbon of fading yellow and black that marked the San Juan River Valley. His mind was on Janet Pete, who had been ir-ritated with him—but not nearly as ir-ritated as he had expected her to be. He decided, tentatively, that this was because

Hosteen Pinto had told him nothing incriminating. Still, she should have been furious because he'd tried to take advantage of her. That could be explained if Janet didn't give a damn how he behaved. Chee didn't like that explanation. It was true, perhaps, but he rejected it. More and more, he was giving a damn about Janet.

He retrieved his pickup from the airport parking lot and drove down off the mesa into the heavy after-work traffic on 550. He'd stop at the police station in Shiprock and see if the captain was in. Largo had been around a lot longer than Chee and knew a lot more people in this part of the Reservation. He might have heard of the Tse A'Digash that Ashie Pinto had mentioned. It would be somewhere south of Shiprock, Chee guessed. Somewhere in the volcanic outcrop country. Probably not too far from where he'd arrested the man. And if Largo didn't know, he'd be likely to know some old-timer who would.

But Largo wasn't at the station.

Angie was at the desk.

"Hey, man, how's the hand?" she asked, grinning at him. And without waiting for an answer: "The captain's been looking for you. Like he has something heavy on his mind."

"What?" Chee asked, starting the automatic examination of conscience that such statements provoke. "I'm on sick leave."

"I don't know what. He didn't say. But Lieutenant Leaphorn was with him. Up from Window Rock. And he looked pissed off."

"Leaphorn?"

"Captain Largo," Angie said. "Come to think of it, the lieutenant, too, I guess."

"Was that today?"

Angie nodded. "They left here just a little bit ago."

To hell with it, Chee thought. He'd see Largo when he saw him. The Leaphorn news disturbed him more. Leaphorn had been trying to reach Tagert. There could be just one explanation for that. The lieutenant, the supercop, had invited himself into the Pinto investigation. Not at the invitation of the FBI, Chee guessed. That wasn't likely. More likely he'd guessed Officer Jim Chee had screwed it up. Well, to hell with Leaphorn.

"Angie, you've been here awhile. Do you know any places around this part of the Reservation that people call Tse A'-Digash?"

Angie just looked at him.

Chee persisted. "A place with a bad reputation for witches? Sort of place people stay away from?"

"Sort of place people don't talk about to

strangers, either," Angie said. "I'm from over near Leupp. Over on the southwest side of the Reservation. Three hundred miles from here."

"I know," Chee said. "But you've lived here ten or twelve years."

Angie shook her head. "That's not long enough," she said. "Not to talk about skinwalkers with you."

And it wasn't. Chee knew that.

Chee drove home thinking about who, among his friends, was enough of a Ship Rock territory old-timer to know what he needed to know. He had three names in mind, with Largo the fourth. Largo was sore at him, apparently, at the moment. But that was not unusual. And Largo would tell him what he knew. He wondered what had upset the captain, and Lieutenant Leaphorn. And at the thought of Leaphorn, he was irritated himself.

As he tilted his pickup off gravel and onto the steep track that led downward through the rabbitbrush toward his trailer house, he saw he had a visitor. A car was just pulling away from the trailer, coming toward him. A Navajo Tribal Police patrol car.

It stopped, went into reverse, reparked just where Chee usually parked his pickup. He parked beside it.

Captain Largo was driving, another policeman beside him.

"Glad to see you," Largo said, hoisting himself out. "We've been looking for you."

"That's what Angie said," Chee said. "You want to come in?"

"Why not," Largo said.

The other policeman emerged from the passenger door, putting his uniform hat back on a head of short-cropped gray hair. Lieutenant Leaphorn.

"Yaa' eh t'eeh," Leaphorn said.

The afternoon sun still lit the high side of Shiprock town but here in the cottonwoods beside the river Chee's trailer had been in shadow for long enough to be cold. Chee turned on the propane heater, filled his coffeepot with water, got out three cups and three of the paper filters he was now using to brew the stuff right in the cups. Why had the captain been looking for him? Why was Leaphorn here, so far from his desk at Window Rock? Chee lit the fire under the coffeepot, conscious that he was more cautious with fire than he used to be. The captain and the lieutenant occupied his two chairs. Chee took a seat on the edge of his bunk.

"We have to wait until the water boils," he said. "Just takes a few minutes."

Largo cleared his throat, producing a rumble.

"We had a man killed here in Shiprock today," Largo said. "Shot."

This was not anything like what Chee had expected.

"Shot? Who?"

"Fellow named Huan Ji," Largo said. "You know him?"

"Wow," Chee said. He sat stock still, digesting this. Digesting how he was learning it, too. "Yeah," he said. "I don't exactly know him, but I've talked to him. Once. Last week. It was his car I saw out there where Delbert was killed." Then another thought. "Who shot him?"

He noticed Leaphorn sitting, arms folded across his chest, watching him.

"No suspects," Largo said. "Apparently somebody came to his house this afternoon. It must have been very soon after he got home from school. Or maybe they were there waiting for him. Anyway, whoever it was shot him twice. Left him on the floor in the front room."

"Son-of-a-bitch," Chee said. "Any idea why anybody'd shoot him?"

"None," Largo said. He was leaning his chair back against the wall, looking at Chee over his glasses. "How about you? Any ideas?"

"None," Chee said.

"What did you talk to him about?"

"About what he might have seen that night Nez got killed."

"What did he see?"

"He said he didn't see anything."

"He left a note," Largo said. "Wrote it on the wallpaper there where he was lying. He wrote 'Take care of Taka' and under that he wrote 'Tell Chee I lied.' He put his finger in his own blood and wrote it."

"Be damned," Chee said.

"What do you think he meant?"

Chee hesitated. "Well, I knew he lied about one thing. He said he didn't see any other cars. He had to have seen my police car. He was coming toward me, his Jeepster was, and he did a right turn just before we met. My siren was going and the flasher. And my headlights were right on him. No way he wouldn't have seen me."

The three of them considered that.

Leaphorn said: "Odd thing to lie about."

"I thought so, too," Chee said. "I wondered why."

"Did you ask him?"

"No."

"Why not?"

"I didn't think it would lead anywhere."

Leaphorn considered this, and nodded.

He said: "Why did you go talk to him? You're on convalescent leave. And it's a federal case."

Chee felt himself flushing. "The FBI hadn't talked to him," Chee said. "I thought he might have seen something."

Leaphorn didn't comment on that. He said: "The water's boiling for your coffee."

Once Joe Leaphorn had been addicted to cigarettes—smoking unfiltered Pall Malls at a rate of two packs a day and, when he shifted to filters in response to Emma's concern, three packs a day. He had broken that habit early in Emma's terminal illness. He had bitten the nicotine deprival bullet as a sort of offering to her, who loved him. And to the gods—that this small, lovely woman would be left with him. As the yearning for cigarettes faded he had found it replaced by a delight in coffee. Now he awoke each morning in his lonely bed anticipating that first sip and savoring it. His working day was measured out in the intervals between the cups. Being Leaphorn, being logical, he'd known that this obsessive affair with coffee represented a flaw in his character, a weakness, as well as a risk to his health. He'd made a logical compromise: no more than four cups before noon and nothing but decaffeinated stuff after lunch. With that he lived fairly happily.

But today he'd had almost no coffee. He had drunk his usual two cups with what was left of last night's mutton stew for breakfast. He had stopped at the store beside the highway at the Newcomb junction for another cup. But none had been available. At lunch in Shiprock the product served had been a reheated stale brew obviously left over from breakfast and undrinkable even by Leaphorn's relaxed standards. And then the homicide of Huan Ji had interfered. Now, as Jim Chee poured boiling water through the coffee grounds, the aroma that reached Leaphorn's nostrils was indescribably delicious.

He'd never seen coffee made that way before. Chee had arrayed three mugs beside the sink, put a little black cone-shaped gadget atop one of them, inserted a paper filter into it, dumped a spoonful of Folger's into that, and poured the water through. Then he replaced the grounds and repeated the process in the other cups. Wasteful, Leaphorn thought, and time-consuming. But when he tasted the results, he was impressed. Downright fine. As good as any he'd ever tasted. He studied Chee over the rim of the cup. Odd young man. Good-looking in a way, with the sort of long, sensitive face women seemed to like. A fairly good cop, excellent in some categories, weak in others. He remembered that Largo had tried him out as an acting sergeant once. It hadn't lasted long for some reason he had forgotten or, more likely, had never known. But he could guess the reason. Chee wasn't an organization man. He was a loner. Liked to freelance. A man who worked inside the system only until the system interfered. One of those who marched to his private drummer. This business of trying to be a *hataalii* and a policeman at the same time, for example. It wasn't just impractical. How the hell could a cop get time off at the drop of a hat for a nine-day sing? It was incongruous. It was like being an investment banker and a Catholic priest at the same time. Or a rabbi and a clown. People wouldn't accept it. They expect a shaman or a priest to be different from ordinary humans, expect him to live in the shadow on the dangerous mystical fringe of the supernatural.

Now Chee was refilling the pot, the heavy bandage on his left hand making it a clumsy project. The fruit of freelancing, Leaphorn thought. But in fairness he should say a dead policeman was the result of the rules-bending, the burned hand the product of Chee's bravery. He wondered if he would have walked into that fire, gripped that red-hot door handle, to save another man's life. He wasn't sure he would have. He might have stood there, calculating the odds of success—trying to do what was rational.

"Is it still painful?" Leaphorn asked. "The hand?"

"Not much." Chee sat on the bunk again. "Not if I'm careful."

"You mentioned one thing Ji lied about when you talked to him. Do you think that's what the message was about?"

Chee was tucking a stray end of the gauze back into the bandage—concentrating on that.

"No," he said. "I doubt it."

Smart, Leaphorn thought. Of course it wasn't that. "What do you think it was?"

Chee hesitated. "This is new to me," he said. "I need a minute to get it together."

Leaphorn sipped, enjoyed it. Wonderful coffee.

"Take your time," he said.

Chee looked up from the bandage. His face was full of anger.

"I have a question for you. What pulled you into this? Into the Delbert Nez homicide?"

Leaphorn considered Chee's expression, the anger in his voice. "Somebody shot Huan Ji," he said. "That pulled me into it."

"No," Chee said, shaking his head. "Last week you were looking for a professor named Tagert. What's up? You think I arrested the wrong man? You think I screwed that up, too?"

Captain Largo shifted in his chair. "Take it easy," he said.

Chee's emotion was interesting. What motivated it? Leaphorn turned his cup in his hands.

"I wondered how Pinto got where you found him," he said. "The FBI didn't check it out. They didn't see any reason to, I guess, since you gave them the man with the smoking gun." Leaphorn was silent a moment, looking into Chee's anger. There was absolutely no reason for him to tell this young man anything. No reason except the bandaged hand and what it represented.

"I wondered about that," Leaphorn continued, "and then Pinto's niece came to see me. She's Turning Mountain Clan. A relative of my late wife. She wanted to hire a private detective to find out who gave the old man the ride. I decided to do it for her."

Chee nodded, unmollified.

"You wondered, too, I noticed," Leaphorn said. "You went to the trouble of finding out about Tagert hiring him, too."

"Did he hire him?" Chee said. "All I knew was that Tagert had used him in the past. As a source for old legends. That sort of thing. Had Tagert hired him this time?"

"Yes," Leaphorn said. He told Chee about the letter Old Man McGinnis had written, about the vehicle seen driving away from Pinto's place. "How did you make the Tagert connection?"

Chee told him about Janet Pete, about climbing into the formation where the crazy painter Nez hoped to catch had been defacing the rocks. He told him what they had seen there, that the painter had carried a ladder into the formation, painting high places, ignoring low ones, painting part of the surface of one formation, skipping the next one. He told him about the car with the REDDNEK plate, about going to the library at UNM to listen to Pinto's tapes, noting who had taped them. He told Leaphorn about what he had learned from Jean Jacobs and Odell Redd.

"You think Tagert is chasing down something about Butch Cassidy then?" Leaphorn asked.

"They think so," Chee said. "That seems to be his connection with Pinto.

That old story about the horse thieves and the two whites."

"So what do you think Ji lied to you about?"

The abrupt change of subject didn't seem to bother Chee.

"I don't think Ji was driving the car," Chee said. "I think he lied about that."

"Why?" Leaphorn asked. "Why do you think that?"

"He didn't see my car. He didn't see the fire. He was very cautious about the way he answered questions. He didn't volunteer anything that would catch him out. He just waited for a question and then gave a very careful, limited answer."

"Why would he lie about that? You have any theories?"

"What else did you say he wrote on the wall?" Chee asked.

Captain Largo answered that: " 'Take care of Taka.' "

"No," Leaphorn said. "It was 'Save Taka.' "

"That's his kid?" Chee asked. "Right?"

Leaphorn smiled slightly, approving of the way Chee's mind was working. "So you're thinking that Taka was driving the car? I think that's not a bad guess. He was driving it after school today. He drives it a lot, I think. He told me he even has his own key to it."

"I suspect he didn't want the boy pulled into a police investigation," Chee said. "I don't know why."

"He seems to have been a special friend of the Central Intelligence Agency. Back from his days in Vietnam," Leaphorn said. He explained what Kennedy had told him.

"So maybe Colonel Ji was just the nervous sort. Is that what you're thinking?" Chee asked.

Leaphorn shrugged. "A man makes a career out of playing hard games, it would be difficult to get over that sort of thinking. A policeman gets killed. You don't want your child touched by something like that." He shrugged again. "Good a guess as any. We just don't know enough."

"No," Largo said. "We don't know a damned thing. Except homicide is a felony and we don't have jurisdiction in any of this. Nez nor Colonel Ji."

"We have jurisdiction in a vandalism case," Leaphorn said. "Tell me about that?"

Largo looked puzzled. "What vandalism?"

Chee said, "You mean the painting on the rocks? You know what was in the report. Well, Delbert noticed this maybe two or three weeks earlier. Somebody putting white paint here and there in a rock formation out there between Ship Rock and the Chuska Range. He got interested in it and he started swinging past there whenever his patrol would allow it. He was hoping to catch the guy. But he never did."

"And he thought he saw him that night?"

"That's what he said."

"And it sounded like he was going after him?"

"That's how it sounded."

Leaphorn put down his coffee cup. He glanced at the stove. Steam was jetting from Chee's pot, but this wasn't the time to break this chain of thought.

"What do you think?" Leaphorn asked. "You see any connection? Was Ashie Pinto painting rocks? That seems totally unlikely. Did Pinto being there have something to do with the painting? Anything at all to do with it? Or was it just that Nez, thinking he was chasing his painter, turned out to be chasing Pinto? And he catches himself a homicidal drunk. Or what? What do you think?"

Silence.

Largo got up and turned down the burner under the coffeepot. He picked up the funnel that held the grounds. "How do you make this stuff?" he asked. "And as far as the painter and Ashie Pinto are concerned, I pick number two. Nez thought he was chasing his nut and he catches Pinto."

Chee scratched the back of his neck. "Yeah," he said slowly, "that sounds the most probable."

"No connection otherwise, then?" Leaphorn said. "Neither of you can think of any?"

Chee got up, collected the cups, lined them beside the sink, and picked out a fresh filter.

Another cup of coffee would be fine, Leaphorn thought. And then he would go and pick up Professor Bourebonette and be on his way. She had come up with a graceful way to get out of his way when he'd come out of Ji's house and returned to the car.

"You're going to be busy for a while," she had said. "Just drop me off at the community college. I have a friend in the library there I'd like to see."

Nothing more was going to come out of this conversation. He would drink his coffee, drop by the library to pick up the professor, and then head back to Window Rock. Neither Chee nor Largo seemed to be able to think of any connection between a rock painter and a policeman's murder. But there must be one. Because Leaphorn's logic told him that somehow Colonel Ji had tried to tell them that with his blood-smeared finger. The man must have known he was dying. Protect his son, he'd told them, and then that he had lied to Chee. There must be a connection, and the connection—as Chee thought, too—must be that the boy had been driving his car that night. Driving it out where an old drunk was killing a policeman and a madman was painting random patterns on an outcrop of lava.

Random, Leaphorn thought. Random. When he was a young man, a junior at Arizona State, running around, drinking, chasing the girls, he had gone to a sing-dance once over between Kinlichee and Cross Canyon. It had rained that night, and he and Haskie Jim, his father's older brother, had watched the first drops pattering into the dust. He had been full of the mathematics he was studying, and of his own wisdom, and he had talked to his old uncle of probabilities and of randomness. He had always remembered the scene.

"You think these raindrops are random?" his uncle had asked. And Leaphorn had been surprised. He'd said of course they were random. Didn't his uncle think they were random?

"The stars," Haskie Jim said. "We have a legend about how First Man and

First Woman, over by Huerfano Mesa, had the stars in their blanket and were placing them carefully in the sky. And then Coyote grabbed the blanket and whirled it around and flung them into the darkness and that is how the Milky Way was formed. Thus order in the sky became chaos. Random. But even then . . . Even then, what Coyote did was evil, but was there not a pattern, too, in the evil deed?"

That had not been the time in Leaphorn's life when he had patience for the old metaphysics. He remembered telling Haskie Jim about modern astronomy and the cosmic mechanics of gravity and velocity. Leaphorn had said something like "Even so, you couldn't expect to find anything except randomness in the way the rain fell." And Haskie Jim had watched the rain awhile, silently. And then he had said, and Joe Leaphorn still remembered not just the words but the old man's face when he said them: "I think from where we stand the rain seems random. If we could stand somewhere else, we would see the order in it."

After he had thought about the meaning in that, Leaphorn had looked for order in everything. And he usually found it. Except in the events of insanity. Joe Leap-

horn didn't think a man—or a woman—
who carried a ladder along with a paint
gun into the hills would be insane.

There was a pattern there, and a motive, if he could only find them.

16

DEPUTY T. J. BIRDIE was on duty when Jim Chee arrived at the San Juan County jail at Aztec. T. J. said he was just too busy right now.

"We're short-handed. I got the desk and the telephone switchboard, and the radio and everything all to myself. Just George back there in the jail and me. Come in tomorrow during regular hours and somebody will do it for you. It's not as easy as you make it sound. All that sorting around. Putting stuff back where it was."

"Come on, T. J.," Chee said. "Don't act like a horse's ass. All you got to do is pull the file on booking Ashie Pinto and let me take a look at the inventory of what stuff he had."

"Can't leave the phone," T. J. said. "Sheriff'd hang me up by the balls if he calls in here and I'm not on it." Deputy Birdie was a stubby young man with his black hair cut short—half Apache. It was gossiped in political circles that the sheriff had hired him in the interest of attracting votes from the nearby Jicarilla Apache Reservation and still didn't know Birdie was a Mescalero, whose numerous kin-folks and clansmen voted two hundred miles south and east in Otero County. Chee knew that Birdie was actually White Mountain Apache whose folks voted in Arizona and he was pretty sure the sheriff had hired him because he was smart. Unfortunately he was also lazy.

"Come on, damn it," Chee said. He came around behind the counter. "Just get in there and pull out the Ashie Pinto file. I'll answer the telephone for you."

"Well, hell," T. J. said. "What's the big hurry?"

But he left, muttering. And when he returned five minutes later he handed Chee the folder.

The inventory of Hosteen Ashie Pinto's impounded possessions was short:

wallet containing:
two fifty-dollar bills
photo of woman
photo of two men
one pocketknife
one comb
one tin chewing tobacco
    containing corn meal
one leather pouch (jish) containing:
    two crystals
    feathers
    mineral stones
    bull durham pouch of pollen
    assorted small jish items

Chee handed the folder back to Birdie.

"That it?" Birdie said. "Can I get back to doing my duty for San Juan County now?"

"Thanks, T. J.," Chee said.

"What were you looking for? Did you find it?"

"His *jish*. The old man is a crystal gazer," Chee said. "I wanted to see if he was working. If he had his medicine bundle with him."

"Well, hell," Birdie said. "I was here the night they brought him in. I could have told you that. Saved me all that work if you'd just asked."

It was late but Chee decided to make

the four-hour drive to Albuquerque, turning the new information over in his mind. First, there was the fact that Tagert had hired Pinto. Presumably he'd picked up Pinto at his hogan and taken him to the vicinity of whatever he was hunting. Pinto had taken along his crystals—the tools of his profession as a finder of the lost and seer of the unseen. Some white men around the Reservation used crystal gazers but Tagert didn't seem the sort. He guessed the historian was more interested in the old man's memory than in his shamanistic powers. Memory of what? Logically it would be connected to Tagert's interest in two white men who seemed to have died a long lifetime ago in a rock formation on the Navajo Reservation. Presumably Tagert would be hunting their bodies, for evidence that one of them was the notorious Butch Cassidy. Logic suggested that the rock formation would be somewhere fairly close to where he'd arrested Pinto. There were plenty of them around—the product of the same paroxysm of volcanic action that cracked the earth and formed the basaltic spires of Ship Rock. It might be the same formation into which he and Janet Pete had taken their stroll to study the work of Delbert Nez's nutty vandal. If all else failed, he might search that formation again. Given a day or two to cover it better and more daylight he might find something. Or get snakebit. But Pinto's old tale suggested witches were involved. First he would see where that could lead him.

And then there was the business of Colonel Ji. Who? Why? Probably Ji had lied to protect his son, Chee guessed. What had his son done? Or was it just a father's concern that his kid might be involved in something dangerous?

He turned it over, and over, and over. And the thinking kept him awake while he drove the endless miles of N.M. 44 toward Albuquerque. He had relied on a translator's transcript of Hosteen Pinto's tale of horse theft and homicide. He wanted to hear it for himself in the old man's own voice.

17

THE YELLOW TAPE used to isolate the scene of a crime dangled loosely across Colonel Ji's front gate. Leaphorn detached it, ushered Professor Bourebonette through, and reconnected it behind them.

"You're sure this is all right?"

"The people from the Bureau are all finished in here," Leaphorn said. "But keeping your hands in your pockets, not moving anything—that's a good idea."

Actually, it wasn't exactly all right. It would be better if Bourebonette waited in the car. Better still if he had made this recheck of the colonel's darkroom before he picked her up at the library. But he hadn't thought of it until too late for that. And then the idea pressed on him. A feeling of urgency that he couldn't really understand.

He unlocked the door, felt the little sigh of cold air that empty houses release when he opened it. It was a familiar sensation to Leaphorn—one he felt each evening when he unlocked his own house in Window Rock.

Nothing had changed in the front room, except it was silent now and the sills and surfaces bore the faint gray stains of fingerprint powder. He noticed Professor Bourebonette looking at the chalk lines that marked where the colonel's body had been. He noticed the colonel's messages were still on the wall, looking blacker now under the artificial yellow glare of the ceiling bulb. He noticed the professor's expression. Strained? Sad? Mournful? Obviously this is unpleasant for her. Why was she here?

Everything in the darkroom was as he remembered it—a cramped, airless space, musty, nostrils filled with the acid smell of print-developing fluids. The prints were where he had seen them but now they also wore traces of gray powder. Would an FBI lab technician be sorting out Joe Leaphorn's fingerprints? He checked his memory. No, he had handled everything carefully, by the edges.

Now he spread the prints on the cabinet top in two neat rows and examined them methodically. They were all the standard eight by ten inches on black-and-white glossy paper. All seemed to be exposures of parts of the same dark basaltic outcrop. They seemed to have been shot from a considerable distance through a telescopic lens. Or perhaps they had been magnified in the enlarger. The same negative had been used to make several of the prints, each blown up to a different magnification. But the angle in all was almost exactly the same—as if all the negatives had been exposed from the same location, but had been made by using lenses of different focal lengths and by shifting the camera on the tripod. All included the same segment of that outcrop. Some more of it, some less, depending on the lens. But in all, the same features were near the center of the print.

Leaphorn showed them to Bourebonette and explained what he was thinking.

"Why telescopic?" she asked.

"Notice this juniper in the foreground here in this one? Here it is in this other one. Notice how the relationship in size has changed. A telescopic lens compresses the distance like that."

Bourebonette nodded. "Sure," she said. "That's the way the optics would work."

"You know the Reservation pretty well. Does this look familiar?"

She studied the prints. "They're all the same place, obviously. But we don't get enough of it to put it in the landscape."

"Have you seen it?"

She laughed. "Probably. Or something like it. It could be about forty places in the malpais down around Grants. Or maybe out in the Bisti badlands, or in the Zuni Mountains, or on the Black Mesa side of Monument Valley, or down around the Hopi Buttes, or out here beyond Shiprock toward Littlewater or Sanostee. Or one of those volcanic throats east of Mount Taylor, or—" She shook her head, and handed the prints to Leaphorn. "Hard to tell. Any place that lava bubbled up through the cracks during a volcanic period. And that happened a lot out here."

"It would be near here someplace, I think," Leaphorn said. "We can presume Ji or his son shot them. Do you have any idea why either one would do that? Or make all these prints?"

"No idea," she said. "But they certainly weren't taken for the beauty of the landscape. Could you call the boy and ask him? Didn't you say he was staying with some friends here?"

"They decided against that. They're taking him to Albuquerque to stay with some relatives instead. He won't be there yet. But let's see if we can locate the negatives. Maybe they'll include enough background to tell us where this is."

They spent almost thirty minutes sorting negative files without finding anything useful.

Leaphorn pulled the wastebasket from under the sink, sorted through it, and extracted a crumpled sheet of photographic paper. It was part of the same scene, blown up larger on an eleven-by-fourteen-inch sheet. The print was much darker. Overexposed in the enlarger, Leaphorn guessed, and thrown away. He spread it on the cabinet, looked at Bourebonette, raised his eyebrows in a question.

"I don't know," she said. "Maybe big enough to work with." She looked at Leaphorn and grinned. "But work on what?"

"I think maybe we're just wasting our time," he said and put the picture back in the wastebasket.

"I'm thinking you're in a strange business," she said.

"Oh, not usually," he said. "All this is an oddity."

"A single-minded photographer," she said. "Rocks and this girl." She touched the portrait of the teenager Leaphorn had noticed earlier. "Several of these. Probably the boy's girlfriend, I'd guess."

"It looks like it's a photocopy," Leaphorn said. "Not very good."

"Out of this, maybe," she said. The Shiprock High School yearbook was on the shelf behind the enlarger.

They found the girl's portrait among the cheerleaders. She was a junior. Jenifer Dineyahze.

"I think we should go find Jenifer Dineyahze," Leaphorn said. "Maybe she can tell us something useful." But even as he said it, he doubted it.

Jenifer Dineyahze proved to be a rider of the Shiprock school bus.

"It's a little tough to tell you exactly where the Dineyahzes live," the acting assistant principal told them, and he dug a map out of his desk drawer and showed them which school bus she rode and just about where the bus picked her up. "Back in here," he said, putting the tip of his pencil on the slope of Beautiful Mountain. "Or here, maybe." And he moved it a little toward Sanostee. "You'll see the place where the track takes off to the left."

Before they left Shiprock, Leaphorn filled the tank of his patrol car—as he always did on junkets that would take him onto the back roads. But at least this errand took them south and west, toward Window Rock and home. And it would take them past the place where Jim Chee had arrested Ashie Pinto. It would give him a look at the rock formation where the painter had done his vandalism.

"What do you think you're going to learn?" Bourebonette asked.

"Frankly, nothing," Leaphorn said. "I think tomorrow I'll get on the telephone and try to get hold of the boy in Albuquerque and I'll ask him about the pictures. But it's sort of on the way home—or back to your car. And you never know."

They turned west off Route 666 toward Red Rock on Navajo 33.

Bourebonette pointed south toward Rol Hai Rock and then toward Barber Peak across the highway. "Those pictures," she said. "It could be a little piece of either one of those."

"Or even of some of those rays that run out from Ship Rock," he said. "Any new ideas by now of why he took them?"

"No. Not even an old idea. How about you?"

"I have an old idea," Leaphorn said. "I'm thinking that when we get to that rock formation Nez's vandal was painting, maybe it will turn out to be the same formation Ji, or Ji's boy, was photographing."

Bourebonette thought about this. "Why?"

Leaphorn chuckled. "I was afraid you'd ask me that," he said. "I think it's because since my wife died I've started watching television. That's the way the plot ought to work out."

Bourebonette didn't comment for a while. And then she said: "Well, there had to be some reason for somebody to shoot Colonel Ji. He was up around where the painter was working the night Mr. Nez was killed. At least his car was. And he took pictures of the rocks. So maybe there's a connection."

Leaphorn glanced at her, caught her looking at him. She shrugged. "Sounds silly, but the same rocks—" she said, "—that would be some connection."

Leaphorn made a left turn off the asphalt onto a dirt road which hadn't been on this year's road grading schedule. They bumped down it, raising dust. "Well," he said. "We'll soon know."

Leaphorn parked at the place the car of Officer Nez had burned. It had been hauled away—an unusual fate for a derelict vehicle on a reservation where they commonly rusted away where they died— but the place was marked by the skeletons of partially burned junipers and scorched cactus.

"There it is," Bourebonette said, pointing. "See the painted places?"

The formation rose to the southeast, one of many old volcanic extrusions scattered along the flanks of the great upthrusts that form the multitude of mountain ridges of the southern Rockies. "Where?" Leaphorn asked and, as he said it, saw a stripe of white, and another, and another, where no white should be.

"Ah," he said, and reached behind the seat of his car for his binoculars. But before he used them, he studied the formation, looking for the same pattern of shapes he memorized from the photographs. He didn't see it.

The formation seemed to have been produced by a series of eruptions. In some places the basalt had been worn smooth by eons of time and softened by growths of lichens—its cracks sprouting buffalo and bunch grass, cactus, and even scraggly junipers. Elsewhere it was newer, still ragged and black. A couple of miles long, Leaphorn guessed, with a smaller formation beyond it extending perhaps another quarter of a mile.

Through the binoculars the formation seemed even rougher and more complex.

In places the upthrust seemed to have forced overlying sandstone upward, producing broken walls and leaning slabs in a chaotic labyrinth. There, in the highest part of the ridge, the painting had been done.

Done carefully. Despite what Chee had told him, that surprised Leaphorn. At the point where the binoculars were focused, the black of the basaltic surface and the white of the paint formed a slight curve, not perfect but generally clean-cut. He shifted his vision to the next spot. The shape seemed irregular. Perhaps that was because of his perspective. But here, too, the margin was clean. He could see too little of the other painted surfaces to form a judgment.

He handed the binoculars to Professor Bourebonette. "Notice the edges. Notice how carefully done," he said. While she looked, he thought about what she was seeing. As he did he understood exactly where the photographs had been taken.

His uncle had been right. Things seem random only because we see them from the wrong perspective.

He told Bourebonette about it as they drove down the bumpy road toward the Dineyahze place.

"It still sounds crazy as hell," he said,

"but I think either Ji or the boy took all those photographs and blew them up to plan where to put the paint."

Professor Bourebonette looked suitably surprised. She considered. Leaphorn slowed, let the car roll across the borrow ditch and onto a road, which quickly became simply two parallel tracks through the bunch grass and snakeweed.

"Okay," Bourebonette said finally. "If you wanted to paint something regular on a totally irregular surface, I guess that's how you could do it."

"I think so," Leaphorn said. "You'd pick the spot you wanted to see it from, and take the photographs, mark out the places where the paint had to go. Little bit here on this corner of this slab, and then back here, and up there and so forth."

"That leaves the really big question, though," she said. "The big question is why anybody sane would want to paint something out here. And what it would be." She looked at him. "You have that part of it figured out?"

"Afraid not," Leaphorn said.

"I think that would take some real genius."

The patrol car eased up a long slope, jolting over rocky places. The windshield was coated with dust, but the sun was low in the southwest now, out of their faces. Leaphorn shifted down, and up, and down again. And suddenly he found another answer. Or maybe he did.

"I have another thought," he said. "About 'what.' Or more about 'why.' "

Bourebonette looked at him, waiting.

Leaphorn considered whether he would look stupid if he was wrong. It occurred to him that he was showing off. And enjoying it. He considered that. Why would he be showing off? Why enjoying this?

"Are you going to tell me?" Bourebonette asked.

Leaphorn shifted up again as the tracks leveled off. "When we get to the top of this ridge here, we're going to be able to see that formation again. From a different perspective now. I think we're going to see those painted spaces coming together. Forming a unity."

"Oh? Like what?"

"Something to do with this little girl we're going out to visit." And as he said it, realized that it sounded absurd. It would be wrong. The painting would remain, forever, a crazy jumble.

They reached the summit of the ridge. The shoulder was wide here, blocking their view of the formation. But they could see the Dineyahze place. It was built on the slope opposite them. The Dineyahze outfit included a small oblong of house with a tarpaper roof weighed down against windy weather by a scattering of old automobile tires, a hogan built of stone, a mobile home set on concrete blocks, and the usual brush arbors, corrals, and storage sheds.

"If I'm guessing right, the Ji boy took those photographs from the ridge above the house. He wanted the same view that Jenifer would have from her yard." He glanced at Bourebonette, who was looking impressed.

"If I am guessing wrong," he added, feeling sudden embarrassment, "then I have made myself look foolish."

"Right or wrong," Bourebonette said, "I'd say you have made yourself look like an innovative thinker. None of that occurred to me at all."

The rock formation emerged slowly into view as the car moved along the ridge. And then they could see the paint.

Leaphorn stopped the car. He pulled on the parking brake. He stared.

Jubilation!

It wasn't perfect from this perspective. But you could easily make it out. The white-against-black read:

"Can you see it?" he asked. "Can you read it?"

"How about that?" Professor Bourebonette said. "Congratulations to you, Lieutenant Leaphorn."

Her smile engulfed him with warm approval.

"I should have thought of it sooner," he said. "I had all the information I needed. As soon as I knew where the girl lived, I should have guessed."

"Modesty," Bourebonette said. "I think that was right out of Sherlock Holmes."

"To tell you the truth, I'm sort of proud of it myself," he said.

"I wonder what the girl thinks?" Bourebonette said. "I think I'll ask her."

"I don't see much need to bother her now," Leaphorn said. "We were going to ask her if she had any idea what would be going on with Taka. Now we know."

"We sure do," Bourebonette said.

She was silent while he backed the car around. Then she said: "What we don't know is why somebody shot his father."

"No, we don't," Leaphorn said.

But he was beginning to think he might know that, too.

CHEE HAD HOPED to catch Janet Pete before the federal court session convened. But there was the problem of finding a parking place in downtown Albuquerque. So he emerged from the elevator just in time to see the U.S. marshals ushering Hosteen Pinto into the courtroom.

"Jury selection today," the receptionist at the Federal Public Defender's office had told him. "She'll be over in Judge Downey's court in the new Federal Building. On Gold."

"How long will that take?" Chee had asked, and the answer had been "Maybe all day. Maybe tomorrow. Probably you can catch her before it starts. If you hurry."

He'd hurried, but not quite enough. Maybe, he thought, there would be a recess and he could talk to her then. He nodded to the bailiff at the door and started in.

"You'll have to sit over by the wall, and about the fourth row," the bailiff told him. "All the front rows are for the jury panel, and they use the back rows until their names get called."

Chee sat against the wall in the fourth row and watched the panel being ushered in. There would be sixty of them if he remembered the procedure—men and women from around New Mexico with nothing much in common except that they lived in this judicial district and had registered to vote. Thus their names had been drawn for this duty.

When the last one was seated a middle-aged woman in a dark blue dress began spinning the bingo cage on a table beside the judge's bench, pulling out names. An elderly Hispano named Martinez was first. He came down the aisle through the gate in the railing, turned right, and took the first chair in the row inside the railing.

"Mrs. Eloise Gibbons," Blue Woman read, and a slender young woman in a gray pantsuit came down the aisle and took the chair next to Martinez.

"Mr. William Degenhardt," Blue Woman said, and a conservative-looking man with a conservative haircut and a conservative gray suit took the chair to her right.

Blue Woman continued the litany, filling the row of chairs inside the railing, and then the two rows behind it. Slightly more women than men, Chee estimated. Altogether, seven Anglos and Hispanics, a Vietnamese or Cambodian, a middle-aged Navajo woman, a man who might be an Apache, and two who were clearly Pueblo Indians, although Chee couldn't identify which of the Pueblos.

Janet Pete and a man who Chee guessed must be the federal prosecutor assigned to this case were standing in front of the high desk where the judge sat. The three were discussing something with her. Would that be an advantage? Woman judge, woman lawyer? Chee doubted it. It would be fairly common these days.

Chee felt tremendously drowsy. It was warm in the courtroom and he'd slept very little last night. He thought of his hand, which was itching under the bandage. How much use of it would he recover? He thought of what he wanted to tell Janet

Pete—about Ji's son being the driver of the car he'd seen the night Nez was killed. About Ji's message on the wall. He thought of how Janet Pete looked. She was wearing something dark green with a skirt that came far below her knees. She had pretty knees, not that he'd seen them often, and pretty ankles.

Janet was standing facing the jury panel now and the judge was asking if any panelist knew her, knew her family, had had any dealing with her. A very classy woman, Chee thought. He felt a wave of affection, and of chauvinistic Navajo pride in her. And more than that, he felt a hunger for her. And a sense of failure. Since the day she'd come to the hospital to see him he'd lost ground with her. He was sure of that. She liked him less now than she did that morning.

The prosecutor was standing, undergoing the same scrutiny from the jury panel. One man on the front row put up his hand, and said he knew the man. They were members of the same church. He was excused.

Then Ashie Pinto stood. The business suit issued by the Bernalillo County jail for this appearance was too large for him, making him look even thinner than Chee had remembered.

"Face the jury panel, please, Mr. Pinto," the judge said.

Hosteen Pinto reacted to his name. He looked back at the judge, puzzled.

"Interpreter!"

The interpreter responded to the impatience in Judge Downey's voice. He awoke from whatever had been occupying his thoughts, stood, said something in Navajo too low for Chee to understand.

Hosteen Pinto looked at the man, cupped a hand behind his ear.

"She wants you to look out at those people," the interpreter said, much louder now. "So they can see you."

Pinto looked out at them, his expression sometimes embarrassed, sometimes determined. Pinto's eyes moved across the courtroom, hesitating a moment when they came to the Navajo panelist, hesitating another moment when they met the eyes of Jim Chee.

Chee looked away, down at his itching hand.

No one knew Hosteen Ashie Pinto. The whites didn't know him, nor the Hispanics, nor the Apache, nor the Pueblos, nor the Asian. *Nor Janet Pete, nor me. He is a shaman. He is a stranger to us all.*

The prosecutor looked at his notes then looked up. "Mrs. Greyeyes, I believe you live at Nakaibito. On the Navajo Reservation. Is that correct?"

"Actually, closer to Coyote Canyon," Mrs. Greyeyes said.

"But on the Reservation?"

"Yes."

"Are you a Navajo?"

"Yes."

"Do you have any clan relationships with the defendant?"

"I don't know what he is."

The prosecutor looked at his notes.

"I have two clans written down here. Turning Mountain Dinee and the Bitter Water People." He looked at the interpreter. "Is that right? Two clans?"

"Mother's and father's," the interpreter said. "Two clans."

"I am born to the Sage Brush Hill People," the woman said. "And born for Towering House Clan."

"So there is no connection? Correct?"

"We're not kinfolks," the woman said.

Judge Downey leaned forward and stared at the interpreter. "Miss Pete," she said, "do you think your client should know what is going on here? Shouldn't it be interpreted for Mr. Pinto?"

Janet Pete looked abashed.

"I would like to have it interpreted," she said.

"So ordered," said Judge Downey.

The interpreter was a man of perhaps forty with a disheveled look that was probably genetic. He explained in loud and precise Navajo the exchange between Mrs. Greyeyes and the prosecutor.

Chee began to doze. Snapped awake. The man with the conservative look was being questioned now by Janet Pete.

"Mr. Degenhardt, I want you to tell me if you have ever had or if anyone in your family, or even a close friend, has ever had any unpleasant experience involving a member of the Navajo Tribe. Have you ever been in a fight with a Navajo? Anything like that?"

Mr. Degenhardt thought about it.

The interpreter said: "She asked him if he ever been in a fight with a Navajo."

Mr. Degenhardt shook his head. "No."

"Can you think of any reason why you could not give this gentleman here, Mr. Pinto, a fair trial?"

"She say you be fair?" the interpreter said.

"No, Ma'am," Degenhardt said.

"He say yes, he be fair," the interpreter said.

Chee stopped listening. Who was the interpreter who translated Ashie Pinto's words from the tape to the transcript? Had he been as lazy as this one? Skipping? Summarizing? Or, if he was a traditional Navajo, perhaps leaving out unpleasant parts about witches and skinwalkers? He was remembering he'd decided yesterday to hear Hosteen Pinto's story in Hosteen Pinto's very own words. This business of selecting a jury would take hours. Chee got up and moved quietly out the door.

Finding a parking place near the Federal Building downtown was child's play compared to finding a place to park anywhere near the university library. Finally Chee left his pickup in a POLICE VEHICLES ONLY space behind the campus police station. He identified himself to the duty sergeant, explained his business, and got reluctant approval to leave it there.

By the time he climbed the stairs to the Reserve Room in Zimmerman Library, checked out the tapes and transcripts, and went to work, it was almost noon. He was hungry. He should have stopped for lunch.

He started with the horse thief tape. He'd listened to some of it already, with a lot of skipping around, and he'd read a copy of the transcript in Tagert's office. Now as he listened to Pinto's voice droning the same story into his earphones his sleepiness returned. But he fought it off, checking what he was hearing with the library's copy of the transcript. When he came to a discrepancy, he stopped the tape and replayed it. The revisions tended to be minor corner-cuttings or sometimes eliminations of repetition. By one P.M. he'd found nothing that changed the meaning or left out anything significant.

Sleepiness was almost overpowering. His stomach grumbled with hunger. He put down the transcript, took off the earphones, yawned and stretched. The air around him had the deadness common to rooms without open windows, common to rooms where old things are stored. The silence was absolute, the place empty except for himself and the young woman who sat behind the desk at the entrance, working on files.

He would walk across the mall to the Union and get something to eat. No, he would walk across Central Avenue to the Frontier and have a green chile enchilada. But first he would skip ahead and see if the translator had cheated when the subject became witchcraft. When he'd read the transcript before, it had seemed that Pinto had said remarkably little about why the Ghostway cure had been needed for Delbito Willie. Perhaps he'd actually said more.

He ran the tape fast forward, listening

to Pinto's old voice quacking in his ears until he found the proper place.

"... And then the two white men rode their horses out into a place where there was a lava flow. It is dangerous to ride a horse in there, even in daylight, because, you know, he might get his hoof in one of those cracks—just a little slip, you know, and break his leg and throw you onto the rocks."

Chee stopped the tape and checked the translation. Just as he remembered, the copy he'd read omitted the digression about the horse breaking its leg. He started the tape again.

"... The Yucca Fruit Clan men followed very slowly. The lava was rough there and they kept way back anyway because of the man with the yellow mustache. They say he was a very good shot even riding on a horse. Finally they found where the white men had tied up their horses and went up into the rocks. Right there, Delbito Willie and the Yucca Fruit Clan men they stopped, too, because they knew Yellow Mustache would be protecting his horses with his rifle and because they saw then where it was the white men had gone. It was up there in the place where the witches gather. It was up there in the cave where the evil ones come to make somebody into a skinwalker. Some of those Yucca Fruit Clan men knew about it. They lived over on the other side of the Carrizo Mountains, but they had heard about this place. And you could tell it was this place because of the way the rocks were formed there. They say it looked like the ears of a mule sticking up. If you looked at it from the west, that's the way it looked. Two sharp spires with a low saddle between them. They say it looked like a saddle, like one of those McClellan saddles, with the steep rise up the back side and the horn sticking up on the other side. Reminded people of a saddle."

Chee stopped the tape. None of this, not a word of it, was in the transcript he'd read at Tagert's office. He turned the pages of the library copy. None of it was here, either. Two pages were missing, cut out with a very sharp knife or a razor blade.

He ran the tape again, hearing how Delbito Willie wanted to go in after the white men, to see if they were dead. If they were he would take the rifle of Yellow Mustache—a very fine rifle. The argument had lasted two days, with all of the Yucca Fruit men against it until finally, when they all agreed the white men must be dead by now, one of the Yucca Fruit Clan agreed to go partway with Willie—but not as far as the witches' cave. And Willie had gone in and had come out with the rifle of Yellow Mustache, and the word that both men were indeed dead.

He checked the tape and transcript in at the desk.

"Is there a way to find out who did the translating? Any record kept of that?"

"Just a minute," the woman said. "I think so."

She disappeared into a door marked STAFF ONLY.

Chee waited, rechecking his reasoning. He thought he knew who the translator would be.

He was right.

The woman reappeared, holding a file card.

"Someone named William Redd," she said.

19

LEAPHORN WAS HAVING one of those frustrating mornings which cause all bureaucrats to wish the telephone had never been invented.

At first, he got nothing but a no answer at the number of Mr. Doan Van Ha, the Albuquerque uncle to whom Taka Ji had been sent for safekeeping. Finally, when someone did pick up the phone it proved to be an elderly woman who identified herself as Khanh Ha. Her command of English was barely rudimentary. After a few minutes of total failure to communicate, Khanh Ha said: "You stay. I get boy."

Leaphorn stayed, telephone receiver held to his ear, listening to the silence in the home of the Ha family. Minutes ticked away. He noticed his windows were dusty. Through them he noticed that one of the crows that used the cottonwoods across the road from the Justice Building had lost some wing feathers and flew out of balance. He noticed that the high clouds he had seen when he came to work had thickened and spread from the northern horizon across most of the sky. Maybe it would snow. They needed it. It was late. He thought of Emma, of how she gloried in these days when time hung stalled between the seasons, urging winter on, then cheering for spring, then happily announcing that tomorrow it would be summer and thunderstorm season. Then pleased to see the summer die, anxious for the peaceful gold of autumn. Emma. Happiness was always on her side of the horizon, safely in Dinetah, safely between the Sacred Mountains. She never felt any need to learn what lay beyond them.

A door slammed faintly in distant Albuquerque. Then came the sound of footsteps on a hard floor, and a boyish voice said: "Hello?"

"This is Lieutenant Leaphorn, Taka," Leaphorn said. "Remember? We talked at your house in Shiprock."

"You have the wrong number," the boy said. "I think so."

"I am calling for Taka Ji," Leaphorn said.

"This is Jimmy Ha," the boy said. "I think they took Taka to my aunt's house. Down in the South Valley."

"Do you have that number?"

Jimmy Ha had it, but it took another five minutes to find it. Then, when Leaphorn dialed it, he got another no answer.

He fiddled ineffectively with his paperwork, passing enough time to make another try sensible. Again, no answer. He hung up, dialed the Federal Public Defender's office in Albuquerque.

No, Jim Chee wasn't there. He had been in this morning but he'd left.

"To go where?" Leaphorn asked.

To the federal courthouse.

"How about Janet Pete? Is she in?"

Janet Pete was at the courthouse, too. A jury was being selected.

"When she comes in would you tell her that I have to get a message to Jim Chee. Tell her to get word to him that I have to talk to him. Tell her it's important."

When he hung up, he made no pretense of doing paperwork. He simply sat and thought. Why had Colonel Ji been killed?

He swiveled in his chair and stared at his map. It told him nothing. Nothing except that everything seemed to focus on a rock formation south of Ship Rock. Nothing made any sense. And that, he knew, was because he was seeing it all from the wrong perspective.

He thought about Professor Bourebonette.

He thought about Jim Chee. Unreliable perhaps. But a good mind.

He noticed his wastebasket. The maintenance man who had been neglecting to wash his windows had also neglected to empty it. Leaphorn leaned over and fished out the brochure describing the wonders of the People's Republic of China. He spread it on the desk and studied the pictures again.

Then he threw it back in the wastebasket.

20

ODELL REDD WAS NOT at home. Or if he was, he didn't respond to Jim Chee's persistent knocking. Chee gave up. He found a vacant parking place in a loading zone behind the Biology Building and walked over to the History Department.

No, Jean Jacobs hadn't seen him, either.

"Not this morning. He came in yesterday. We went out to lunch." Jean Jacobs's expression made it clear that this was a happy event.

"No idea where he is?"

"He should be working on his dissertation. Maybe in the library."

The idea of hunting through the labyrinthine book stacks at Zimmerman held no appeal to Chee. He sat down.

"How about your boss? Still missing?"

"Nary a word," Jacobs said. "I'm beginning to seriously think he died someplace. Maybe his wife killed him, or one of his graduate students." She laughed. "They'd draw straws. Stand in line for it if they thought they had any chance of getting away with it."

"What kind of car does he drive?"

"I don't know." She opened a drawer and extracted a file. "I've seen him driving a white four-door sedan, and sometimes a sexy sports car. Whorehouse red."

She extracted a card from the file.

"I think that's when his wife gave up on him, after he bought that red one. Let's see, now. Oldsmobile Cutlass. Nineteen ninety. Corvette coupe. That's a 1982 model. But cool, you know. Impresses the cute little coeds looking for a father figure to take them to bed."

Jean Jacobs laughed when she said it, but it didn't sound like the thought amused her.

"That's his application for a parking permit?"

"Right," Jacobs said. "It covers both

cars. You just hang it on the one you're driving."

Chee looked down at his hand which was itching furiously. He resisted an impulse to rub it, adjusted the bandage instead. Jacobs was watching him.

"Healing up okay?"

Chee nodded. He was thinking about a low-slung Corvette, or a brand-new Oldsmobile, banging over those tracks south of Ship Rock.

"Which car did he drive mostly? Which one was he driving that last day you saw him, that evening when he came in to pick up his mail? You have any way of knowing what he was driving?"

"No," Jacobs said. She hesitated. "He just came in and got his mail. And stuff."

"Stuff?"

"Well, he took some stuff he'd collected for a paper he was doing. It had been on his desk there. And a couple of letters that were in his out-basket."

"Was he all right? What did he say?"

Jacobs sat looking out of the window. She glanced at him and back out the window again.

"Were you here when he came in?"

"No."

"Just the next day you noticed he'd been in and picked up stuff?"

Jacobs nodded.

They considered each other.

"But he left me a note," she said. She rummaged in her desk drawer, extracted a salmon-colored WHILE YOU WERE OUT slip, handed it to Chee.

Scrawled across it was:

"Jacobs—Call admissions. Get class lists on time for a change. Tell maintenance to clean up this pigpen, get windows washed."

"He doesn't sign his notes?" Chee asked.

Jacobs laughed. "No please. No thank you. That's Tagert's signature."

"But it's his handwriting?"

She glanced at the note. "Who else?"

He used Tagert's telephone to call the Federal Public Defender's office for Janet Pete. The receptionist's voice boomed in his ear, telling him that Miss Pete was still at the courthouse. He held the receiver away from his ear, frowning.

Jean Jacobs was smiling about it. "The professor is hard of hearing," she said. "He kept complaining to the telephone people about their equipment mumbling so they came in finally and put in that high-volume phone."

"Wow," Chee said.

"Just hold it a little way from your ear.

It's easy once you know how to handle it."

The receptionist was talking again, less painfully now that he was following Jacobs's advice.

"But there's a message for you," she was saying. "For her actually. She's supposed to tell you to call Window Rock. 'Please tell Mr. Chee to call Lieutenant Joe Leaphorn at his office.'"

Chee called.

"You in Albuquerque?" Leaphorn asked.

Chee said he was.

"We've got sort of a funny situation," the lieutenant said. "It turns out that Taka Ji is the rock painter that Delbert Nez was after."

"Oh," Chee said. He digested the thought. "How'd you find out?"

Leaphorn told him.

"Has anyone talked to him?"

"I can hardly hear you," Leaphorn said. "It sounds like you're standing out in the hall."

Chee pulled the mouthpiece closer to his lips. "I said has anyone talked to him? He was out there the night Nez was killed. Maybe he saw something."

Leaphorn explained that the boy had been taken to Albuquerque to stay with relatives. He gave Chee the name and the number. "Nobody home when I called. But I think somebody should talk to him in person."

"Did you tell the FBI?"

Chee's question provoked an extended silence. Finally Leaphorn chuckled. "The Bureau was not particularly interested in a vandalism case at the moment."

"They don't see the connection?"

"With what? The agent handling the Ji killing is new out here, and pretty new in the business for that matter. I got the impression that he'll talk to the boy one of these days but I don't think he could see how painting his romantic message on rocks had anything to do with somebody shooting the colonel. I think they see some sort of link back to Vietnam. And what he did there."

"How about with somebody shooting Officer Delbert Nez?" Chee asked.

Another pause. Then Leaphorn said: "Yeah. That's what troubles me, too. I think that's the key to it. Have you got it figured out?"

Chee found, to his surprise, that being asked that question by Lieutenant Joe Leaphorn pleased him. The question was clearly serious. The famous Joe Leaphorn, asking him that. Unfortunately he didn't have an answer. Not a good one.

"Not really," he said. "But I think once we understand it, we're going to find there was more to the Nez homicide than we know about."

"Exactly. Has the trial started yet?"

"They're picking the jury. Maybe they'll start it tomorrow. Or the day after."

"You'll be one of the first witnesses, I'd say. That right?"

"I'm under subpoena. The prosecutor wants me to tell about the arrest. What I saw."

"So you'll be in Albuquerque," Leaphorn said. "I know you're on leave but I think you ought to go see the Ji kid. See what he'll tell you. See if he saw anything."

"I was planning to do that," Chee said.

"Unofficially," Leaphorn said. "Not our case, of course." There was a pause. "And get that telephone fixed."

21

THE ADDRESS LEAPHORN had given him for the Ha residence was in the opposite direction from the Tagert address. But Tagert's house wasn't far from the university campus and Chee made the detour. He had a hunch he wanted to check.

It was a single-story, brick-fronted house on the lower end of the middle class—the sort of house history professors can afford if they are frugal with their grocery buying. Chee parked on the street, walked up the empty driveway, and rang the bell. No answer. He rang it four times. Still no answer. Then he walked across the yard and peered through the garage window. It was dirty, but not too dirty for Chee to see a red Corvette parked inside and beyond it a white Oldsmobile sedan.

The Ha residence was neat, standing out for its tidiness in a weed-grown neighborhood which was on the upper end of the lower class. There was no car in the driveway, but as Chee parked his truck at the curb, an elderly blue Chevy sedan pulled up beside the carport. The boy sitting beside the young woman who was driving was Taka Ji.

They started their talking in the driveway, Chee leaning on the sedan door, the boy standing stiffly facing him, and Miss Janice Ha, the driver, standing beside Taka—a silent, disapproving observer.

"I was the officer who made the arrest out there that night," Chee told the boy. "I saw you driving your father's car. I was in the police car you met just before you turned off the pavement toward Shiprock."

Taka Ji simply looked at him.

"Now we know some more," Chee said. "We know you're the one who painted those rocks. It might help us catch the man who shot your father if you tell me what you saw."

Janice Ha put her hand on the boy's

shoulder. "I think we should go inside," she said.

The front room of the house was almost as small as Chee's own cramped lodgings—but there was space in it, between the two front windows, for a shrine. The shrine featured a foot-tall plaster statue of the Blessed Virgin in her traditional blue-and-white robes looking down serenely at two small candles and two small pots of chrysanthemums. A woman who reminded Chee of a smaller, slightly older, and female version of Colonel Ji was sitting on the sofa beside it.

She was Thuy Ha, and she bowed deeply to Chee when Janice Ha introduced him.

"Taka's father was my mother's younger brother," Janice Ha explained. "Her English is not yet good. It was a long time before we could get her released by the Communists. She joined us only last year."

"I hate to intrude at this bad time," Chee said. He looked at Taka Ji. "But I think Mr. Ji here might be able to help us."

Janice spoke to the woman—translating Chee presumed—and Thuy Ha said something in response. "She said he will help you any way he can," Janice Ha said.

The older woman spoke again, a longer

statement this time. The girl responded briefly and the older woman responded. Her voice sounded angry.

"Mrs. Ha asked me to tell you that the Communists killed Colonel Ji," Janice Ha said. She looked embarrassed. "She said I should tell you Colonel Ji worked faithfully for the Americans, and made many enemies because of that, and the Communists sent someone all the way over here to America just to kill him."

The woman was watching Chee intently.

"Would you ask her if she knows who might have done it?"

Janice Ha translated. Mrs. Ha spoke a single word.

"Communists," Janice Ha said.

Taka Ji broke the brief silence that followed that.

"I didn't see very much," he said. "It was getting dark, and the storm was coming."

"Just tell me what you saw," Chee said.

First he had heard a car. He had climbed down from the ladder and was sitting on the sand beside it, looking at the blown-up photograph of the rocks, deciding exactly where he should add the next section of paint. He had heard the engine of a vehicle, revving up, driving in very low gear, coming in closer to this formation than vehicles usually come. He had folded up the ladder and put it out of sight. Then he had hidden himself. But after a while he heard voices, and he climbed up to where he could see what was going on.

"There were three people. They had left the truck, or whatever it was, parked back behind some of those junipers on the slope. I could just see the roof. And three of them were walking toward the formation. Not toward me, but more toward the west. At first I thought it was one man and two women because one was larger than the other two. But then I saw when they got a little closer that one of them was a real thin old man."

"Ashie Pinto?"

"Yes," Taka Ji said. "I saw his picture in the Farmington *Times* that Sunday, after he was arrested. It looked like the man who killed the policeman."

"The other two? Did you recognize them?"

The boy shook his head.

"Could you, if you saw them again?"

"One of them, I think. The bigger one. I got a better look at him. The other one, I don't know."

"But the other one was a woman?"

"I don't know. I think I thought that just

because of the size. They had on a dark-colored felt hat, and a big jacket, and jeans." Taka stopped, looking doubtful. His aunt said something terse in Vietnamese.

"Okay," Taka said. "After that, they disappeared up into the rocks. I just stayed there awhile, where I was. I was thinking I should go, because I didn't want anybody to know what I was doing." He stopped, glanced at his Mrs. Ha, said something haltingly in Vietnamese.

She nodded, smiled at him, reached over and patted his knee.

"He said he was afraid people would think what he was doing was silly," Janice Ha said. Her expression said she agreed with her cousin. They would think it was silly.

"I thought if I left now, they would maybe see me driving away. I always left the car down in the arroyo where nobody could see it, but they would see me driving away. So I decided I would wait until they left." He stopped again.

"Go on," Janice said. "Tell us what happened." She looked at Leaphorn. "We didn't know anything about this either. He should have told the police."

Taka flushed. "My father told me not to tell anybody. He said it sounded like something I should not be mixed up in. He said to just be quiet about it."

"Well, better late than never," Janice said. "Tell us."

"I wondered what was happening over there, so I decided to get closer so I could see. I know that place real well by now, or the part of it where I was working anyway. It's full of snakes. They come in there when the weather starts getting cold because those black rocks stay warm even in the winter and the field mice move in there too. And, normally, those snakes hunt at night because that's when the kangaroo rats and the little mice come out to eat, but in the winter it's cold at night and the snakes are cold-blooded reptiles so they stay in their holes after . . ."

Taka had noticed Janice's expression—impatient with this digression into natural science.

"Anyway," he said hurriedly, "I know where to walk and how not to get snakebit. So I went over in the direction I had seen the three people go and in a little while I could hear voices. Talking up there in the rocks. So I moved around there—it was just beginning to get dark now and there was lightning up in the mountains. And then I saw the one who killed the policeman. He hadn't gone up in there with the other two. He was sitting out by a piñon tree on the ground. I watched him awhile, and he didn't do anything except once in a while he would drink out of a bottle he had with him.

"I thought about that for a while and I decided that if that one was drunk, then when it got just a little darker, I could get down to the arroyo and get my car and slip away without being seen. I just sat there and waited a little while. I heard the two who went up into the rocks yelling. It sounded like they were really excited. I thought they had stirred up some of the snakes back in there."

Taka Ji stopped, looked at his aunt, and at Janice, and finally at Chee. He cleared his throat.

"Then I heard a shot," he said. "And I got out of there and got the car and went home."

The boy looked around him again. Finished. Waiting for questions.

Janice Ha was looking startled. "A shot! Did you tell your dad? You should have told the police."

Mrs. Ha said something in Vietnamese to Janice, got an explanation, responded to that. Then Janice said to her mother: "Well, I don't care. We're living in America now."

"Where did the sound of the shot come from?" Chee asked.

"It sounded like from back in the rocks. Back in there where they had been yelling. I thought maybe they had shot at a snake."

"Just one shot?"

"One," Taka said.

"Were you still there when Officer Nez came?"

"I heard the car. I heard it coming. There's a track that runs along there west of that rocky ridge where we were. It was coming along that. Toward us."

"Did he have his siren going? His red light on?"

"No, but when I saw it, I saw it was a Navajo Tribal Police car. I decided I better go. Right away. I got away from there and went to the arroyo and got the car and went home."

"Do you remember meeting me?"

"It scared me," Taka said. "I saw your police car, coming fast, toward me." He paused. "I should have stopped. I should have told you I heard the shot."

"It wouldn't have made any difference," Chee said. But he was thinking that it might have saved Colonel Ji's life.

Mrs. Ha was watching them, listening to every word. Chee thought that she must know a little English.

"I want you to give me some directions," Chee said. "I have a big-scale map out in my truck. I want to show you that and have you mark on it exactly where those people were in that rock formation."

Taka Ji nodded.

Mrs. Ha said something in Vietnamese, said it directly to Jim Chee and then glanced at her daughter, awaiting the translation.

"She said: 'We have a saying in Vietnam—'" Janice Ha hesitated. "I'm not sure of the word for that animal in English. Oh, yes. The saying is that fate is as gentle with men as the mongoose is with mice."

Chee shook his head, nodded to the woman. "Would you tell your mother that Navajos say the same thing in different words. We say: 'Coyote is always out there waiting, and Coyote is always hungry.'"

It was obvious when the elevator doors opened that federal district court was recessing for lunch. People were milling in the hallway. Janet Pete was hurrying for the elevator, directly toward him. He let her in, along with twenty or thirty other citizens.

"I found Colonel Ji's boy," Chee told her. "I just came from talking with him."

He explained what Leaphorn had learned—that Taka Ji was the elusive painter of stone, that Taka Ji had been out on the basalt ridge the evening Delbert Nez was killed.

"You're going to tell me that you have your witness now. That that boy saw Ashie Pinto shoot Delbert Nez."

She was pressed against him, sideways, in the jam-packed elevator. All Chee could see was the top of her head and part of her cheek. But if he could see her face, the expression would be disappointed. He could tell that from her tone.

"No," Chee said. "As a matter of—" The fat man with the briefcase and the Old Spice cologne leaned against his hand, causing Chee to suck in his breath. He raised the hand gingerly and held it above his head, preferring looking silly to risking the pain.

"As a matter of fact, I wanted to tell you I may have arrested the wrong man. Could you get the trial postponed a little? Maybe a few days?"

"What?" Janet said, so loudly that the buzz of competing conversations surrounding them hushed. "We shouldn't be talking about the case in here," she said. But then she whispered, "What did he see?"

"Before Nez got there, there were three

people out there. Pinto and two other people. Maybe two other men, maybe a man and a woman."

Janet had managed to turn herself in the crush of people about forty-five degrees—a maneuver which Chee found most pleasant—and looked up at him. Her face was full of questions. He went on, "He said Pinto sat down by a tree on the grass and was drinking from a bottle. The others climbed up in the rocks. He heard them yelling up in there, and then he heard a shot. He thought they'd killed a rattlesnake. Remember those?"

Janet's face expressed distaste. She remembered them all too well.

"Then he heard Nez's police car. And he left."

Chee had his chin tucked against his chest, looking down at her. He was conscious of her faint perfume, of her hip pressed against him, of hair which smelled of high country air and sunshine. He could see her face now. But he couldn't read her expression. It baffled him.

"You think that helps prove you caught the wrong man? Helps Hosteen Pinto?"

"Helps Hosteen Pinto? Well, sure it does. Somebody else had the pistol, or at least a gun of some kind, before Nez was shot. All Pinto had, as far as the boy could see, was the bottle. Sure it helps. It creates a reasonable doubt. Don't you think so?"

Janet Pete had put her arms around his waist and hugged him fiercely.

"Ah, Jim," she said. "Jim."

And it took Chee, bandaged hand held high over his head, several seconds to realize that everyone on the elevator who faced the right way must be staring at them. And when he realized it he didn't care.

22

TAKA JI PROVED to be as efficient at marking Jim Chee's map as he had been plotting out his romantic signal to Jenifer Dineyahze. Chee drove almost directly to the site and found the place in the adjoining arroyo where Taka had hidden his father's vehicle. He climbed out of his pickup and stood beside it for a moment, stretching cramped muscles and plotting the most efficient way to climb into the outcrop.

Somewhere back in those black rocks was what Professor Tagert was looking for—probably the skeleton of Butch Cassidy. There was also something that had caused Redd to change a translation to foil Tagert, something that eighty years ago had caused a stubborn Navajo to undergo a cure for exposure to witches. Back in there two *biligaana* bandits had probably died a long time ago. And back in there, Taka Ji last month had heard someone shoot a snake, or perhaps another human, or perhaps nothing.

Since leaving Albuquerque in the early afternoon, Chee had been racing against the weather as well as the sun. As far south as the point where Highway 44 entered the Jicarilla Reservation, he'd been conscious of the darkness on the northwestern horizon. "A slow-moving storm, this one, and that means we might get some substantial snow," Howard Morgan had told them on the Channel 7 news. "But of course, if the jet stream moves north, it could miss most of New Mexico." The storm had indeed moved slowly, much more slowly than the reckless seventy to eighty Chee had been pushing his pickup in defiance of law and common sense. Even so, by the time he passed the Huerfano Mesa two-thirds of the sky was black with storm and the smell of snow was in the air.

His nostrils were still full of that aroma

of cold wetness as he stood beside the truck. The sun was almost on the horizon, shining through a narrow slot not closed in the west between cloud and earth. The slanting light outlined every crevasse in shadowy relief, making apparent the broken ruggedness of the ridge. It rose, ragged and tumbled shapes in black and gray, out of a long sloping hummock—what a million years or so of erosion had left of the mountain of volcanic ash that had once buried the volcano's core. From where Chee stood there seemed to be dozens of ways up into the ridge. Most of them would dead-end at walls of lava.

He found what traces of Taka Ji's tracks the rain that night had left and followed them—helped by the angle of the light. Then he found other tracks, easy-to-follow high-heeled cowboy boots among them. They led up into the malpais.

They led, as Chee was thinking, into Tse A'Digash. That was the term Hosteen Pinto had used—the rocks where witches gathered. There was that to think of. That, and the variety of rattlesnakes which would have been accumulating here since the first autumn cold snaps, taking advantage of a final few days of warmth from the rocks before hibernating for the winter. Maybe they would already be in hibernation. Chee doubted it. The old shamans watched such things closely. And they would not have yet started scheduling those curing rituals which could only be held when the snakes were safely asleep. Ah, well. Snakes preyed on animals small enough to be swallowed, not on men. But snakes struck men in self-defense. With that thought in mind, with the reputation this place had earned—even a hundred years ago—for witches, Chee moved cautiously.

The first path he chose led into a pocket of rocks with no exits. The second, after he climbed a difficult tilted slab of stone, led him higher and higher into the ridge. The dying sunlight no longer reached this path but the going was relatively easy. Obviously this walkway had been used for many years by animal and man. Here a cactus had been broken by a careless step, and healed with time. There a clump of buffalo grass had been distorted by the pressure of footsteps. Now and then, where the rocky formation fended off the rain, Chee picked up recent boot prints. The high-heeled boot marks were no longer evident. They must have been Ashie Pinto's boots. Ashie Pinto had been too wise to enter here. Pinto had sat beside a piñon on the grass, not taking any chances with destiny. But Coyote had been waiting out there, too.

Chee was high in the rocks before he saw his first snake. It was a smallish prairie rattler which had been moving slowly across the pathway just as he turned a corner between shoulder-high boulders. Chee stopped. Snake stopped. It formed itself into a coil, but the motion was lethargic. Chee stepped back to where his human smell would be less likely to reach the reptile. Waited a moment, looked around the rock. The snake was gone.

Chee paused as he stepped over the snake's track across the sand and took time to erase the zigzag marking with his toe. He couldn't remember the reason for this action, just that it was one of the litany of taboos and their counters his grandmother had taught him—a small courtesy to Big Snake.

Not fifty feet beyond where the snake had been, he found the place he had come to find.

In some forgotten time, a great upsurge of molten magma had produced a cul-de-sac walled in by slabs of weathered, lichen-covered basalt. At the wide end, a bubble of this molten rock had burst—forming a small cave. Eons of migrating sand, dust, and organic material had been trapped here, borne directly in by the wind or washed down from the rocks above. It had formed a flat floor on which bunch and needle grass grew when enough water seeped in from above. At the near edge of this little floor, Chee saw the weathered ruins of what had been a saddle.

Chee stopped and studied the place.

Even from where he stood, yards away, he could see the floor had been disturbed by foot tracks. He heard a scraping sound. Or thought he did. When he had left his truck there had been a breeze, the edge of what weather people call "proximity wind" stirred up on the edges of a storm. Now that had died away, leaving the dead calm that so often comes just as the first flakes fall.

Had he heard something? Chee couldn't be sure. Probably just nerves—the proximity of witches. Witches. That caused him to think of Joe Leaphorn, to whom belief in witches was superstitious anathema. Chee had come to terms with them in another way. He saw what the origin mythology said of them as a metaphor. Some choose to violate the Way of the People, choosing incest, murder, and material riches over the order and harmony of the Navajo Way. Call them what you like, Chee knew they existed. He knew they were dangerous.

Now Chee listened and heard almost

nothing. A meadowlark somewhere out of sight ran its soprano meadowlark scales. Down near the arroyo where he'd parked, the crows were quarreling. He heard nothing to explain his nervousness.

The sun was down now just below the horizon, and was coloring the bottom of the storm cloud a dazzling yellow in the far west and dull rose over Chee's head. Reflected light washed the rocky landscape with a dull red tint—making vision deceptive. No time to waste.

He walked past the old saddle into the cul-de-sac. And stopped again.

First he saw the hat. Sand had drifted over most of it, but part of the brim and much of the crown were visible. Apparently a very old hat of once-black felt now faded into mottled gray. Beyond the hat, over a low partition of sloping rock, he saw a pant leg and a boot—also mostly buried under the drifted dust.

Chee drew a deep breath and let it out, steadying himself. Apparently, old Hosteen Pinto's story was true. At least one man had died here a long time ago. In a moment, he would check for the second one. No terrible hurry. Chee, like most Navajos who hold to the traditions of the People, would avoid a corpse as diligently as an orthodox Jew or Moslem would avoid roast pork. They were taboo. They caused sickness.

But there were cures for such sickness if it couldn't be avoided. Chee walked over to inspect the corpse.

The man who wore the pant leg lay mostly far under an overhang of stone—seeking shade probably when he was dying. Now, too late, it protected him from wind and weather. But the desiccating heat had converted him into a shriveled mummy swaddled in faded clothing.

There should be another man, Chee thought. He found him in the little cave.

This had been a bigger man, and he, too, had been partly mummified by the dry heat. His hat had been placed on his face but under its brim Chee could see a long mustache, bleached a gray-white. This body had been moved, pulled out flat on the sand. It still wore a gun belt but the holster was empty. Here seemed to be Professor Tagert's famous Butch Cassidy. Here was Tagert's revenge upon his detractors.

He stood studying the body. Part of the man's vest had been torn away and part of the other clothing had pulled apart when it had been dragged from under the sheltering rocks. Or perhaps, totally rotten, had fallen away by its own weight. Or perhaps Tagert had gone through Mr. Cassidy's pockets in search of identification.

Had Tagert been here? He must have been one of the two people Taka Ji had seen. Chee checked for tracks. They were everywhere. Tracks of two people. Flat-heeled boots with pointed toes, about size ten, and something much smaller made by patterned rubber soles.

Where were their saddlebags? One had been strong enough to carry his saddle up. Surely he would have brought the bags. He looked for a place they might be hidden. The shelf behind him—the most logical place to toss them—was empty. He noticed a deep slot about shoulder high between two layers of rock. He peered into it—cautiously, because it was a perfect place for a snake to rest. Indeed, a snake was coiled back in the crack. It looked like a full-grown diamondback rattler. To the left of the snake, where the slot was a little deeper, Chee could see the tannish-gray color of old canvas. A saddlebag had been pushed back there out of sight. He could reach it, he thought, if he didn't mind risking irritating the snake.

He looked around for an adequate stick and settled for a limb broken from an over-hanging juniper.

"*Hohzho,* Hosteen Snake," Chee said.

"Peace. Live with beauty all around you." He moved the stick into the slot. "Just take it easy. Don't mean to trouble you."

He could reach the saddlebag without getting his hand in range of the snake. But he couldn't move it.

The snake tested the air with its tongue, didn't like the human aroma it detected, and began readjusting its coil. The tip of its tail emerged. It rattled.

"Hohzho," Chee said. He withdrew hand and stick and looked around, seeking something more suitable for extracting the saddlebags.

Then he noticed drag marks.

They were fresh. Something large and heavy had been pulled across the sandy space to his left and into the rocks.

Chee followed. He turned the corner.

William Odell Redd was standing there. He had an oversized revolver in his hand, pointing more or less at Chee's knees. And there, at Redd's feet, was the body of a small man, face up, as if Redd had dragged him by the shoulders.

"I wish you hadn't come back here," Redd said.

Chee thought, So do I. But he said: "What are you doing here?"

"I came after some things of mine," Redd said. "I guessed you'd be coming. I was going to be gone before you got here."

"I guess Jean Jacobs mentioned it to you," Chee said.

"A great girl," Redd said. "Really."

"I thought so too."

Redd was looking down at Tagert. "He treated her like dirt," Redd said. "He treated everybody like dirt. The son-of-a-bitch."

"Is that why you shot him?"

"No," Redd said, still looking down at the professor. "Probably should have. Long ago."

Chee was looking at the pistol. It looked about a hundred years old. It probably was. Probably it had come from the holster of Butch Cassidy, or whoever the bandit turned out to be. What mattered was whether it would still work. It looked ancient and dusty. But not rusty. It was cocked. The hammer had gone backward so it would probably come forward. Fast enough to detonate the cartridge? Maybe. Would the cartridge still be good after all these years? It seemed doubtful, but this arid climate preserved almost everything. Taka had heard a shot up here. This pistol? Shooting Professor Tagert? Chee found it difficult to think of anything but what Redd planned to do with the weapon. But he didn't want to ask.

It was snowing now. Small dry flakes drifted in, hanging in the air, disappearing. Chee found his mind working in an odd way. It had deduced why Colonel Ji had been killed, which was not at this moment a high-priority question. He and Janet had talked about Ji in Redd's house, about Ji being the owner of the car seen leaving this area after Nez's death. Redd must have seen it that night, too. Must have presumed the murder of Tagert had been observed. Must have gone to Shiprock and killed Ji as soon as he'd learned from them (or thought he had learned) the identity of the witness. And killed the wrong person. But there was no right person. Taka hadn't seen the killing either.

Now, suddenly, Chee saw how this information might be useful. If he could be subtle enough. He said:

"Did you see the boy in here that night? The boy who was painting the rocks?"

"What boy?" Redd looked surprised.

"The Shiprock High School boy," Chee said. "He saw your car in here. Saw you with Hosteen Pinto and," Chee glanced at the body, "with the professor. Climbing up here. The two of you, he said. Not Pinto. He said Pinto stayed behind and got drunk."

Redd looked stricken. "It was the math teacher," he said. "Not a boy."

"We were wrong about that. It wasn't the math teacher. It was a high school kid."

"Ah, shit," Redd said. "Ah, shit." He leaned back against the rock. "So they'll be after me, then. No matter what."

"Best thing would be to turn yourself in," Chee said.

Redd wasn't listening. He was shaking his head. "Weird," he said. "Weird. The way this all started."

"How did it?"

"I was just going to squeeze a thousand bucks out of the old bastard. Just what he owed me for the overtime he was always working me and not paying me for."

"By holding out part of the translation?" Chee asked. "You knew he wanted to find this place. These dead cowboys, or whoever."

"Butch Cassidy," Redd said, absently. "Yeah. I left that part of the story out. The part that located this place. Then I told Tagert that since I know Navajo and can talk to people I'd be able to find it. He gave me a five-hundred-dollar advance." Redd looked up at Chee, and laughed. "I found this ridge all right. That was easy enough with the details Pinto had in his story. But I couldn't find this spot. The son-of-a-bitch wanted his money back. Then I got the idea of hiring Pinto. As a crystal gazer, you know. Sometimes that works, I heard, especially if the shaman knows something he's not telling."

"So Pinto found it for you?"

"We brought him here. He looked in his crystals. Put 'em on the ground, used pollen, did some chanting and looked into them and told us where to climb up into here. He was very vague about it at first but Tagert poured the whiskey into him. Loosened him up."

"So why did you kill Tagert? He wouldn't give you the other five hundred bucks?"

Redd was staring at him. "You said the boy saw me shoot Tagert? That's right?"

Chee nodded.

"You bastard," Redd said. "No he didn't." He laughed. Relieved. Delighted.

"What do you mean?"

"I mean I didn't kill the son-of-a-bitch. I didn't shoot Tagert. The boy couldn't have seen that. I'll bet he didn't see a damned thing."

"He saw you," Chee said, but Redd wasn't listening.

"I do believe this is going to work out after all," Redd said, half to himself. He stepped over Tagert's body, looked down at it.

"I'll tell you why I should have shot him, though. Not for any five hundred dollars." He poked Tagert's shoulder with the toe of his boot. "For lots of money."

The pistol was now pointed directly at Chee and Redd was looking at him over it.

"Do you know about the robbery? The one these two bandidos were running from?"

"A train robbery, I think. Up in Utah, wasn't it?" Chee asked. But he was asking himself what Redd meant. That he hadn't shot Tagert. If he hadn't, who had?

"Right," Redd said. "Not much money in it, and they lost most of that because the third man in the bunch was carrying it and he got shot. But the train was making stops at all the little post offices out here, stocking them up with stamps and stuff. There were just twenty or thirty silver dollars and some five-dollar gold pieces in the bag they had. But there were a dozen or so packages of stamps. You know what that means?"

Chee was remembering the stamp collector's book he'd seen in Redd's house.

"I'd guess it means a lot of money," he said.

"A lot of money! Dozens of sheets of uncancelled stamps. All kinds. I'm no stamp man but I looked some of them up. Five-cent William McKinleys worth like four hundred dollars for a block for four. Ten-cent Louisiana Purchase memorials worth eight hundred bucks for a block of four. Some of those one-centers worth over a hundred bucks apiece. I didn't add it all up, but we're talking about three or four hundred thousand dollars."

"Lot of money," Chee said, but he was thinking about whether the old pistol Redd was pointing at him would work, about how the hell to get out of here. And he must not have sounded properly impressed.

"It may not sound like much to you, with a regular job. But if you're starving your way through graduate school, it sounds like a hell of a lot," Redd said. "It sounds like an escape from never having a dime and doing slave labor for bastards like this one."

"What was the problem, then? Did Tagert want to keep it all?"

Redd laughed. "He didn't need money. He had it. He needed fame. And getting even with the other historians who don't agree he's God. No. He was going to leave it all here—just like I found it for him. Then he was going to call in the authorities. Most especially he was going to call in somebody important from the U.S. Post

Office. He wanted official certification that this mailbag and all in it came off that Colorado and Southern train."

"Oh," Chee said. "I guess I see. He wanted a solid connection between these bodies here and that identification of Cassidy as the train robber. To make those other historians eat crow."

"I think he'd found some sort of identification on the body. And he measured it. Can you believe that? Laid it out straight as he could and measured it. He said Cassidy was five foot nine inches and so was the mummy with the mustache. He said Cassidy had a scar under one eye. And two deep scars on the back of his head. He claimed he found those, too, but the thing's so dried-up I couldn't tell."

"I say it would be safe to say he's Cassidy without all that. How you going to prove it isn't?"

"You don't know historians," Redd said. "And Tagert's a single-minded bastard. I told him what it would do—if he called in the authorities. The Post Office would claim the mailbags, and the stamps. Face value of those stamps to them, maybe a hundred dollars, and we lose a fortune."

"What did you want to do?"

"Split it," Redd said. "Just split it. Fifty-fifty. That would be fair. After all, he never could have found it without me."

Chee was thinking, How about thirds? How about Ashie Pinto sitting out there under his tree with his bottle? You wouldn't have found anything without Pinto. But he said: "What did Tagert say?"

"He just sneered at me. Said I had made a deal for a thousand and I had five hundred coming out of that."

"So you shot him?"

"I didn't shoot him. I grabbed the mailbag and it turns out he had a pistol in his coat pocket. He pulled it out. Said he would shoot me if I didn't leave things alone." Chee watched Redd's face register surprise at this manufactured memory. "You know, I think he would have done it too."

Play along, Chee thought. Play along. "I wouldn't be surprised. What I've heard about him."

Redd laughed. "No," he said. "Talk about irony. Old Ashie shot him."

Of course. And Nez, too. Lay the blame on old, drunk Ashie Pinto.

But Chee said: "Pinto. What's ironic about that?"

After the first flurry, the snow had stopped. But now it began again, brushing Chee's cheek with flakes and swirling them around the knees of Redd.

Redd had been thinking, not listening.

Sorting things out in his mind. He motioned Chee with his pistol.

"Let me have your gun," he said.

Chee shrugged. "No gun," he said. "I'm off duty."

"Don't bull me," Redd said. "You cops always carry guns."

"No we don't. I'm on convalescent leave." He held up his left hand, displaying the wrappings. "Because of this."

"You have a gun," Redd said. "Lean up against that rock there. Use your good hand. I'll see."

"No gun," Chee said. Which, unfortunately, was true. Chee's pistol was where it always seemed to be when he wanted it— in the glove box of his truck.

Redd checked his pockets, his pant legs, the tops of his boots.

"Okay," he said. "I noticed you looking at this old hogleg. If you're thinking it won't work, it will. I tried it."

"What are you planning to do?" Chee asked. "You didn't shoot anybody. So, why not turn yourself in?"

Redd had walked to the cleft in the basalt where he had hidden the saddlebag. He was pointing the pistol at Chee, reaching in, leaning against the stone, trying to give his fingers a grip on the canvas, eyes still on Chee, a sardonic grin on his face.

"Turn myself in for what?" he asked. He grunted as his fingers slipped off the canvas. "Damned thing's jammed back in there," he said. "I didn't want somebody to happen in here and find it. Like whoever was watching."

"Why didn't you take it with you?" Chee asked. Every nerve was tense. When Redd pulled the bag out, that would be the time to make a run for it. He had ruled out jumping the man long ago. Redd outweighed him by forty pounds and had two good hands.

"Because that goddam cop car came rolling up. First it was Nez. And then you." Redd pulled the arm out, empty-handed again. "I didn't have time to decide what to do. I just wanted to get away from here."

"Why burn him?" Chee's voice was strained.

"That crazy bastard," Redd said, and Chee presumed he meant Pinto—not Nez. He stared into the crevice, estimating distance. "I shouldn't have pushed it in there so far," he said, half to himself. "The cop was already dead. The fire—he was shooting . . . I don't know what happened. Dealing with a drunk, I guess you could call it an accident. Everything that's happened has been sort of accidental when you think about it." He laughed. "Kismet," he said. "Fate."

"Fate," Chee said. "Yeah. Blame it on old Coyote."

"Like you and the girl coming out here the day I came back to pick up the mailbag. I figured the cops would find it and stake the place out. And when I finally decided that hadn't happened and came out to get it, it was the same day you and that woman came out. So I thought I'd just leave it until after the trial. Get it when everything got cooled down and forgotten."

While he talked, he was looking around for something to pry the saddlebag with. He looked at Chee's stick and rejected it. "It had been here like almost a century. What's another few months?"

"What did you mean, ironic that Pinto shot the professor?" Chee asked.

"Well, hell," Redd said, and leaned into the cavity as far as he could reach. "I meant Tagert gave the old man the whiskey. Coaxed him. Had him smell it. Told him he'd brought a really sweet kind because he knew Pinto liked it sweet." He laughed. "I think he put Nutrisweet in Scotch." Redd raised his voice, mimicking Tagert. " 'Just taste it. You don't have to get drunk. Just take a taste.' Just to make him drunk so he'd tell us more than he wanted to. When we were driving over to pick

Pinto up, Tagert told me he did that. He said: 'The old devil always tries to leave stuff out when you hire him to tell you something, but he can't handle whiskey. So when he starts getting coy, I get him started drinking and once he's drunk he tells me—' " Suddenly Redd grunted. He was leaning into the cleft, straining to reach. "Ah," he said. "Now I got it."

Just then the rattlesnake struck.

Redd jerked away from the rocks, gripping the saddlebag by some sort of reflex action. The great gray snake dangled, writhing, from the side of his neck, its fangs hooked through the neck muscles just below Redd's left ear. Redd screamed, a terrified, gargling sound. He dropped the bag, grabbed the diamondback by its flat, triangular head, pulled it loose, and threw it back among the basalt boulders.

Chee wasted perhaps two seconds watching this—first too startled to move and then thinking Redd would drop the pistol. He didn't. Chee ran.

Moving fast over rough country comes naturally to young men raised in a culture in which skill at running is both respected and useful. Within a minute, Chee was sure enough that Redd couldn't find him, so he stopped, looked back, and listened. It was snowing hard now, the flakes no longer tiny or dry. They stuck to the black rocks for long seconds before warmth from the stone converted them to water.

Redd wasn't following him. Chee hadn't really expected him to. Redd didn't seem to know much about snakes but he'd know a rattlesnake when he saw one. And he'd probably know the neck was a hell of a poor place to get bitten. The venom had only a few inches to move to reach the brain. Redd would be running for help.

Chee climbed, looking for a place from which he could see something. He found one, and he saw Redd almost immediately despite the blowing snow. He was out of the ridge formation, running down the grassy slope toward the arroyo, and then up the arroyo. Probably to his Bronco II, Chee thought. He was still carrying the saddlebag.

Chee climbed down, found the path, and found his way through the snow to his pickup truck.

The driver's-side window had been broken out.

Chee climbed in and tried the starter. Nothing happened. He pulled the hood release, climbed out, and found exactly what he had feared he'd find.

Redd had torn loose the wiring.

Chee stood beside the truck, creating a

map of this landscape in his mind. Where would be the nearest telephone? Red Rock Trading Post. How far? Maybe fifteen miles, maybe twenty. If he walked all night he could be there about opening time tomorrow morning.

23

CHEE PUSHED THE UP BUTTON of the elevator in the Albuquerque Federal Building a little after ten thirty. He looked like a man who had spent a sleepless night walking out in the snow, which he had. The minuscule amount of nighttime traffic that Navajo Route 33 normally carries had been cut to zero by the storm. A disappointing storm as it turned out, depositing less than two inches of snow across the arid Four Corners landscape, but enough to keep people at home. Chee had finally reached Red Rock Trading Post and got to a telephone a little after dawn. He'd called the station at Shiprock and reported everything that had transpired. Then he called Mesa Airlines and reserved a seat on its nine A.M. flight. Finally he'd persuaded an early-rising Navajo rancher who'd stopped for gasoline to give him a ride to his trailer and from there to the airport. From the airport, he'd tried to call both Janet Pete and Hugh Dendahl, who was prosecuting this case for the U.S. attorney. Both of them had already left for the courthouse. He left messages for them both.

A U.S. marshal in a suit that had been big enough last year spotted Chee as he headed for the courtroom door.

"Where the hell you been?" he asked. "Dendahl has been looking for you."

"He get my message?"

The marshal looked blank. "No message. He was making sure all his witnesses were ready."

"He said he wouldn't need me until this afternoon," Chee said. "Maybe not then if they had trouble getting a jury." Maybe not at all when he finds out about Redd, Chee was thinking. They'll have to start over on this one.

"They got themselves a jury," the marshal said. "Opening arguments this morning. He may need you right after lunch."

"Well, I'm here," Chee said.

The marshal was looking him over. No sign of approval.

"You live close?" he asked. "Maybe you could go home and clean up a little. Shave."

"I live at Shiprock," Chee said. "Let me borrow your pen. And have you got a piece of paper?"

The marshal had a notebook in his coat pocket. Chee wrote hurriedly. Two almost identical notes to Janet Pete and Dendahl. He was thinking that as a witness they wouldn't want him in the courtroom now. But what the hell. This trial wasn't going to be held now anyway.

"Thanks," he said, and handed the marshal his pen. "I have to get this note to Dendahl."

The bailiff stopped him at the door.

Chee folded the notes, handed them to the bailiff. "This one goes to Dendahl," he said. "This one to Janet Pete."

Something was going on in the courtroom. The jury was being brought in. Janet, Dendahl, and another assistant district attorney who Chee didn't know were huddled in front of Judge Downey. The judge looked irritated.

"What's going on?" Chee asked.

"I don't know," the bailiff said. "I think the old man's going to change his plea, or something. But he demanded that the jury be in here to hear it. He wants to make a statement."

"Change his plea?" Chee said, incredulous. "You mean plead guilty?"

"I don't know," the bailiff said, giving Chee a "you dumb bastard" look. "She has him pleaded not guilty, so if he changes it, I guess that's what you'd get."

"Look," Chee said. "Those notes are important, then. They have to get that information right away."

The bailiff looked skeptical. "All right," he said, and waddled down the aisle.

Chee moved inside, found a back-row seat, and watched.

Hosteen Ashie Pinto was sitting, too. Waiting. He noticed Chee, looked at him, nodded. The conference at the bench ended. Janet sat next to Pinto, whispering something to him. Pinto shook his head. Judge Downey tapped tentatively with her gavel, looking out of sorts with it all. The bailiff waited patiently for the proper opportunity to deliver his messages.

"The record will show the defendant wishes to change his plea," Judge Downey said. "Let the record show the defendant, after consultation with counsel, requested that the jury be brought in. The record will show defendant wishes to make a statement to the court."

Janet Pete motioned to Ashie Pinto. He

stood, looked around him, wiped his hand across his lips.

"I am an old man, and ashamed," Hosteen Pinto began. His voice was surprisingly strong. "I want everybody to know, all of you to know, how it was that I killed that policeman. And how it was—"

Pinto's interpreter signaled him to stop. He stood, looking surprised and uncomfortable, and converted Pinto's confession into English, and nodded to Pinto when he was finished and said: "Go on now."

Chee sat stunned. Did the old man kill Nez? Not Redd? He'd presumed Redd was lying. He'd presumed—

"And how it was when I was a young man," Pinto continued, "I killed a man in my father's clan at a sing-dance out at Crooked Ridge. Every time it was the same thing. Every time it was whiskey." There are several words in Navajo for whiskey in its various forms. Pinto used the one that translates to "water of darkness." Then he stopped, stood, head slightly bowed, while the interpreter translated.

Chee was watching Janet Pete. She looked sad, but not surprised. Pinto must have finally confided in her. He had wanted to do this and she had arranged it. When?

Pinto was talking again, to a silent, intent audience.

". . . When they came out of the rocks there, Mr. Redd and the man I would kill, that man had a pistol in his hand. He was pointing that pistol at Mr. Redd. Now that man with the pistol was the man who gave me the whiskey. He gave it to me some other times. Before, when I worked for him. He knew how it was for me. This whiskey. He knew that when I drank it I would do wrong things. I would tell him what I didn't want to tell him. He knew it made my tongue loose and he knew that when it was in me it took over my mind. It made the wind that blows inside me blow as dark as night."

The interpreter was tugging at Pinto's sleeve.

"Going too fast," he said, and Pinto stopped.

Pinto had gone too fast. The interpreter missed a little of it, cut some corners.

Pinto told them Redd was a good young man, that Redd had signaled him to get the man's pistol, and when they were all three getting into his car to drive away, he had gotten it.

"So I shot him," Pinto said. "By the car. Then I shot him again."

The interpreter translated.

"Then Mr. Redd he carried the body of that man away. I think he didn't want the police to find it. The man I shot is a very little man and Mr. Redd is big and he carried him back up into the rocks where nobody would find him. And I was waiting there by the car when the policeman came. He was talking to me about painting things. I didn't know what he was talking about but he acted like he wanted to arrest me so I shot him, too."

The interpreter translated but Chee didn't wait to hear it. He still wondered why Pinto had set the car on fire. Maybe the old man would explain that, but he didn't want to hear the answer. Not now. He hurried out the door and down the elevator.

He'd taken a taxi from the airport. This lack of wheels was an oddity he had little experience dealing with. He stopped in the main-floor coffee shop, ordered a cup, and thought about it. He had a headache, which was as unusual as the lack of transportation. Probably the product of lack of sleep last night. Or maybe lack of breakfast. He wasn't really hungry but he ordered a hamburger.

Redd would be arrested by now, probably. Or dead. If he hadn't checked into a hospital fast to have that venom dealt with it had probably killed him. Chee considered that. That and the value of three or four hundred thousand dollar's worth of old stamps. What would Redd have bought with it that he didn't now have? A better car? A better house? Then he faced the fact that he was thinking of this because he didn't want to think of the note he'd sent to Janet. To Dendahl, too, for that matter, but to hell with Dendahl.

"Ask for a recess," he'd told them both. "I don't think Pinto did it. Redd was there. He killed Colonel Ji. I think he killed Tagert and Nez. I think we can prove all of it."

Wrong again. Redd had killed Colonel Ji because he thought Ji had seen too much. Ji would find the bodies, and the stamps.

Wrong about it all. Looking foolish. Feeling foolish.

He ate his hamburger slowly, thinking of Janet hugging him in the elevator. Was that before or after Pinto had told her? Something about his memory of the moment made him think it was after. That she already knew Pinto was guilty. But why, then, the hug? Quite a hug it was, with her pressing against him like that. The hug was about the only bright spot of this whole business.

Then Janet came hurrying up.

"I saw you in here," she said, and sat beside him in the booth. "How much of that did you hear before you left?"

"Up to where he said he shot Delbert," Chee said. "I left then. Did I miss anything?"

"You missed part of Mr. Pinto's speech about whiskey. How it destroys everything it touches. He asked the jury to have all whiskey everywhere poured out on the ground. That's what he was waiting for. Why he wouldn't say anything before. He remembered the time he was tried before, and sent to prison. He thought that this would be the time to warn the world about whiskey."

"Good as any, I guess," Chee said. "Anyway, it's just about what you'd expect from a nutty old Navajo shaman. The spoken word has great power, you know." He sounded bitter.

She was grinning at him. "Don't be sarcastic. It does have power. Did you notice the press was here? He wasn't so nutty."

The grin disappeared. "I got your note. I want to hear all about that. About Odell Redd."

"All right," Chee said. "You want something to eat?"

"Maybe some coffee." She signaled the waitress. "How did you figure Redd out?"

"You mean about him shooting Delbert Nez? How did I get that wrong, too?"

She noticed his tone. She was serious now.

"You didn't get it wrong. You arrested Ashie Pinto. Hurt as you were, you arrested him. It was me. I thought he didn't do it."

"Yeah," Chee said. "Okay."

"I was wrong about something else, too," she said.

"Like what?"

"Like about you," she said. "You made me think for a while that all you cared about was proving you were right."

"What do you mean?" Chee asked.

"Oh, forget it," she said. And to his amazement Janet Pete hugged him again, even harder this time.

24

LEAPHORN HAD SPENT all morning in his office. By a little after ten, he'd leaned back in his chair and spent a long moment just enjoying the scene—his in-basket was empty, his out-basket full but neat, the surface of the desk bare. Wood visible. Nothing cluttering the blotter except a ballpoint pen.

He picked up the pen, dropped it in the top drawer, and looked at the desk again. Even better.

Then he worked through the Nez homicide again. He fished the Gallup *Independent* out of the wastebasket where it had landed in this paroxysm of housecleaning. He reread the story of Ashie Pinto's confession and his indictment of alcohol. Leaphorn agreed with every word of it. Death in a bottle, Pinto had called it. Exactly. Death, sorrow, and misery. The story said Judge Downey had delayed his sentencing pending a medical and psychiatric examination of Pinto. The worst the law allowed under the circumstances would be life in prison. Downey would probably give him something less. But it wouldn't matter, life or ten years. The story said he was "about eighty."

Satisfaction from the clean desk waned. Leaphorn considered Officer Jim Chee. A screwup, but an interesting young man. Intelligent, the way he had made the connections to tie everything in. But he'd never make a good administrator. Never. Nor a team player, and law enforcement often required that. Maybe he would work better in criminal investigations. Like Leaphorn. He smiled at the thought. Where screwing up didn't matter much if you had a creative thought now and then. He would talk to Captain Largo about it. Largo knew Chee better than he did.

He considered everything about the affair of Delbert Nez.

His mother would have said Coyote was

waiting for Nez. Bad luck. For that matter for Redd as well. All he seemed to have wanted was some decent pay for his skills as a linguist. And he ended his game killing the wrong person for the wrong reason. Anyway, Coyote ate Redd. They'd found the old Bronco in a ditch and got him to the hospital, another Dead on Arrival.

He turned to his map and pulled out the few pins this business had inspired. They hadn't helped much this time.

Even a pin for Professor Bourebonette. The question of her motive. He smiled to himself, thinking of that. Emma had always accused him of being too cynical. She was right this time, as she often was. He had checked on Bourebonette. He'd called an old friend in the anthropology department at Arizona State. Did he know someone at Northern Arizona who would know Bourebonette, the mythologist in American Studies there? Could this person determine how she was coming on her new book? She could. The manuscript was off to the publishers. It should be out early next year. So much for that. He would get a copy. He'd like to read it.

They'd talked of mythology on their way back from Short Mountain Trading

Post that night. She had talked a little, and slept a bit, and when she awoke she was full of conversation. She'd questioned him about his own knowledge of Navajo myth and where he had learned it. And then they had covered the nature of imagination. How the human intelligence works. The difference between mind and brain. It had been a pleasant ride. She had talked, too, of the time she'd spent in Cambodia and Thailand collecting animism myths and working with the shamans who select the exact place where the bones of one's crucial ancestor must be kept to ensure good family fortune.

From his window, Leaphorn could see four cattle semitrailers in a convoy rolling to a stop at the tribal barns across Navajo Route 3. That would be rodeo livestock for the Tribal Fair. He made a face. The fair was an annual problem for every cop on the Reservation. Then, too, it meant winter was coming. This year he dreaded winter.

He would go to lunch. Alone. He picked up his cap, put it on. Took it off again. Picked up the telephone. Dialed information.

She answered the telephone on the second ring.

"Hello."

"This is Joe Leaphorn," he said. "How are you?"

"Very well," she said. "Are you here in Flag?"

"Window Rock," he said. "My office."

"Oh? By the way, I found out you did some checking up on me. About my book."

"I was skeptical about your motives," Leaphorn said. "It's one of my flaws. Cynicism. Emma used to fuss at me about it."

"Well, I guess that's reasonable. For a policeman."

"Professor Bourebonette, I think I'm going to China," Leaphorn said. "Would you like to go along?"